Praise for Nell Dixon's *Things To Do*

Five Stars "You think that all stories are alike? That nothing new can impress you? Well, you HAVE to read Things To Do!"

~ *Anne Chaput, Ecataromance*

"I completely enjoyed THINGS TO DO. It's written in first person, which I love when it's well done, and this is. …The author has a knack for giving a strong sense of character and location without a lot of explanation, leaving it to her characters to do that for her. For a funny, exciting and romantic story, I wholeheartedly recommend THINGS TO DO."

~ *Sue Waldeck, The Road To Romance*

Things to Do

Nell Dixon

A SAMHAIN PUBLISHING, LTD. publication.

Samhain Publishing, Ltd.
2932 Ross Clark Circle, #384
Dothan, AL 36301
www.samhainpublishing.com

Things To Do
Copyright © 2006 by Nell Dixon
Print ISBN: 1-59998-285-4
Digital ISBN: 1-59998-136-X

Editing by Sara Reinke
Cover by Scott Carpenter

This book is a work of fiction. The names, characters, places, and incidents are products of the writer's imagination or have been used fictitiously and are not to be construed as real. Any resemblance to persons, living or dead, actual events, locale or organizations is entirely coincidental.

All Rights Are Reserved. No part of this book may be used or reproduced in any manner whatsoever without written permission, except in the case of brief quotations embodied in critical articles and reviews.

First Samhain Publishing, Ltd. electronic publication: August 2006
First Samhain Publishing, Ltd. print publication: November 2006

Dedication

This book is dedicated with much love to the late Mrs. Betty Warneck. A wonderful mentor and friend.

Chapter One

Things to do:

Try on costume.

Wax my legs.

Book a taxi.

Kill my sister.

Okay, so I added the last one later, after the stupid costume she sent me turned up too late to try on, and once I realized my chances of booking a taxi for the night were about as good as my becoming a lottery millionaire. Better add that to my list *buy a lottery ticket.*

I'm not an uncharitable person. I put money in donation envelopes. I buy flags on flag days and I manned a stall at the church jumble sale. It's just that Fiona, my older sister, is in another league altogether. Fi is the Oscar winner of charity events. I'm more local amateur dramatics on a Saturday night.

"Emma?"

I slid my list under the bundle of paperwork on top of my desk as Rob approached. He knows I make lists all the time, but I wasn't in the mood to listen to any of his jokes about my crap organizational skills.

He stood in front of me, perched against the corner of my desk. "I wondered if you wanted a lift to this charity thing of Fiona's tonight."

What do you know? I thought. A knight in tarnished armor driving a sports car...

Rob's been my friend since we were at college together. He knows me better than anybody, but even Rob doesn't know everything. He got me the job here at the travel agency when I returned to England after my year abroad. Rob's kind, handsome, single the perfect catch for someone.

He's also in love with my sister.

"That would be great, thanks," I said. "I hadn't realized you were going, or I would have asked you for a lift earlier." It would have spared me an hour of working my way through the telephone directory calling *Dodgy Cabs "R" Us*.

When I'd first met Rob I'd thought he looked absolutely gorgeous, but it had been obvious from the start that he only had eyes for Fiona. So I had become Rob's friend, his surrogate little sister. We'd shared a drunken kiss once, back when we were students, but that was all.

"I'll pick you up from your flat, then." He moved away from my desk to leave and I caught him trying to take a sneaky peek at my list, which had poked out from under some invoices.

"I'll see you later." I grabbed a stack of papers and moved them over so he couldn't read what I'd written.

"Half past seven, and try to be ready on time." He flashed me his trademark lazy grin and sauntered off toward the back office.

His love for Fiona is hopelessly unrequited but he never gives up. In the meantime, he serial-dates, discarding his unsuspecting girlfriends the minute they start hinting at the "c" word *commitment*.

I don't date at all, not at the moment. Therefore, in the eyes of my mother and sister, I have no valid excuse for not helping Fiona with her charity work. Tonight, it's the Crystal Foundation with the usual format—expensive dinner in a fancy place to be attended by the great and good, all of whom would pay generously for the privilege.

Fi had organized a raffle, tombola and a bachelor auction all to benefit a foundation helping women with cancer achieve their wishes—trips to Disneyland, balloon flights, parachute jumps, that kind of thing. So Fiona had the bright idea of making tonight's theme *magic*.

It had all sounded okay when she'd asked for my help. Mind you, I'd been at a disadvantage. We'd been eating lunch at Mother's house and I'd drunk several large glasses of chardonnay. Which is why I'd be spending that night—Valentine's—dressed as a fairy and waiting on tables.

The courier had dropped the costume off as I'd been about to close the front door behind me earlier that morning. A few minutes later and he would have had to leave it with Steven and Toby, the couple who live in the flat above me. I might have had trouble getting it back; Steven likes pink.

Fiona planned to go as the Fairy Godmother. Tall, slim and blonde, my sister would look good even if she was dressed as the Wicked Queen. The glimpse of lurid pink tulle escaping from the courier's zipper bag that morning had made me suspect my costume wouldn't be quite as flattering as hers.

The agency supplying the fairy waitresses had hit problems. Apparently most of the girls had dates or flu, which was why Fiona had asked me to help.

"I need fairies for ambience, darling. It's only for a few hours and it's not as if you have anything planned for Valentine's. Do you?"

I didn't, and she knew it. Mother had joined in at that point.

"Fiona wouldn't ask if she wasn't desperate, Emma. Besides, you never know, you might meet someone."

The unspoken follow-up to Mother's sentence went: "Nice, eligible and rich, like your sister's fiancé."

I expected Niall to be there that night too, bless him. Niall's a doctor, the only son of well-connected, well-to-do parents. He's very sweet in many ways but rather dull and Fiona walks all over him. Their wedding—the event of the century—was due to take place in June. I've made a list of things to do by then. Some of them aren't very practical but I don't want to let the side down.

Things to do:
Lose fourteen pounds in weight.
Grow three inches in height.
Achieve minor celebrity status.

I took a nice, comforting bite out of one of the chocolate biscuits I keep for emergencies in the bottom drawer of my desk and right then the phone rang. Why does that happen? People always call when you have your mouth full.

"Hello, Pack and Go travel agency." I tried not to choke on a crumb and hoped whoever was on the other end couldn't tell I had a lump of half-chewed biscuit wedged in my cheek. We weren't supposed to have food whilst at our desks.

"Emma, have you seen the outfit Fiona's sent me for the Foundation auction tonight?"

Sara's my oldest friend. Fiona had managed to rope her into helping tonight, too.

"It arrived as I left for work this morning, so I didn't get a chance to look at it," I said. "The color seemed a bit fierce, though."

"It's awful, like Barbie on acid," Sara pronounced.

"Is your mum still going to baby-sit Jessie for you?" Sara's little girl is nine months old.

Sara groaned. "I don't have much choice. Shay's supposed to be away with the band 'til Sunday, so I've already had two lectures on the unsuitability of my lifestyle now that I'm a mother." She did a perfect imitation of her mother's clipped and disapproving tones.

Shay, Sara's boyfriend, has a reggae band and had secured a few dates at a club in the Midlands. Ever hopeful this might prove to be his big break, he had taken off, leaving Sara holding the baby. Literally.

"Rob's offered me a lift tonight," I said.

"Is Rob going?" Sara sounded surprised.

"Mmm-hmm." I took another bite of biscuit.

"You're eating biscuits. What happened to your diet? Fiona will freak if you can't fit in your bridesmaid dress."

"It's one lousy biscuit. I've got ages 'til the wedding and anyway…oh, hell, Greenback's coming. I'll see you tonight." I managed to wipe the crumbs from around my mouth and put the receiver down before my employer loomed over my desk, staring down at me from behind my computer monitor.

"I hope that wasn't another personal call, Emma." I swear he has supersonic hearing. His name really isn't Greenback; the nickname started as a bit of a joke after Rob pointed out the resemblance between Mr. Grebe and the fat toad that plays the villain in the kids' cartoon series *Dangermouse*. Rob, therefore, was Dangermouse and I was his loyal assistant, Penfold.

Mr. Grebe looked particularly toad-like at the moment as he peered at my mouth. "Eating at your workstation is a disciplinary matter, Emma."

I resisted the urge to lick my lips and tried to look virtuous. "Yes, Mr. Grebe." He still appeared dubious. Half an hour and a lecture on my sales figures and targets later, and I needed more than a chocolate biscuit—I could have done with a large gin.

Working in a travel agency isn't really my thing; the problem is I don't know quite what is. I never had a career plan. I had been one of those kids at school who, when asked what they wanted to be when they grew up, scuffed the ground with their toe and muttered, "I dunno." I'd fancied a job as an international spy but my careers master hadn't been keen.

And I still don't know what I want to be when I grow up. I'd like a job that pays oodles of money and allows me to stay home all day eating chocolate and watching TV, but there aren't many of those about and I don't think I'll find them in the jobs section of the *Guardian*, not even in the "creative" section.

Fiona works as a personal assistant for an advertising agency. She fits the image in their glossy brochure. Of course, when she marries Niall, she plans to give work up and concentrate on her charity events. Niall's mother does heaps of charity work too; she's featured a lot in the glossies, usually next to some famous close friend, so I imagine she and Fi might team up.

My day didn't improve. I think I lack the ruthless streak so necessary for clinching sales. Mr. Grebe glowered at me for the rest of the afternoon as I muffed chance after chance. Eventually, he moved me onto the floor to hand out brochures and took over my desk himself.

Of course, by the time the last customer had shuffled out clutching a pile of color brochures extolling the wonders of the Australian outback, it was late. As the most junior member of staff, I was always the one who had to stay to assist Greenback with locking up, so I never got out on time.

The steel roller shutter went down at last and the shop was secured. Greenback seemed to be in one of his talkative moods and in no particular hurry to go home. I've met Mrs. Grebe a few times, and I could understand why Mr. G didn't want to rush.

"So, any plans for this evening, Emma?" It always puzzled me how he could become so different when work had finished. As soon as the shop closed, he turned into Mr. Congeniality.

"I'm helping my sister out at a charity event for the Crystal Foundation." I resisted the urge to glance at my watch, and sidled a step away.

"No date tonight?" To give him his due, he did manage to look genuinely surprised.

"Too busy, I'm afraid. What about you and Mrs. Grebe?" It felt far safer to change the subject.

Something about the way Mr. G shuffled his feet and the uncomfortable look on his face made me suspect I'd dropped a clanger.

"Well, no. As a matter of fact, Emma, and I'm sure I can rely on your discretion, Mrs. Grebe and I are living apart at the moment."

He cleared his throat and looked at the floor. I must have looked like a stunned mullet, opening and closing my mouth with no words coming out. Of all the couples I knew, I would have sworn the Grebes were rock solid. I mean, they were like Jack Sprat and his wife; he was sort of round and she was one of those women who looked as if a lettuce leaf would add a stone.

"I'm so sorry," I said. Come to think of it, he appeared to have lost a bit of weight recently. One of the other girls had commented on it only the other day.

"I don't suppose you could spare the time to go for a quick drink, Emma?"

Uh-oh. One quick glance at his woebegone expression and I knew I was in trouble. Rob says I'm too soft-hearted and he's right. I had excuses lined up and ready in my brain. You know the ones:

> *I have to get home to feed the cat.*
>
> *I need to visit the little old lady next door to make sure she's not dead.*
>
> *I've undergone a religious conversion which means I can't frequent bars with sad middle-aged men whose wives don't understand them.*

Well, none of them came out. Instead, I heard myself mutter, "Just a quick one, then," and I ended up ambling down the street to the Slug and Lettuce with Mr. Grebe.

The bar seemed quiet with only the usual early evening regulars and a couple of weary shoppers.

Perhaps I have the word "sucker" tattooed across my forehead. I sat cradling my gin and tonic and tried to look sympathetic as Mr. Grebe, or rather "call me Ian," unburdened his soul. Trouble was, time had crept on and I still needed to get home, shower and change into the fairy outfit in time for Rob to pick me up.

"So, what do you think I should do?"

Mr. Grebe—Ian—looked hopefully at me.

"I'm not sure. It's a very tricky situation isn't it?" I hedged my bets and hoped he would throw me a few more clues about what he'd apparently just told me.

"I see what you mean," he said, his voice heavy with gloom as he stared at the bottom of his empty pint glass. "You don't think I should rush things, then? I should give her more time to work out what she really wants?"

"I'm sure it's the best thing to do." I drained the remainder of my gin in one swallow and stood up, ready to go. Mr. G blinked at me.

"I have to go. Fiona will murder me if I'm late." Drat, why did I feel so guilty? Before I knew it, those sad, baggy eyes got the better of me again.

"Tell you what," I said. "I've got a spare invitation to the auction tonight. Why don't you come along?" Me and my big mouth. I pulled the card out of my bag, threw it on to the table, left the pub and sprinted like a mad woman toward the tube.

Hell, it was really late. I'd barely have time to make it in through the front door before Rob arrived and I didn't know what had possessed me to invite my boss to the auction. Squashed in like a sardine on the train, I hung onto a strap and ran over in my head what bits of conversation with Mr. Grebe I could remember.

From what he'd been saying, it appeared Mrs. Grebe—Esme—had become bored of married life and taken herself off to Scotland to stay with her mother and think about the future of her marriage. I could see that Mr. Grebe might not be the most exciting husband in the world but Esme, on the few occasions I'd met her, hadn't struck me as Miss Wonderful, either.

I fell through my front door and reckoned I had about ten minutes before Rob turned up. The light blinked red on my answering machine. I hit the button as I whizzed past on my way to the kitchen. A large gin and tonic is not a good idea on a stomach that only contains chocolate biscuits.

While I weighed up the options of a very brown banana or a slightly out-of-date diet yogurt, my message played.

"Emma, you haven't forgotten about tonight, have you? Don't be late. See you later, bye." Fiona's voice. Pulling a face, I continued to search for something quick to eat. I pounced on a forgotten tube of Pringles and stuffed a handful in my mouth as the second message started.

"Emma, are you there? I'll call you later." My husband's voice, once so familiar with his low sexy accent, sent the air whooshing from my lungs and I sat down heavily on the sofa with another handful of Pringles halfway to my lips.

The tape clicked off and whirred back to the start. I played it again. Hearing Marco's voice after all this time shook me up more than I cared to admit.

It was him, all right. No one else ever had the same effect on me and even now my hand trembled as I deleted his message the way I'd tried to erase him from my life. Why had he decided to phone me now? And on Valentine's

Day? Although common sense told me Marco would have no idea of the significance of the date.

The ring of my doorbell brought me back to reality. Throwing the Pringles can onto the kitchen counter, I brushed the crumbs from my shirt and hurried to answer the door.

Rob leant on the door frame, his thumb hovering over the bell push. "You took your time."

"I've only just got home," I said.

"Well, you'd better get a move on," he said. "You're not even changed yet."

Rob's monkey suit fitted him well and I had to admit he looked good. Some men are born to wear a tux, and Rob was one of them. He also smelled very delicious; a waft of musky aftershave hit me as I squeezed past him to get my costume from the back of the sofa where I'd dumped it.

"Look, I'll only be a few minutes," I said. "Sit down or get yourself a drink or something."

I escaped inside the bathroom and shut the door. I wouldn't have time to shower or do my legs now. I slipped my uniform off and prayed my legs weren't too hairy. Thank goodness I'd only done them a few days ago; I'd be able to get away with them under tights.

After the quickest wash and touch-up of my make-up in my life, I unzipped the costume bag. Sara hadn't been kidding about the awfulness of the outfit and, what's more, it looked a very small size twelve.

All right, so I always told everyone I took a size twelve and in some clothes I did. But those were the ones with Lycra stretch or a generous cut, not a skimpy, low necked, lurid pink all-in-one fairy costume.

I cursed under my breath and sucked in my stomach before starting to struggle into the outfit. I heard Rob crashing about in the kitchen.

"When did you last go to the shops?" he complained. "I can't find a single thing in these cupboards."

"There's a can of Diet Coke in the fridge," I called back.

Well, the bottom half of me was in, although I needed to pause for a breather. Heaven only knows what Fiona had been thinking when she ordered this costume for me. Perhaps she had decided to call my bluff over the amount of weight I claimed to have lost so I would be able to fit into the bridesmaid's dress she had on order.

Rob hammered on the bathroom door. "We're late! Fiona's threatened me with dire consequences if we don't get there on time."

"I'm trying," I said. "I can't get the zipper to close." Hah, there's an understatement. I couldn't see what I was doing. Even trying to look at my reflection in the bathroom mirror while I struggled with the fastener almost had me pitching myself face forward into the bath.

"Well, come out then and I'll give you a hand." Rob sounded exasperated. I felt pretty ticked off myself. I grabbed hold of the top of the costume in a vain attempt to preserve some shred of dignity and banged the bathroom door open.

Rob took one look at my face and decided discretion might be the better part of valor. "Turn around and hold your hair up out of the way."

I presented him with my bared back and gritted my teeth as he attempted to tug the edges of the zipper together. "Ouch!"

"What?"

"That was my skin." I would have glared at him but given I had one hand holding up the front of my dress and the other hand lifting my hair clear of the zipper, it proved a bit difficult.

"It would be a lot easier if you'd stop fidgeting," he said.

"I can't help it. It hurts!"

"Look, do you want me to help you or not?"

"Yes." I didn't care if I sounded sulky. Who wouldn't under the circumstances?

Rob gave one final tug on the zipper and I was in. I couldn't breathe, but I'd done it. I let go of my hair and the top of the costume, then took a chance and cautiously straightened up.

"Blimey, Emma!" Rob exclaimed.

The one advantage (or disadvantage) of tight corsetry is it does give the wearer rather impressive cleavage. In my case, if I turned around too fast I would probably take someone's eye out.

Rob's eyes were now transfixed on my bosom and he had to be chivvied along the hall while I grabbed a coat and my bag. The only coat that fitted over the top of the wings sticking out of my back was an old Mac which had last been in fashion when I was in high school.

At least I had a lift. If I'd been out on the street dressed like this I would have been arrested. Rob had parked his car right outside the flat. It had turned frosty and the pavement glittered silver with ice. I tested it with one stiletto, a bit slippery. Rob went out into the road and unlocked the car door. I took as deep a breath as my costume allowed and tottered after him, but as soon as my heels hit the ice I slid forward. With my arms waving like a dervish in an attempt to keep my balance, I careened toward the car and crashed inelegantly into the passenger door.

"Sorry," I said.

Rob glared at me. "I hope you haven't damaged the paintwork."

His car is his pride and joy. He spends an inordinate amount of time and money on caring for, what to my eyes, is an old-fashioned, inconvenient, gas-guzzling go-kart.

I opened the car door and tried to figure out how I could get into the low-slung front seats without doing myself a serious injury. To hell with dignity, let's face facts; even supermodels struggle to enter and exit those kind of seats without flashing tomorrow's washing.

I resigned myself to the inevitable, closed my eyes and toppled backwards onto the seat, hoping I hadn't really heard the sound of tearing fabric. The pained expression on Rob's face as I wiggled into position meant I must have demonstrated my complete lack of feminine finesse yet again.

"So, what has Fiona persuaded you to do this evening?" I wondered if Rob might be helping with the raffle. He had the gift of the gab, so he'd be certain to sell loads of tickets. Plus, in his tux, he looked James Bond-ish and there would be lots of attractive single females around this evening. Or maybe Fiona needed more men to balance the tables up.

"I'm not sure. She mentioned something about being short of men for the auction."

I stopped trying to fix my hair. "You're going to be one of the bachelors?"

Rob changed lanes and slid the car out into the city traffic. "What bachelors?"

"One of Fi's bachelors. In the auction."

The gears crunched and a stream of expletives filled the air.

"You did know it was an auction of dream dates?" It was pretty obvious from Rob's reaction he didn't. "I can't believe she didn't tell you!"

Rob scowled. "I didn't ask her. I thought this auction would be like the one she did in November, when she sold those celebrity cast-offs."

We were both silent for a minute. For the pre-Christmas auction, Fiona had persuaded lots of well-known people to donate clothes, and then sold them to the highest bidders. It had gone extremely well, raising shed-loads of money for the Foundation.

"It's not too late to back out," I said, but knew Rob wouldn't. Like me, he'd feel obligated to see the evening through, but I felt I ought to make the offer anyway. After all, it didn't sound as if Fiona had exactly been honest with him.

Rob growled something under his breath and slid the car into a freshly vacated, metered space outside the gallery where the auction was to be held. Despite the cold weather, plenty of people were heading up the impressive stone steps of the building and in through the automated glass doors.

"What's he doing here?" Rob looked up from sorting out coins for the meter to glower at someone standing at the bottom of the stairs. I struggled to sit up from my semi-reclined position to see who he meant.

"Oh, um, I invited him." Ian Grebe waved at us.

Rob stared at me. "Good move, Penfold!" His voice sounded heavy with sarcasm.

"He seemed so down, and I felt sorry for him." Still fighting to release my seatbelt, I could only watch helplessly as Rob stalked off to feed the meter and Greenback Grebe trotted across the pavement to meet us.

Chapter Two

"May I assist you from the car, Emma?" Mr. Grebe swung the door open and offered me his hand. I think I would still be stuck in there like a stranded whale if he hadn't hauled me out.

I popped out of the car at speed and managed to poke him in the eye with my cleavage. It had to be either the shock of his nose landing in my bosom or the sheer hideousness of my lurid pink costume which rendered him speechless.

We made our way up the stone stairs through the throng. The inevitable groups of photographers from the glossies were in position at the top ready to accost any passing celebrities. Fiona cuts deals with the tabloid magazines as it raises more money and ups the profile of the charity.

Mr. G and I made it past the press without incident but when I turned around Rob had been spirited off into a side room accompanied by Fi's future mother-in-law and a posse of paparazzi.

Fiona clearly planned to advertise Rob as one of the bachelors for the night's auction. I hesitated for a moment, torn between attempting to stage a rescue or trying to find where to go to report for waitress duty. Mr. G remained glued to my side and I began to worry about where I could park him for the rest of the evening.

"Emma!"

My heart sank. A familiar Prada handbag waved imperiously at me from across the lobby.

"Hello, Mummy. I didn't know you were coming tonight." I air-kissed her cheeks so as not to spoil her make-up. Her eyes narrowed at the sight of my ratty coat and I knew she would be unable to resist commenting on the fit of my costume. "Where's Fiona?" I asked. "She didn't tell me where I had to check in."

Mother tutted (she has a good line in tuts). "I imagine she has far more important things to do than worry about you. I expect you'll be needed in the kitchen."

"I didn't realize this charming lady was your mother, Emma."

I'd forgotten all about Mr. G.

"It is you, isn't it, Charlotte?" he asked, looking past me toward my mother.

Much to my surprise, she turned rather pink and began to flutter her false lashes at Mr. G. "Ian! What a surprise to meet you here."

Mr. G looked a little flushed, too.

"Do you two know each other?" I asked. Silly question, given the goofy looks being exchanged. I tried to recall what I'd ever told my mother about my boss. I had a horrible feeling none of it had been flattering.

"We met a few months ago, at Jemima's wedding," she told me. "You remember, the one with the ghastly little bridesmaids in pea-green chiffon."

Mother can never resist adding fashion footnotes to something, even when she means to be telling you something serious. I had a hazy memory of having to listen to all the fashion minutiae from a wedding Mother had been to before Christmas. The daughter of one of her old school friends, I think. I'm sure I would have noticed if she'd mentioned anything as important as her fraternizing with my boss.

"You never pay attention, Emma," she complained.

"Exactly." Mr. G nodded in agreement.

Good grief, they were even ganging up on me now!

"You ought to go and do some work," my mother said. "Your sister is counting on your support. This is a very important event for her and why you're wearing that hideous coat I can't imagine."

Well, that put me in my place. Fortunately, I spotted Sara in her bright pink outfit, jumping up and down at the back of the crowd and pointing toward a door in the far wall.

"You're absolutely right, Mummy. I'll see you both later." Giving her cheek another quick air-kiss, I worked my way through the masses and over to the door.

"Where have you been?" Sara hissed at me. "Fiona's been on my case ever since I got here."

Her costume fit much better than mine did. She pulled me through the doorway into a kitchen at the back of the bar. Fairies of all shapes and sizes collected silver trays loaded with champagne glasses while shirtless, muscle-bound men in bow-ties, waistcoats and devil horns carried out platters of hors d'oeuvres.

"What's Greenback doing here?" she asked.

My face gave me away. I'm not brilliant at fibbing and Sara knows me too well, anyway.

"Oh, Emma! You are such a soft touch. Don't tell me Esme's here as well?" She glared at me.

Sara used to work with Esme Grebe; they had been on the same cosmetics counter but not on the same wavelength.

"No. That's why I asked him."

Sara rolled her eyes. "Spare me the sob story. Come on, you'd better get your coat off and get going or Fi will be on the warpath."

I had a bit of trouble getting out of my coat. Too much movement and my costume threatened to perform a very painful kind of surgery on a delicate bit of my anatomy.

"Wow, Em, what are you going to do if you need the loo? You'll never get your outfit back on." Sara giggled.

"If I have to spend too long wearing this, I may never need to go to the loo ever again," I replied.

One of the bow-tied waiters thrust a couple of trays full of champagne flutes at us. "There are people dying of thirst out there," he said. I swear he flounced as he walked away from us.

"Get a load of her!" Sara muttered darkly.

We each picked up a loaded tray and made our way out into the reception area. The noise level hurt my ears as soon as the door swung open. The raffle and tombola ticket sellers were in full flow and the place looked packed with people.

On the wall above the crowd hung large black and white photographs of the bachelors taking part in the auction. I recognised the picture of Rob. It had been taken a couple of years ago after we had graduated. He'd given one to Fiona, but I hadn't realized until now that she'd kept it.

Mother and Mr. G were nowhere in sight. I looked for Rob but he must still have been in 'celebrity central.' My fairy costume soon attracted a certain amount of unwanted attention and my bum got pinched twice before I managed to dispense all my glasses. I retreated back to the kitchen to refill. Four more trips and my feet were hurting and worse still, I had been ogled, propositioned and bruised by a hundred different elbows.

I drank the last glass of champagne on the tray myself, ignoring the affronted gazes of the assembled society guests. To be honest, I didn't care. I don't think a single part of me didn't ache. And dinner had still to be served, or the auction held yet.

Guests started to file through the polished double doors into the dining area and take their places at snow-white, circular tables. I found it hard to believe the gallery wasn't a proper restaurant. Fiona had transformed the floor-space into an incredible fantasy setting, like the inside of a posh chocolate box. I hobbled around the bar as it emptied, collecting up dirty glasses and wishing I'd worn shoes with a lower heel.

Fiona and Niall stood near the doors while Fiona did her hostess-with-the-mostest bit. Something about her stance caught my attention. She looked as lovely as ever, with her long blonde hair twisted up under a little twinkly tiara and her silvery, fairy-godmother dress fitted in all the right places, but something didn't appear to be right.

A bright spot of color lit each cheek and she seemed a touch too animated. Niall didn't look at all comfortable; he raised his hand as if to touch her arm and then dropped it back down again, as if having second thoughts. I maneuvered myself nearer, even though almost everyone else had been seated in the dining area and I should have been helping to serve the first course.

"Niall, will you stop fussing! I am perfectly all right."

Fiona's voice carried over to where I skulked with my tray. I expected her to notice me, but she and Niall must have been wrapped up in their dispute. I didn't catch Niall's answer but Fiona gave him one of her famous looks, (she's inherited the talent from Mummy), then sailed off into the dining room, leaving him to trail along behind in her wake.

The diners had already begun to tuck into their soup before I caught up with Sara. She'd slipped out of the fire exit to have a crafty ciggy.

"Where did you skive off to?" Sara sucked at her cigarette with the same fervor Jessie, her baby, reserved for her dummy.

"I wasn't skiving! I was collecting up the glasses in the bar." I told her about Fiona and Niall. Any other couple having a spat wouldn't be news, but Fi and Niall never disagree on anything ever. For one thing, Niall is not that brave. My sister in full flight is not something any sane man would want to experience more than once.

"So, what do you think it was about?" Sara ground out her cigarette butt with the toe of her stiletto and popped a breath mint into her mouth.

"I don't know," I replied. "Unless pre-wedding nerves have set in."

The fire door banged open and the same waiter who'd had a go at us earlier stuck his head out.

"If you two ladies would like to honor us with your presence, I think you'll find there's work to be done." He scowled and flicked a disapproving glance at my cleavage. "Oh, and may I remind you the champagne is reserved for the guests." He disappeared back inside and Sara looked at me with one eyebrow raised.

"It was only one little glass. My feet hurt." I tried to look pathetic.

"Did I say anything?" Sara said. "Oh, well, back to work, Cinderella, before the wicked stepmother comes back!"

By the time the coffee cups had been placed on the tables, my feet throbbed and I longed to take off my shoes. The last event of the night, the bachelor auction, was about to start and the atmosphere in the room pulsated with energy. With a few glasses of champagne, the well-heeled, decorous society ladies had miraculously transformed into a rampant hen-party.

Pheromones mingled with expensive perfume as Fiona tapped her spoon against her glass to obtain the attention of the crowd. I slipped behind a huge slab of marble labeled 'Reclining Nude' and eased my aching feet free from my shoes. Sara sidled up next to me, tucking her mobile phone up the leg of her fairy costume.

"I called Mum a minute ago. Jess is really miserable; I think she's cutting another tooth." Sara had dark smudges of fatigue under her eyes and even her blonde ponytail had drooped.

"Why don't you go home, Sara? I'll get your money off Fiona."

Her face lit up for a second then fell again. "I can't. The auctions about to start and Fi asked me to work 'til one."

"There's not much to do now and it's already gone half-eleven. Go home, Sara."

She didn't put up much of an argument. I snuck her out of the fire door and waved her off before creeping back to my hiding place behind the statue where I'd left my shoes. Fiona handed the mike over to the professional auctioneer, ready to start conducting the bidding.

The bachelors sat on tall chrome stools in a row along the centre of the stage. Rob's skin paled when the first guy was helped off his stool by two tall, skinny fairies and led to the front of the stage.

The crowd went wild. The first bachelor was announced as a Right Honorable somebody-or-other and the dream date offered was a hot air balloon ride over his estate followed by a candlelit supper. As an offer, it seemed to go down well with the ladies and the bidding flew along.

The final sum ended up more than my annual salary and I wondered how much Rob's date would fetch. An impoverished travel agent with a clapped-out sports car wasn't about to reach the same level of bids as a Hooray Henry with a title. I couldn't bear to watch.

Bachelor Number Two stepped up to the mark while the first chap was claimed by the winning bidder, a sturdy, horse-faced woman in blue taffeta. Number Two turned out to be a dot-com tycoon who offered to pilot his date in a private jet for lunch in Paris. His bids rose even higher than the first bachelor, proving money is more important than a title these days, I suppose.

Rob was led from his seat by the twiglet twins and the auctioneer read the spiel from her little card. I peered through the gaps between my fingers as she did her stuff.

"Bachelor Number Three is Rob. Twenty-four years old, Rob likes fast cars and foreign travel. His lucky date can look forward to a special moment aboard his yacht in Spain followed by a romantic dinner for two in an exclusive restaurant. So if you'd like a bit of yo-ho-ho, this sexy sailor is the man to bid for!"

I laughed. Rob doesn't have a yacht; he doesn't even own a lilo. I can only guess Fiona had persuaded a friend to loan him their yacht...although somebody other than Rob would have to sail it. I mean, Rob wouldn't know where to start. I expected someone had to go along on these things anyway to act as a chaperone.

The bids started to come in, not as high as the other two, but then again, Rob isn't a millionaire and doesn't have a title. He is much better in the looks stakes, though. The hammer went down and a tall, familiar-looking brunette whose face I couldn't quite place crossed the stage to claim him. Fiona's mother-in-law-to-be shepherded them both away to have more photographs taken.

My feet pulsated with pain and I needed to pee. I hoped Rob wouldn't forget he'd promised to take me home. My mother and Mr. G had been absorbed in each other's company all night. I thought I'd seen them holding hands when I served the desserts and I'd dropped two chocolate profiteroles on some poor bloke's lap.

I eased my poor, puffy toes back inside my shoes and slipped out from my hiding place. The last bachelor had been auctioned and Fiona began her speech praising the generosity of the bidders. The snarky head waiter gave me a nasty look as I emerged, so even though my bladder felt about to rupture, I hobbled about collecting glasses from the tables and half-heartedly tidying up.

A huge round of applause signaled the end of the event and people started to head for the cloakrooms to collect their coats. Fiona moved to the door with the chairman of the Foundation to see them out. I couldn't see Niall or his mother.

One of the twiglet fairies gave me a nudge. "We can collect our money; it's ready for us in the kitchen. We should get a decent whack for working Valentines."

I needed to collect Sara's money before anyone noticed she'd gone. Fortunately Mr. Snarky (who seemed to be in charge of the envelopes) got distracted by one of the other fairies so I forged Sara's signature on the pay list and picked up her envelope before he could realize she had gone missing.

The lobby looked deserted by the time I'd managed to collect my coat and head back out in search of my lift. Mother and Mr. G stood talking to Fiona. At least, Mother stood; Mr. G swayed from side to side like a sailor on the high seas. My bladder hurt so much, it took all my concentration not to plait my legs as I teetered across the lobby to join them.

"Darling, you mustn't panic. Listen, come home with me tonight and you can talk to Niall in the morning." Mother sounded distressed.

Something was wrong. Fi dabbed at her eyes with a soggy tissue and Mummy's face looked as if she'd been struck by lightning.

"What's the matter?"

Neither of them answered me. Fi hiccupped and patted at her eyes even harder than before.

"What's going on?" I asked. "Where's Niall?"

Fiona shrugged her shoulders and Mother glared at me. "I'm taking your sister home with me. She and Niall have had a slight difference of opinion."

At this, Fiona let out a wail and bolted down the stairs toward the exit.

"Now, see what you've done!" Mummy dashed off after Fiona, leaving me and Mr. G staring at one another.

"It's been a very *pleassshant* evening," he slurred. "Thank you so much for your kind invocation, Emma."

Mr. G must have enjoyed a little too much champagne. And where the hell had Rob gone? I hoped he hadn't run off with his date and forgotten me. God, I needed to pee.

"I wonder if you and Rob might be good enough to give me a lift home…? I think I may be a touch over the limit." Greenback swayed sideways and, catching hold of his elbow, I propped him up against a pillar before he fell over.

"Psst, Emma!" I heard someone hiss. Thank heaven it was Rob and at last we could go home. He peered round the edge of the cloakroom door, almost as if he didn't want to be seen.

"What are you doing?" I said. "Come on, I want to go home!"

"Has she gone?"

"Has who gone?"

Mr. G started to slide down the pillar so I pulled him back upright again. "Will you stop pratting about and take me home!"

"Only if you're sure she's gone," he said.

It wasn't like Rob to avoid Fiona.

"There's no-one here except me and Mr. G," I told him. "Now, please take me home before my bladder bursts and my feet catch fire."

Rob emerged from the cloakroom and after a quick look around, came over to us.

"Who were you hiding from?" I asked. "Fiona?"

Rob looked at me as if I'd gone mad. "No. It's Gilly, the date from hell."

"Tell me on the way home," I said, trying to steer him toward the door.

"What's he doing here?" Rob stared at Mr. G, who grinned beatifically at him in return before sliding down the pillar again.

"He needs a lift home; he's had too much champagne."

Rob sighed and slipped an arm around Mr. G's waist. "You'll have to give me a hand, Em."

Mr. G smiled at me, breathing alcohol fumes in my face. We supported him between us and staggered together down the steps. After the suffocating warmth of the gallery lobby, the icy air hit me like a bucket of water. I wanted to cry from the pain in my feet, my full bladder and the raw bits of my body where the fairy costume had dug into my flesh and rubbed.

We slipped and slid our way across the frozen pavement and, panting from the exertion, leaned Mr. G against the side of Rob's car. "How are we going to fit him in?" I asked.

Rob's pride and joy is primarily a two-seater. There is a back seat but it's designed for very short people or Gucci-clad poodles, not sixteen stones of inebriated male boss.

It's a good thing glares aren't deadly or I would be pushing up daisies now (I must be immune from years of living with my mother). Rob stalked around to the driver's door, muttering something unpleasant under his breath. With a click of the switch, he started to lower the folding roof.

"What are you doing? We'll freeze to death." The words hung in a vapor in front of my face to emphasize my point.

"Do you have a better idea?"

Even if I did, from the look on Rob's face, I could see this might not be the best time to mention them. And my bladder hurt so much all I could think of was home. Between the two of us, we managed to wedge Mr. G in the tiny space behind the front seats. I heard a few sinister ripping noises from under my coat when we heaved him into the car but to be honest, I didn't care.

We drove back to my flat at a nice sedate speed. Rob didn't want to attract any police attention as we were overloaded, and let's face it, we made an odd enough sight already—a sports car with the top down on what felt like the coldest night of the year, containing an indecently dressed fairy, a bloke dressed up like James Bond and a fat man wedged in the back singing old Duran Duran songs. If the police did see us they would think the circus had come to town.

"If he throws up I'm holding you responsible," Rob warned me.

Mr. G moved on to the chorus of "Rio."

"Why is it my fault?" I tried to turn around to check on Mr. G, but my knees were under my chin from where Rob had pulled the seats forward. I didn't dare risk moving; I didn't think the costume had any stretch left in it, not that there had been much to begin with.

"You gave him the invitation!" Rob exclaimed.

"I didn't know he'd get so drunk."

For heaven's sake, how come I got to be held responsible for the antics of a fifty-year-old man?

From the dismissive snorting sound on the driver's side, Rob obviously felt I had to be the one at fault. I tried to distract myself from the agony in my bladder. I'd have joined in with Mr. G's singing but I didn't know all the words. I'd never realized there were so many traffic lights in London before and how come they were all on red? If we didn't get home soon Rob would have a puddle on his front seat. I tried to make a list in my head of what I needed to do when I got home.

Things to do:

Go to the loo.

Burn this stupid costume.

Rub the free samples of Clarins lotion Sara had given me all over my sore bits.

"So, who placed the winning bid for you?" Thank God we were almost there.

"Didn't you recognize her?" Rob asked incredulously.

"I thought she looked familiar but I wasn't close enough to see." I didn't tell him I'd been hiding behind a sculpture resting my feet.

"Do you remember the girl I saw in the summer? The one who dragged me past every jeweler's window in town?"

I tried to remember, but Rob has had quite a few girlfriends. "Is she the one who took you to meet her family and got you property details?" Of course, now I knew why I'd recognized her! Rob used to hide in the office storeroom when he saw her coming, leaving the rest of us to make excuses for him.

"That's the one—Gilly, mad as a box of frogs."

Mr. G switched to Roxy Music and the mournful strains of "Jealous Guy" wafted from the back seat. Thankfully, we pulled up outside my flat. I almost cried with relief when I saw the familiar outline of the scrubby, overgrown bushes in the front garden.

"Have we stopped?" Mr. G popped his head up from the back, breathing stale alcohol over me while I fumbled in my coat pocket for my key.

Rob flung open his door and strode around the car, ready to help pull me out. I couldn't do it on my own; my knees were wedged under the dashboard and between my ill-fitting costume and dire need for the bathroom, I wasn't in any fit state to even try.

Mr. G tried to clamber out from the back seat before Rob managed to tug me free.

"We're just dropping Emma home. You can get in the front in a minute." Rob didn't sound very happy as he wrapped his arms around my waist and yanked me out of the car. I hung onto him for a moment, letting the blood circulate back down to my poor, swollen feet while I got ready to make a dash for my flat and the loo.

Mr. G stumbled out of the car behind me and I heard the tinny sound of something scrape along the bodywork of Rob's beloved motor. I winced and hoped it wasn't anything serious.

"We going in for coffee, then, eh? Jolly good idea." My boss swayed alongside me.

I wanted to get inside the flat and out of my fairy outfit as fast as humanly possible. Clutching my key I took a step towards the front door.

"Wait!" Rob grabbed hold of my arm.

"What's the matter?"

He peered into the darkened area near the front door. The bulb had gone in the outside light and we'd been meaning to replace it.

"Wait here."

Rob darted off down the path.

"'Wos he doing?"

Mr. G staggered up against me knocking me off balance so I slipped on the frosty pavement. Crashing noises came from the shrubbery in front of the house, followed by muffled shouts and the sound of scuffling. A light clicked on in one of the upstairs windows and Steven from the flat above emerged from behind the blind.

"What's going on?" Toby, his partner came to join him.

"Rob?" I felt really scared now. What was he doing? It could be a burglar; he might pull a knife on him or anything. "Rob, be careful!"

"Shall I phone the police?" Toby leaned out of the sash window trying to peer into the shadows.

"Keep still." Rob's voice emerged from the bushes as if he was giving orders to somebody. I crept a bit nearer, with Mr. G hanging onto me for dear life.

"We'll come down." Steven and Toby left the window and a few seconds later, a light appeared in the hallway, spilling out shards of colored light through the glass half-moon in the top of the communal front door.

It swung open and illuminated Rob, who looked rather disheveled, sitting on someone who lay half-covered by the bushes.

"I found this bastard lying in wait by the front door," Rob panted triumphantly.

"For God's sake, Emma," cried the man beneath Rob. "Tell him who I am!"

The world ceased to turn and air stopped entering my lungs.

"Marco?" I gasped.

Four pairs of eyes turned towards me.

"You know this guy?" Rob demanded.

The man underneath him jerked and Rob rolled off on to the floor.

"Of course she knows me," the man said. "She is my wife."

Chapter Three

Oh, fuck!

Steven and Toby gaped at me open mouthed. Rob looked at me as if I'd grown two heads, and even Mr. G straightened up to stare at me, wide-eyed.

What could I do? I took the only reasonable course of action open to me. I ran past Toby and Steven, unlocked the door of my flat and bolted myself in the loo. At least with an empty bladder and wrapped up in my comfy fleece dressing gown, I could think.

The utter bliss of freedom from my awful costume and having a pee that felt like Niagara Falls! Once finished and undressed, I heard the rumble of male voices inside my flat so I wrapped my dressing gown around me more securely and went in to the lounge to face the music.

They were all in there. Steven and Toby had made themselves mugs of tea; Mr. G sat slumped in the corner on a kitchen chair while Rob and Marco glowered at one another from opposing armchairs.

Marco. His dark brown eyes met mine and my heart developed the funny irregular beat that always seemed to happen whenever he came near me.

"Is it true, Emma? This guy's telling the truth?" Rob still looked as if he was about to haul Marco off to the police station at a moments notice.

"Emma is my wife. We married while she was working in my country." Marco looked at me to confirm his answer.

Steven and Toby's faces were alight with interest. I can't explain how I felt; this had to be happening to someone else. Not me, Emma Morgan, reluctant travel agent, crappy fairy waitress, girl who couldn't get a date on Valentine's Night.

"It's true," I said.

Even my voice didn't seem right or sound as if it belonged to me. I sat down next to Toby on the settee, my legs wobbling as if someone had extracted my kneecaps and replaced them with marshmallows.

I couldn't stop looking at Marco. I couldn't believe he was here, and he'd found me. God knows what he must have thought when I'd turned up blue-chested and red-nosed, crammed in the front of Rob's car with a musical drunk sitting in the boot.

"What was he doing skulking around the front door?" Rob asked. "And why have you never mentioned him before, Emma?" He drummed his fingers on the arm of the chair. Bits of twig still clung to his trousers.

What could I say? How do you tell people you were married months after the event? Especially when the marriage has been the biggest mistake of your life. Anything I said now would make me sound even more pathetic and sad than I really am.

"Emma did not know I was coming here, so when I arrived and she was out, I decided to wait for her." Marco gave a careless shrug as if everything was all quite normal. He dominated the room. He seemed more alive, vibrant, and colorful than anyone else I'd ever met.

Rob looked at me and I knew he must be trying to assess what was going on, attempting to make sense of it all.

"I had reasons." I sounded defensive.

"Does your mother know?" Rob's eyes continued to bore into me, making me squirm in my seat.

"You are such a dark horse, Emma." Steven hugged himself with delight.

"Mmm, and I can see why you wanted to keep him all to yourself," Toby added.

Rob switched his glare to them.

"Look, I didn't tell anyone, okay?" I said. I'd wanted to. I'd wanted to shout it from the rooftops the day Marco and I married. Funny, isn't it, how things turn out? My memories of our wedding are a bit like Marco himself—vivid, Technicolored and larger than life. God, I'd been so stupid.

Rob snorted and shook his head in disbelief.

"Does Sara know?"

I gave a reluctant nod. Sara had been the one person I had told, the exception to the rule.

A gentle snore came from the corner of the room. Mr. G slid down on his chair and slept, his jowls resting against the wall as he dribbled open-mouthed onto the woodchip.

Rob's expression said it all: hurt that I hadn't told him, confusion about Marco's status in my life, and worst of all betrayal.

Marco stretched out in his chair, his long, denim-clad legs spreading out on to my favorite Ikea rug.

"It's so romantic, a secret wedding." Toby sighed and sipped his tea.

"It wasn't meant to be a secret," I said. "It's just…well, everything happened so fast." It sounded feeble even to my ears. The wedding had taken place over six months ago and getting married wasn't the sort of event you forgot to mention.

"I think," Marco leaned forward in his chair, "Emma looks very tired and we have many things to talk about." His eyes met mine and my heart gave an involuntary squeeze.

"Emma?" Rob still looked dubious about leaving me alone with Marco.

"It's fine, really. I'll see you tomorrow." *And try to explain*, I added silently.

Rob enlisted Toby and Steven to help him get Mr. G back into the car. Toby looked reluctant to leave. I think he hoped for more gossip and I knew he'd be back down in the morning on some pretense so he could find out all the juicy details.

The door closed and Marco and I were alone together for the first time since the aftermath of our wedding. Of all the times I'd imagined meeting him again, I had never pictured it like this. He looked as good as ever—better, even—while I wore a tatty fleece dressing gown with my hair a mess, and I didn't want to think about what my make-up must have looked like.

"My beautiful Emma." He caressed my cheek with a large brown thumb and my heart wobbled. "Why did you run away?"

The rat! He knew full well why I'd done a bunk! I turned away before the touch of his hand undid my irritation or anything else for that matter.

"More to the point, what are you doing here?" I folded my arms and tried to look indifferent.

"To see you, of course. You left in such a hurry, we had no time to talk, for me to explain." He lifted his hands as if to reach out and hold me and I stepped back to avoid his touch.

"You didn't exactly rush." I'd been back in England for over six months and until last night, I hadn't heard a thing from Marco. No phone call, letter, e-mail...not even a Christmas card.

"I didn't know where you were."

Damn, how did he manage to inject that injured tone into his voice?

"I have been so sad without you." He reached out to stroke my hair, twisting it gently around his fingers.

"Don't, Marco." I put my hand on his to stop him. Bad move.

"I love you, Emma."

God knows I wanted to believe him.

"I'm tired, Marco. We'll talk about this in the morning, okay?" It occurred to me that I didn't know where he was staying. Did he plan to spend the night here? Where had he left his luggage?

He leaned forward and kissed my forehead, his lips delicate on my skin. "Of course. I'm sorry."

"Where are you staying?"

"I left my bags at a friend's house." He paused, and I realized he wanted me to ask him to stay. A mental image of Marco lying in bed next to me flickered temptingly through my mind.

"There are some blankets and a pillow if you want to sleep on the settee." I squished the thought flat and bolted for the safety of my bedroom.

✔ ✔ ✔

When I woke the next morning, my mouth felt like the bottom of a birdcage and my eyelids were still glued together as I tried to read the time on my watch. I gathered up what remained of my wits and tried to figure out what had woken me. The overly loud, prolonged ringing of my front doorbell had to be a pretty good clue.

I stumbled through the living room past the hunched up bundle of blankets covering my husband, who still snored blissfully on my sofa. As I yanked open the front door, I half expected to find Toby standing on the mat, eager for a chat. Instead, Sara's partner, Shay, who had been leaning on the door, nearly plowed into me, knocking me to the floor.

Now, ordinarily I'm very fond of Shay. He's great company, good humored and devoted to Sara and Jessie. But why he'd landed in my hall at some un-Godly time on a Sunday morning I wasn't quite sure.

"Hi, Em. Sorry, did I wake you up?"

I tried the family death glare but I don't think I've mastered it.

Shay looked at me, his dark eyes sympathetic. "Late night, huh? You look rough."

I gave up on the glare. "What do you want?"

"I'm looking for Sara and Jessie. I couldn't get any answer at home or on Sara's mobile. I didn't want to trouble Ma-outlaw unless I really had to and I remembered you had the spare key. Any chance of a coffee?"

We trooped back past Marco and into the kitchen.

"Sara and Jess probably stayed at her mum's. Jessie wasn't feeling too great last night. Sara thought she might be teething again."

Shay nodded. "Where's the coffee, Em?" He rummaged through the cabinets. I handed him the jar of instant crystals, though there were only dregs left in it. I needed to add coffee to my list.

Things to do:

Tell mother I'm married.

Get a divorce.

Buy more coffee.

"How did the gig go?" I asked, as he poured hot water from the sink into his cup. Apart from Sara and Jess, Shay's great love in life had to be his music.

"Hard to say. The record company guy didn't show." He took a slurp of coffee and grinned. "How was the auction? Sara's promised me a private showing of her costume."

I wouldn't be giving mine another outing, that was for sure. The very thought of trying to squeeze into it again made me feel sick.

"It seemed to go well. I think Fiona raised quite a lot of money." I told him about Rob and about Fi's row with Niall. A cough came from the sitting room. I'd forgotten to tell him about Marco.

"Another friend of yours, Emma?" Marco appeared in the doorway, and I felt my face burn. He leaned on the doorframe wearing just his white Calvin Klein's and looking as if he slept here every night of the week.

Shay didn't as much as bat an eye—as if he walked in on me with male houseguests in their underpants every day of the week. "Thanks for the key, Emma. I'm sorry I disturbed you, I didn't realize you had company." He nodded at Marco as my husband stepped aside to let him pass. The front door banged shut and a few seconds later, I heard the dull roar of the exhaust on Shay's van accompanied by the 'thump thump" of his stereo as he pulled away.

Marco moved into the kitchen and filled the kettle. My kitchen is much too small to contain me and an almost naked man. Particularly a man I found physically way too attractive, even if my brain told me he wasn't good for me.

"Help yourself to coffee. I'm going to take a shower." Preferably a nice cold one. I didn't bother explaining about Shay. I figured I might as well let Marco think what he liked. I got a bit of a buzz giving him the illusion that I might be considered a desirable and sought-after woman.

Minutes later I stood under the tepid trickle of water passing as my shower and tried to come up with a plan. I needed to talk to Marco. I had to find out if he intended to stay in England. I had to find out if he intended to stay married to me.

After switching off the shower, I wrapped myself in a towel. I sat on the loo seat wanting to bury my head and blub like a two-year-old. The only thing stopping me was the thought that I'd already cried enough tears over Marco to last me a lifetime.

"Emma, are you finished in there? I need to use your bathroom."

I pulled my dressing gown back on and opened the door. He darted past me and pulled the door shut behind him before I had time to answer. From the sound of running water a moment later, I guessed he wasn't wasting any time in using up the last of the hot water. Marco had always been very particular about his hygiene and appearance.

The phone rang as I finished drying my hair. I toyed with the idea of letting the answering machine take it but then, thinking it might be Sara, I picked it up.

"Emma, you have to come and talk to Fiona!" my mother cried. No greeting, no how-do-you-do-today-darling, just this loud, plaintive screech. I moved the receiver away from my ear, wincing.

"What's the matter?" I asked. I don't know what good Mother thought my speaking to Fiona about something would do. Fiona would never listen to anything I said.

"It's Niall. Fiona won't tell me what's happened but she's dreadfully upset."

I'm not being unkind, but Fi only has to break a nail to be dreadfully upset, so I didn't feel unduly concerned.

"Perhaps it's private, Mummy."

She snorted. "Fiona never has secrets from me."

I wriggled guiltily on the edge of the bed. "If she doesn't want to tell you, I'm not sure she'll tell me, either."

"At least you could try. She's locked herself in her bedroom."

I sighed. Fiona always locks herself in her bedroom when she's put-out about something.

"What music is she playing?" When Fi's upset, the music she plays gives the best clue as to how serious the problem is. A mild upset and she plays soul; angry mood and its rock music.

"I don't know. It's some sort of racket."

"Put the phone near her door. Let me listen."

Mother did and I heard the distinctive sound of Bros. "I'll be right over," I said. Fi only dug out her old albums when she felt really, really upset. Bros meant it must be serious. I managed to get Mummy to calm down and told her to put the kettle on.

Marco had dressed and was posed, styling his hair in the sitting room mirror as I walked through to the kitchen to collect my bag and keys.

"I've got to go out for a while. When I get back, we need to talk." I hoped he wouldn't ask me where I intended to go. He might take it into his head to come with me.

"Okay. What time will you be back?" He turned to face me.

"I'm not sure, probably in a couple of hours." I wondered what he planned to do in my absence. I didn't like to tell him to go but I didn't trust him enough to let him stay in my flat while I wasn't there.

"I have to go to my friend's house. I'll see you later."

He left the house with me, kissing my cheek goodbye at the tube as if we made the journey together every day of the week. I'd almost arrived at Mother's house when I realized I didn't know who Marco's friends were or where they lived. Worse still, I had no way of getting in touch with Marco again other than waiting for him to reappear on my doorstep.

A crisis always calls for an emergency remedy, so I'd fortified myself with a Big Mac on the way. I wiped "secret" sauce from the corners of my mouth, hid the wrapper in the bottom of my bag and rang Mother's doorbell. Faint strains of "When Will I Be Famous" floated down the stairs into the hall as Mummy opened the front door.

"Oh, Emma, I'm glad you're here. Perhaps she'll talk to you." She ushered me inside and took my coat, her gaze lingering on my hips. "Have you put on weight, darling?"

I ignored her last comment and followed her into the kitchen. "Do you know what Fi and Niall argued about?"

"She won't say. She keeps crying and saying she can't forgive him."

The last time Fiona wouldn't forgive Niall it had been because he'd called a napkin a serviette and told her dinner guests she'd bought the pudding from Harrods' food hall. He had been in the doghouse for weeks over that misdemeanor.

I carried a cup of tea upstairs and rapped cautiously on Fiona's door. She didn't actually live at home any more, but whenever she felt distressed, she fled back to Mother's and took up residence in her old bedroom.

"I don't want to talk."

"It's me, Emma. I brought you a cup of tea."

The door opened a crack and she peered out. I held up the cup.

"I've got a big bag of chocolate buttons in my pocket," I added. I'd picked up a packet of Fiona's favourite comfort food from the station kiosk while waiting for my train. The door opened fully and I went into Fiona's room. She looked awful. Her eyes were red and blotchy from crying and her hair hadn't seen the straightening iron.

"You look dreadful," I said. "What's happened?"

She plopped down on the bed and buried her face in her handkerchief. "Oh, Emma, it's Niall..." She sniffed. "He doesn't want to marry me any more!" The end of her sentence came out as a wail. I sat down on the bed next to her, placed the tea down on the dresser and put my arm around her shoulders.

"It's probably pre-wedding nerves." I couldn't take in what she'd said.

"No, it's not. He doesn't love me." Big sobs shook her body.

"Well, did you argue or something? People often say things they don't mean when they argue." I didn't know what else to offer her. I'd expected a tiff over the number of bridesmaids or the price of the wedding favors, not to hear the wedding had been called off altogether!

Fiona blew her nose. "We were discussing the seating plan and he threw it up in the air and…" She began to cry again. "Oh, Emma, he sounded so nasty!"

I passed her a box of tissues from the dresser. "Well, doesn't that prove what I was saying? He's feeling the stress of all the preparations."

She shook her head fiercely. "When we went to the Crystal Foundation auction, he said he'd been doing a lot of thinking." She paused. "Then he said he'd realized we were making a terrible mistake and he didn't love me anymore."

I gave her a hug. Damn Niall—how dare he do this to Fiona! I know she has her faults but, blow it all, she's still my sister and she loves the idiot.

"What am I going to do, Em? I'll be a laughing stock."

"I can't believe this is happening, Fi. It all seems so strange." I couldn't believe my ears. Niall's never struck me as the impulsive type. Something must have happened to trigger it off. The wedding was all arranged, the organist booked, flowers ordered, everything. I opened the bag of chocolate buttons and popped one in my mouth, needing the sugar.

"You have to talk to him, Fi," I said. "I'm sure you can work things out."

She sniffed and smacked my fingers out of the way before plunging her hand into the bag of chocolate. "I can't, it's too upsetting." She stuffed a pile of buttons into her mouth. "Can't you talk to him, Em? See if he'll listen to you."

43

I started to feel like a U.N. peace envoy. How come I'd been voted the great negotiator all of a sudden?

"What am I going to say?" Fiona is so much like Mother sometimes it's scary. Apparently, I take after Daddy. This, according to Mummy, is not a good thing.

"I don't know!" she cried. "See if you can find out why he doesn't want to marry me anymore! There has to be a reason. I've thought and thought all night but couldn't come up with anything." Fiona leaned towards the dressing table mirror and frantically examined her face for wrinkles. "Oh God, Emma, look at my skin! It's because I'm losing my looks, isn't it?"

There was no answer to that. I left her slapping on fifty-pound-a-jar face cream like it had gone out of fashion and went back downstairs to report to Mother. I found her in the kitchen, industriously cleaning the sink.

"How much did you manage to overhear?" She didn't bother to deny it. We both knew she'd been lurking in the hall with her ears flapping like Dumbo.

"Not a lot. You had the door closed."

"Niall's dumped Fiona," I said. "She says the wedding's off."

"Nonsense!" Mother said. "I'm sure this is all a storm in a teacup. It's probably pre-wedding nerves. Niall and Fiona are a perfect match."

"That's what I said."

She gave me one of her looks. Apparently, having me think the same thing as her wasn't reassuring.

"She needs to talk to him." Mummy peeled off her yellow rubber gloves and draped them over the tap.

"She doesn't want to. She asked me to instead."

From the expression on her face, Mother didn't think much of this idea. "Well, I suppose it's worth a try," she said after a moment. "Poor Fiona has always been highly strung. I expect she'd find it too upsetting." She paused for a moment, her face thoughtful. "In any case, it never looks good to be seen to be running after a man."

I wondered if this might be a good time to tell her about Marco. There would never be a brilliant time to tell her I'd married a Caribbean beach barman in secret over six months ago and now he'd arrived here in England wanting to meet his in-laws.

"Mummy," I began. "I need to talk to you about—"

The doorbell rang and she bustled off into the hall calling, "Tell me in a minute!" over her shoulder.

The sound of voices carried into the kitchen, I wondered if it might be Niall coming to tell Fiona he'd made a terrible mistake, prepared to beg her forgiveness with a huge bouquet of roses.

"You'd better come in," I heard my mother say. "Emma's here."

A huge bunch of flowers had arrived all right, but the man carrying them wasn't Niall. Rob looked a bit sheepish when he saw me sitting on one of Mummy's brushed aluminum Conran stools.

"It's so thoughtful of you to bring Fiona some flowers, Robert, dear," Mother said. "She's a little upset this morning so she's stayed in her room. I'm sure she and Niall will sort things out, though. It's a touch of pre-wedding nerves."

Mummy knows how Rob feels about my sister—we all do—and while she's very fond of him, she's never fancied him as husband material for Fiona. I think she hoped he'd transfer his affections to me, but Rob's never seen me in that way.

Rob raised a questioning eyebrow and tapped his ring finger with his free hand while Mummy had her back turned to me, asking me silently if I'd broken the news of my marriage. I shook my head and mouthed a silent "no." He gave me a disapproving look.

Mother turned around in time to catch me glowering back at him. She pursed her lips and sent me a 'don't be rude to guests" death glare. I wanted to ask Rob how he'd heard about Fiona and Niall's split but I didn't dare while Mummy might hear.

"I'll go up and see if Fiona's feeling better," Rob said as he took the vase of flowers Mother had finished arranging. "Isn't there something you wanted to tell your mum, Emma?"

He disappeared into the hall before I had the opportunity to kill him. Mother fixed me with another look. My stomach rolled with the same sick feeling I used to get whenever I had to present her with my school report card.

"Well, Emma?" she asked.

Chapter Four

All credit to Mummy, she took my news on the chin. Rob came straight back downstairs when he heard the scream and helped Mother into the lounge while I poured her a large gin and tonic.

"I always said you took after your father." She took a fortifying gulp of alcohol. "Well, I suppose I'd better meet my new son-in-law, hadn't I? You can bring him for dinner tomorrow night, Emma."

She fixed me with the look and I knew there would be no point arguing. I hoped Marco would agree to come. Always assuming I could find him, of course.

Fiona couldn't be coaxed from her room to see Rob, so he gave up trying and offered me a lift. He continued the theme of Mummy's lecture in the car on the way home. The paintwork on his car was a sore subject; he insisted Mr. G had scratched it and since it had been me who'd invited Greenback along, then it had to be my fault.

"How did you know about Fiona and Niall?" I needed to change the subject away from me, Marco and the merits of car polish.

The back of Rob's neck turned pink, a dead giveaway that he had something to hide. "Niall told me."

"Niall told you he'd called off the wedding? When?"

"Last night at the auction. He took me to one side and asked me to keep an eye on Fiona as he had something to tell her that she wasn't going to like."

"What else did he say?"

47

The back of Rob's neck turned crimson. "He just said he'd been trying to talk to Fiona for days."

That sounded more like Niall, but I felt sure Rob knew something more that he hadn't told me. He's not very good at keeping secrets, and perhaps deep in my subconscious, this had been one of the reasons I hadn't told him about Marco.

"And what had he been trying to tell her for days?" Whatever this big secret was, I was determined to wheedle it from Rob. If I didn't know what had changed Niall's mind about marrying my sister, then I couldn't set about changing it back again, could I?

"He didn't say exactly," Rob mumbled, making a great show of slowing down for a pedestrian crossing.

"But you know why he's called the wedding off, don't you?" I persisted.

He swerved suddenly into a clear space at the side of the road and jerked the handbrake up. He wouldn't look me in the face.

"Promise you won't go mad."

"Why would I go mad? Oh, my God—he's gay, isn't he? He's selling drugs? He's—"

"Emma! Shut up!" Rob raked his hand through his dark hair, leaving it sticking up in spiky little tufts like a militant hedgehog. "Niall's met someone else."

"No! You're joking!" Fiona never left Niall alone for long enough for him to find another woman. He was the kind of man who needed someone to pick out his underpants; he'd never have the initiative to meet someone else on his own, surely.

Rob shook his head. "It's true. He planned to tell Fiona after the auction but they had a row and well…" He shrugged.

"Do you know who she is?" I tried to think of likely candidates. The daughter of one of his mother's friends perhaps? Niall's mother had always appeared to be nice to Fiona but I got the impression she would prefer someone more blue-blooded. Niall's mother is a terrible snob.

Rob shot me a glance. "Do you know Glenda?"

"Niall's secretary?"

Rob nodded.

Glenda, who looked as genuine and realistic as the plastic rubber tree standing in the corner of Niall's consulting room. Glenda, with her brassy blonde highlights and the wire-framed specs. Miss Hygienically Polished Frosty Knickers. I'd never liked Glenda.

"Niall's fallen in love with her?" It didn't sound any more believable when I said it out loud. Fiona would be devastated. Fiona would kill her.

Rob squirmed on his seat. "There's something else."

I didn't need to be Sherlock Holmes to guess what had to be coming next. "She's pregnant, isn't she?"

He glanced at me. "Sorry."

So, my sister's fiancé had been playing doctor-and-nurse with his secretary. "That sneaky, conniving, two-faced rat," I said. "How long has it been going on?"

"Since Bonfire Night." Rob coughed apologetically.

Fiona had been ill on Bonfire Night and she'd missed the big fireworks party and barbeque Niall's mother held every year for family and friends. I'd assumed Niall had gone alone, but instead, it appeared he'd taken Glenda.

"Oh, hell! Quick, get down!" Rob grabbed me and tried to push me down behind the dashboard of the car. He ducked next to me and tried to look inconspicuous.

"Who are we hiding from?" I hissed, my face squashed against my knees and the peak of my knit cap all bent up. I found traveling in a sports car with the top down did your hair no favors anyway and being shoved under the dash without warning definitely didn't help.

"It's Gilly. She's seen us. She's coming this way!"

I bit my tongue and didn't point out that she would have to be blind to miss seeing a six-foot-two-inch male trying to hide in a roofless, low-slung, distinctive car like Rob's in the middle of winter.

"Rob, darling!"

Calvin Klein's Obsession perfume reached us a fraction of a second before she did. I sat upright, took off my cap and tried to act nonchalant.

"I can't wait for our date," Gilly said. "We'll have to meet up and discuss the arrangements." She blanked me completely. I tidied my hair back into a ponytail, folded my arms and tried to keep from freezing to death while Rob made non-committal noises next to me.

Gilly prattled on; she was quite pretty if you like the doe-eyed, besotted look. Her clothes were expensive and her boots were to die for. You don't live with fashionistas like my mother and sister for years without learning something about clothes. She even had the obligatory rat-sized mini-pooch wearing a little Burberry check coat inside her handbag.

I could see why Rob had dumped her, though. The girl was completely crazy. And boy, could she talk. It felt like being verbally mugged for fifteen minutes. Rob finally managed to shut her up and we escaped, leaving her blowing kisses after us from the curb.

My nose had turned blue. "Why is the roof down? I'm frozen."

"The mechanism jammed last night when we put Greenback in the car."

I couldn't say anything to that otherwise I would end up spending the rest of the day feeling guilty and passing wrenches to Rob while he took the roof to bits.

I spent the remainder of the journey simultaneously worrying about what I would say to Fiona and if our local hospital knew how to treat frostbite. It wasn't until we pulled to a halt outside my flat that I remembered I had other things to worry about.

The light was on in my lounge and I knew I'd turned it off before I'd left. I'm one of those people who obsessively checks switches and locks and things. When I'd been at University, I'd had a bad experience with a tumble drier, something to do with not emptying the lint collector. The firemen that came out were very nice and even returned for a party I'd held the same night but it still wasn't an experience I wanted to repeat.

The front door opened as we came up the path and Toby stepped out, a look of suppressed excitement all over his face. This was not good.

"Emma, I tried to get you on your mobile but you've got it switched off. So I hope it's all right, but we've given your husband the spare key to your flat so he can move his stuff in."

It's also never good when someone tells you bad news and smiles whilst they do it. It's like watching David Blaine doing one of his magic tricks; your eyes tell you one thing while your brain tells you something completely different.

Rob muttered under his breath and Toby stood there beaming at me as if waiting for me to pat him on the head or throw him a stick.

"What time did Marco get back?" Too flipping quickly if you asked me, but I tried to sound casual. Rob appeared to be preparing to go into attack mode again, while Toby, on the other hand, looked smitten by my wayward husband's charm. Someone needed to stay calm and in control, so I guessed that person should be me.

"He got here about an hour ago. We helped him carry his cases in."

I walked inside the communal hall, Rob hot on my heels. The front door of my flat stood ajar and two large blue suitcases and a holdall blocked the way into the lounge.

The alien smell of home cooking filled the air. I don't cook. I can defrost, microwave and make toast, but haute cuisine isn't one of my talents. In fact, shopping isn't one of my talents, either (at least not for groceries) so I guessed Marco must have found time to shop as well as collecting his stuff.

I stepped over the cases; Steven sat in the armchair nearest to the door drinking beer and chatting to Marco. The dull roar of a rugby crowd came from the television in the corner.

"Hey, babe, we were talking about you." Marco stepped forward to kiss my cheek in a practiced move. The kiss undid me; I swear I had been ready to slap the man for his sheer brass neck but somehow the touch of his lips on my cheek sent all my thought processes haywire.

"Supper's cooking. It'll be ready in about half an hour." He cupped my face tenderly between his hands. "You feel cold. Take your coat off and sit down by the fire."

Dazed, I shrugged off my jacket and sat down. Rob immediately bagged the other armchair, leaving Toby to hang about on the other side of the settee.

The loud pop of a cork sounded from the kitchen and Marco reappeared, brandishing glasses of bubbly, which he handed out to everyone, although Rob's sour expression was enough to send the champagne flat.

"Please raise your glasses in a toast to Emma and me, and to the future." Marco stood behind me, his hand resting on my shoulder. The heat from his fingers spread to warm my soul as I sipped my champagne.

Steven and Toby cooed like a pair of turtle doves and gazed soppily into one another's eyes. Rob stood up and muttered some excuse about having to go, then he pushed past Marco, put his glass in the kitchen and left. I didn't follow him. Maybe I should have but I didn't know what to say.

I took an extra big gulp of champagne and choked as the bubbles went up my nose. Marco appeared to be intent on moving into my life again. From the way his hand moved to massage my shoulder and sent little shivers of delight through my body, he was intent on moving back into my bed, too.

Things to Do:

Buy condoms.

Get rid of Steven and Toby.

Find my La Perla knickers.

Steven and Toby picked up on the vibes emanating from our end of the settee and reluctantly made their excuses. The front door hadn't quite closed behind them before Marco slid onto the couch next to me.

I vaguely remember him taking the empty glass from my hand before his lips claimed mine and any coherent thoughts flew right out of my head.

We never got around to eating whatever it was Marco had cooked. I threw the dishes away the next day because the black bits on the bottom wouldn't budge, no matter how hard I scrubbed.

Instead, we finished off the rest of the champagne and ate take-away pizza in bed, which sounds nice but makes the bed clothes crumby.

Curled up in bed next to Marco with my head on his bare chest, as I listened to the rain pelt against the windows, I felt very snug and very smug.

✔ ✔ ✔

I wanted to stay home the next day and spend the time in bed with Marco, but instead, he announced he had some business to attend to and had to leave early.

He left before me, so I stayed in bed for a few more minutes to revel in the smell of the sheets from his cologne and the warmth where his body had been next to mine. Even discovering he'd used all the hot water for his shower couldn't dent my good mood as I set off in the rain for the office.

When I arrived, Greenback was out; he'd gone to check on the staff in one of his other shops, which meant he would be out of my hair for the day. It also meant Rob was in charge. Normally that meant we would have a laugh and lark about a bit more than we would if Mr. G was about. But Rob looked as if he'd sucked on a lemon all night. I thought he'd be as happy as a dog with two tails now that Fiona and Niall weren't an item any more, but he seemed to have other things on his mind.

That reminded me; I needed to call Fiona and see how she'd been coping. Then I could pave the way ready to break the news about Glenda so it didn't come as too much of a shock.

"You're late, Emma." Rob dumped a pile of post on my counter.

"I know." I did my best to smother a yawn.

He looked at me.

"Sorry, I didn't get much sleep last night."

Rob's expression turned even more sour.

"I can live without hearing the details of your love life, Emma." He stalked off into Mr. G's office.

The repairs on his car must have been worse than I thought; he wasn't usually this crabby, even in the morning.

The shop always went quiet before lunchtime on Mondays which gave me a chance to catch up on my paperwork and sneak in a call to Fiona. She had decided to stay at Mummy's.

"How can I show my face? It's so embarrassing. I've had to call so many people and cancel all sorts of arrangements."

"It's better to find out about Niall now though, Fi. It would have been worse to find out after the wedding." Uh, oh, that didn't come out right.

"Find what out after the wedding?"

"Um, that you weren't suited." The hole grew deeper; maybe I shouldn't have rung Fiona after all.

"Huh! Well, you're a fine one to talk. I'm not the one who got married and kept it a big secret for six months!"

"I know and I'm sorry I didn't tell you but I had my reasons at the time. Listen, Fi…about Niall. I'm really not sure it's "

Fiona cut me short. "The rat bag! The bloody rat bag! He's sent me a text to ask for his engagement ring back!" She hung up on me with a sharp click.

I delved in the bottom drawer of my desk for some comfort food, then remembered I'd finished off the last of my secret stash of biscuits on Saturday. The weather was absolutely miserable now outside, so dark it looked more like night-time than midday as the rain pelted down against the windows.

I hoped Marco wasn't out in the wet; he didn't like the cold or rain. Amazingly, he'd agreed to come to Mother's for dinner with me that night. I wasn't looking forward to it at all. Fiona would either still be spitting mad at Niall or sobbing into her soup. Mummy would give Marco the third degree, and if Rob was still in the same mood as this morning, he'd just sit there and glower at everyone.

I wasn't sure why Mummy had invited Rob. I think she must have thought he might distract Fiona or redress the balance of a mostly female table.

Things To Do

God, I needed some chocolate.

The little palm trees on my tropical island screen saver waved their branches enticingly at me, sending me into a lovely daydream involving me, Marco and a secluded private beach.

A frantic knock on the plate glass of the shop window got my attention. Sara huddled under an umbrella outside with Jessie in the buggy, drenched to the skin by the pouring rain.

Once I reassured her Mr. G was safely out of the way, she squelched her way into the shop. The water ran off Jessie's buggy raincover in great puddles onto the floor.

"Shay said he met Marco at your flat yesterday." She collapsed her umbrella, sending another deluge onto the laminate and sat herself down on the chair in front of my console.

"He turned up out of the blue. I didn't even know he was in the country."

Sara stared at me suspiciously for a moment, then leaned forward to undo Jessie's cover. "Well, what does he want? And how did he find you?"

"I'm not sure. He says he loves me and wants us to make a go of things."

Sara snorted. "That's rich! Where's he been for the last six months?" She folded Jessie's cover back and adjusted the sleeping baby's blanket. "He didn't seem very interested in making a go of things when you found him in someone else's bed the day after your wedding, did he? Or when he stole your savings and Rob had to lend you the money to get home?"

I shifted on my seat. "I think he's changed, Sara. He seems to be sincere about getting things right between us."

She pulled a face. "Emma, this is the man who lied to you, cheated on you, stole your money and hasn't bothered getting in touch with you for months!"

The worst thing was, I knew everything she said was true but when I was with Marco, none of it seemed important. Besides, we'd talked a lot last night, in between doing other more interesting things.

"What are you going to do, Em?" Sara's blue eyes bored into mine.

"He's moved in."

"Blimey!" Sara's not often lost for words.

"I'm taking him to meet Mummy tonight. She's summoned us to dinner."

"Is he going to go?"

"Yes." I must admit I felt a bit smug when I told her Marco wanted to meet my mother. Sara had been so negative about Marco's reappearance, it felt nice to be able to say something good about him.

"Blimey!" Sara's vocabulary had deserted her, it seemed, with the news of Marco's return. She kept her eyes fixed on my face. Sara might be my best friend, but she also does a good job as a human lie detector. I know Marco is a rat but he's my rat, or at least he says he is.

I changed the subject and told her about Fiona and Niall's break-up. She didn't look surprised.

"At least you won't have to wear that ghastly bridesmaid frock or have to put up with Niall's mother calling you 'poor Emily' anymore."

She had a point. I hadn't thought about that. Niall's mother always treated me as if I was a bit simple; she even asked Fi once if I was adopted. Fiona didn't tell me about this—I overheard the old bat asking.

Granted, Fiona and I don't look like sisters. She's tall, blonde and supermodelish while I'm short, dark and not. So I can see why Niall's mother might have been a bit skeptical about my genes, but it still hurt.

"I can't believe Niall was stupid enough to ask for the ring back," Sara said.

"Or brave enough. The only way he'll get that rock back from Fiona is to amputate her finger." We were both silent for a moment, as we contemplated Niall's fate when Fiona caught up with him and learned the full story.

The shop door opened and more customers came in. Sara pulled the raincover back over Jessie's pram and stood up, ready to leave.

"Give me a call and let me know what happens." She swiveled the buggy around. "And Emma, be careful. Good sex isn't everything, you know."

The young city stockbroker-type who'd come into the shop out of the rain leered at me as he opened the door for Sara to leave.

I didn't get a lunch break until three o'clock. Rob stayed in Mr. G's office and I'd been too busy with people desperate to get away for Easter to remind him that I hadn't eaten.

Still, the stockbroker chap spent a lot of money booking himself and his girlfriend on a trip to the Far East and I needed the commission. Never mind that he stared down my blouse whenever he thought I wouldn't notice.

Thankfully the rain had stopped by the time I finally escaped down to the deli. There wasn't much food left and the staff had started to wipe the counters down when I got there. Once I'd scarfed down half a slightly dry Mexican wrap, I switched my mobile on. I'd had it on charge all morning; the battery had been completely flat for the last few days, so it wasn't any wonder Toby and Steven hadn't managed to get me yesterday when Marco had moved his stuff in.

Sure enough, all their missed messages popped up, one by one.

"Emma, Marco's here with all his cases. When are you coming back? Give us a call." Toby.

"Emma, would it be okay if we let Marco into your flat? Ring us back." Steven.

"Emma, we've let Marco in with the spare key." Toby again.

"Emma, I'll see you back at the flat later. Love you, baby." Marco's voice, deep and unexpected, sent a pleasurable thrill down my spine. My day suddenly seemed less crappy and I still had a smile on my face when I got back to the office and discovered Mr. G had arrived.

Chapter Five

Rob sat behind my console with Mr. G wedged into one of the customer seats opposite him. The shop was empty; the two girls who work Mondays with me are both part-time and finish early so they can collect their kids from school.

I could tell from the sudden silence as I walked in that they had been discussing me. Mr. G began to shuffle files and looked very Greenbackish while Rob simply appeared uncomfortable.

"Ah, Emma. Nice lunch?" Mr. G asked. "Splendid, splendid. Most interesting evening, Saturday. I'm looking forward to meeting your husband properly tonight. I'm afraid I may have had a little too much champagne at the auction. Alcohol disagrees with my blood pressure medication." He spluttered to a halt with a nervous laugh.

I know Mummy had received two nasty surprises in the last twenty-four hours but, honestly, what was she thinking of by inviting my boss to what might well shape up to be the most awful dinner party of all time?

"It was very kind of your mother to invite me to dinner, Emma. Rob, here's going too, I gather."

Rob didn't say anything; he busied himself with pretending to look up the cost and availability of flights to Alaska in an effort not to get involved.

"Well, that's all...erm...splendid, Emma." Mr. G made a feeble attempt at sounding hearty before vacating his seat with remarkable speed for a man of his size. He bolted for the safety of his private office.

Rob avoided my eyes. Instead, the in-flight catering arrangements of Air Alaska continued to exert a morbid fascination.

"What's going on?" I moved around the back of my console and blocked his exit so he couldn't make a run for it.

"Nothing! We're concerned for you, Em, that's all." He half-turned on my swivel chair, still somewhat engrossed by the views of Alaska's unspoiled wilderness.

I grabbed the arms of the chair and spun him around to face me, forcing him to tear his attention away from pictures of white-water rafting in the great outdoors.

"Well, don't be! I've had a lecture from Sara and I'm sure Mummy will have plenty more to add tonight. Marco and I have a lot of issues to sort out and, yes, we've had our problems, but a bit of support from my friends wouldn't go amiss."

I straightened up and let go of the chair. I know Marco's been a git in the past but if I could give him another chance, then surely so could everyone else. They hadn't even got to know him properly yet.

Rob raked his hands through his hair. "Fair enough, Emma."

I'd expected a fight, so his acknowledgment that I might have a point took the wind out of my sails a bit.

"I called Fiona earlier." Perhaps the mention of my sister's name might cheer him up and stop him meddling in my love life.

"How is she?" He looked concerned.

"Spitting mad. Niall text-messaged her this morning and asked for the engagement ring back."

"You didn't tell her about Glenda, did you?"

"Not yet, but we need to tell her soon. It'll be awful if she hears it from somebody else." I wasn't looking forward to breaking the news to Fi.

Fiona has a terrible temper. Don't get me wrong—I think Niall deserves all he has coming to him when Fi does catch up with him but she deserved to be told properly about his infidelity.

"She might have found out already if she's spoken to Niall," Rob said.

"Do you think he'd tell her? He didn't have the guts to do it when he gave her all that crap about cancelling the wedding because they weren't right for each other."

Somehow someone who can't ask for his engagement ring back face-to-face isn't likely to announce to the fiancée they've cheated on that they've got their secretary up the spout. At least, I didn't think so.

"Niall wouldn't, but Glenda would."

I hadn't thought of that. Of course, if Niall's mobile was switched off, then Fiona would be bound to try his office. The implications hit both of us at the same time and we stared at each other in silence. "Call her," Rob suggested.

I fished about in my handbag for my mobile, dislodging a wad of old receipts and empty cheeseburger wrappers in the process. Rob sighed and picked them up off the floor while I dialled Fi's number and waited for her to answer.

"It's turned off," I said. "She's got it on voice mail. Now what, Dangermouse?"

"Nothing we can do, Penfold. We'll just have to wait until tonight to find out what's happened." Rob's always very practical in a crisis.

Mr. G popped his head out of his office door. "Can I see you for a moment, Rob? Oh, and Emma, by the way, does your mother prefer red wine or white?"

"Red." He was out to impress Mummy all right. It wouldn't surprise me if he turned up tonight with a box of chocolates and a bunch of flowers.

For once, I finished work on time and Rob stayed behind with Mr. G to help lock up. I called the flat on my way home to see if Marco was back, but the answering machine kicked in so I assumed he wasn't there.

Most of the shops had end-of-sale final reductions and I couldn't resist a really cute strappy top in Monsoon's window or a 'to die for' pair of half-price shoes in the store near the tube station.

The shoes squeezed my toes a bit when I tried them on, but I figured that was because my feet were still sore from Saturday and anyway, they were such a bargain, it would be silly not to buy them. I would just have to remember not to walk long distances in them.

Bargain shopping takes time, so when I let myself into the flat, I was later than I'd intended to be. Marco still wasn't home. He'd unpacked all his clothes into my wardrobe (which was a bit of a squash), and his flight bag still cluttered up the hall. I tripped over it when I let myself in.

It contained something heavy, judging by the rapidly-developing row of bruises on my shin. If it was duty-free booze then I could use a drink. Fortification with alcohol looked likely to be the only way I would survive dinner at Mummy's that night while retaining any degree of sanity.

Marco and I had finished all the champagne the other night and the dregs of white wine in the fridge door that had been there so long it had nearly turned to vinegar. A bottle of duty-free gin would be a very nice find.

I opened the zipper along the top of the bag and couldn't see any bottles inside, only a layer of carrier bags. I delved down under them. Whatever weighed so much had been wrapped carefully into brick-shaped bundles and sealed up with duct tape.

There had to be a perfectly innocent explanation. It couldn't be what it looked like. Marco wouldn't leave something criminal like a stash of drugs right where I would fall over them, would he? I had to be rational about this. This was my husband.

The sound of a key in the front door lock made me jump and I pushed the mystery parcel back inside the bag and scuttled into the lounge in the nick of time.

Marco strolled in. "You not ready yet, babe? I thought we had to be at your mum's in an hour." He flicked a glance at his watch before stooping to kiss me on the mouth.

"Um, no, I just got in. I did a spot of shopping on the way home." My heart pounded like mad and guilt burnt in bright red spots on my cheeks. I shouldn't have looked in his bag. "So how was your day?"

"Good." He grinned and kissed me again. "You'd better get moving Emma, or we'll be late and I don't want to make a bad impression." He hustled me out of the lounge and into the bathroom.

I heard him move around the flat as I turned the taps on. Whatever was inside those packages couldn't be too suspicious, could it? Or otherwise he wouldn't have left the bag out in the hall—and he must have carried it through customs. The parcels probably contained something stupid like his boxing trophies. I had obviously watched too many episodes of *Murder She Wrote*.

It didn't take me long to get changed. I could set world records for the speed in which I can get ready to go out. A lifetime of running late means I can change clothes and re-do my make-up in five minutes flat.

"…yeah, man, no problem. I'll take care of it tomorrow. Later, okay." Marco snapped his mobile shut as soon as I entered the bedroom.

"Who was that?" On the one hand I really wanted to know, but on the other hand, after finding the packages, I felt a bit scared.

"I'll tell you about it later, babe. Let's just say I've got some good news for us." He reached inside the wardrobe and pulled out a jacket. "Come on, let's go and you can introduce me to your family."

Marco refused to tell me any more about his news even though I begged and pleaded all the way to Mummy's house. His expression darkened when the taxi stopped and he noticed Rob's beloved rust heap parked in the road.

"I didn't know your friend would be here tonight."

"Mummy asked him to try and cheer Fiona up. She's devastated over splitting up from Niall."

I slipped my arm through Marco's, pinned a smile on my face and waited for Mummy to answer the bell, but Fiona opened the door instead.

"Emma. And this must be Marco!"

I was left to stand on the front doorstep with my mouth open while my sister grabbed my husband and pulled him into the house.

"I thought you said she was devastated?" Marco muttered when I caught up with them in the hallway.

Fiona must have better powers of recovery than I suspected. Her hair had been restored to its normal, glimmering blonde perfection. Somehow she'd found time for a manicure, and I didn't remember seeing that particular dress before.

Marco seemed impressed as we followed her into the dining room. Mummy stood by the fireplace, gin in hand, as she talked to Rob and Mr. G.

"I see marriage hasn't improved your timekeeping, Emma." She gave Marco a swift assessing glance, and stepped forward to greet him with a kiss on the cheek. "So, this is my new son-in-law."

"I'm delighted to meet you, Mrs. Morgan," Marco said.

Mummy raised an eyebrow. "I doubt that, but welcome to the family. Help yourselves to a drink; I need to check on dinner."

Fiona poured large splashes of gin into Mummy's Waterford crystal glasses. She waved a bottle of tonic water over the tops with careless abandon before handing a glass to Marco and another one to me.

"Cheers and good luck to both of you." We all clinked glasses and Fiona swallowed the contents of hers down in a single swallow, then poured herself another one.

"That's better!" she declared. "Now Marco, come and sit next to me and tell me how you and Emma met." Fiona settled herself down on the settee, crossed her long slim legs in front of her and patted the space next to her invitingly.

"I'll go and see if your mother needs any help." Mr. G excused himself and disappeared off toward the kitchen.

"How many drinks has Fi had?" I muttered to Rob.

"I'm not sure, but that's her third since I've been here."

I glanced over at the sofa where my sister sat chatting animatedly while Marco hung on her every word. I took a generous swig from my own glass. It looked as if it would be a very long evening.

"Fiona knows about Glenda," Rob warned.

"Oh, hell! Since when?"

Mr. G wombled back in, carrying a tray of nibbles. "Dinner will be ready in about twenty minutes."

Rob and I grabbed a bite to eat while Fi and Marco continued their conversation without a pause.

"She's taken the news better than I thought she would." I tried to keep a snippy note out of my voice. My green-eyed jealousy monster had raised its head at Marco's blatant male appreciation of Fiona's legs.

"Don't be so sure."

The warning note in Rob's voice stopped me mid-bite. "What do you mean?"

Rob sighed and shot a worried glance in Fi's direction. "Well, you know Niall asked for the ring back and Fiona planned to try and track him down?"

"Yes."

"She found Glenda at the office."

My eyes widened. "And?"

"That's all I know—except she's not wearing the ring any more and she's been out shopping." He took a sip of his drink.

"She gave the ring back and went shopping?" I asked. "No scene? No attempt to stuff Glenda into the paper shredder, nothing?" I could see what he meant. This wasn't like Fiona and she had certainly been out for Niall's blood when she'd received his text.

"I don't know what happened. When I asked her, she smiled at me and said everything was under control."

My drink went down the wrong way and Rob thumped my back. Fiona was up to something and if I was Niall, I'd be worried.

"Dinner's ready, come and sit down. Marco you sit here next to me." Mother bustled in and shooed us all toward the table where the starters were ready.

Fiona wobbled on her heels a little when she stood up. "Whoops." She had to steady herself on Marco's arm until she reached her seat.

Mr. G sat on the other side of Mother with Fiona next to him. I ended up seated in between Marco and Rob.

Mummy is a superb cook and so is Fiona. I think it may be another genetic trait I missed out on. I would have enjoyed the delicious goat-cheese starter much better, though, if Mummy hadn't given Marco a grilling all the way through the first course the Spanish inquisition would have been proud of.

Marco took it quite well. One thing that working in a bar teaches you is the art of making conversation with anyone and Marco's a good talker.

Finally all the plates were empty and Mummy stopped the interrogation. Fi stood up to help take the plates into the kitchen and fetch the second course but teetered on her heels again and sat back down in her chair with a thump.

"Allow me, Charlotte." Mr. G leapt to his feet and accompanied Mummy into the kitchen. Fi shrugged and helped herself to another glass of wine from the bottle on the table.

"So what are your plans for the future, Marco?" Rob leaned back in his chair and took a sip of his drink. I don't think Rob likes Marco. Rob's always been a bit protective, kind of like a big brother and I think his ego took a dent when he learned about my marriage.

Marco didn't look up from fiddling with his dessert spoon.

"I've got a few business options coming up with some friends of mine, so Emma and I can make a proper start to our married life." He flicked a glance at me and my tummy flipped over.

"That's nice. Marriage is a wonderful thing." Fiona beamed glassily at us, and even though I knew she was pissed, I wondered if she'd lost her mind.

"Fiona, are you okay?" Rob asked.

"Never better." She downed the rest of her drink and refilled the wine glass again, spilling a few drops onto Mummy's antique lace tablecloth.

Mr. G came in with the second course, followed by Mummy with tureens of vegetables. Rob and Marco both got up to help them and ended up having a mini tug of war over the sauce boat.

Eventually we all settled back down again. We politely passed one another the serving spoons and complimented Mummy on the food.

"Is that a new dress, Fiona?" I felt sure I'd seen an identical model in one of the snooty little boutiques I'd visited on my way home and it had carried a very hefty price tag.

Fi looked pleased with herself. "Yes, I couldn't resist it. I did a spot of shopping this afternoon."

Rob raised an eyebrow warningly at me.

"I thought you said Niall had texted you? What did he say?" I couldn't help myself; I had to ask.

Mummy clattered her knife loudly onto her plate with disapproval.

Fiona shrugged, picked up her wine glass, and took a sip. "Oh, I had the dubious pleasure of cornering his floozy." She contemplated her immaculate nails with a satisfied smile.

A bad feeling settled in the pit of my stomach. "Did you give the ring back?"

I only just heard Mummy's indignant intake of breath. I was too intent on Fiona. She had loved her engagement ring.

"Kind of." She looked like the cat that'd swallowed the canary.

"What do you mean, kind of?" Rob took the words right out of my mouth.

"Well, it was a very valuable ring and if I'd seen him personally, then naturally I would have given it to him."

We all stopped eating and watched Fi with a kind of morbid fascination.

"I could hardly entrust something so expensive to a mere secretary to pass on to him," Fiona continued. "So what could I do?" She lifted her chin defiantly and smiled at us.

"What did you do?" Marco leaned forward and looked into my sister's eyes. Fiona blinked and shook her head a little as if to clear it of some of the alcohol she'd drunk.

"Well, I didn't know what to do at first. I mean, I couldn't get hold of Niall and it wasn't something I could pop in the post."

Mummy put down her knife to reach along the table and squeeze Fi's hand.

"Then as I was walking along looking for a cab, I saw it. The perfect solution." She brightened momentarily.

"What solution?" I was frightened to ask. What on earth had she done?

Fiona beamed triumphantly. "I pawned it!"

Chapter Six

We all gaped open-mouthed at Fiona.

"I saw one of those shops that have a sign in the window that says they give you money for jewellery or electrical things" she said. "So I took in the ring and they gave me the money."

A low appreciative rumble of laughter came from Marco's direction, so I kicked him hard on the shin.

"I posted the receipt through Niall's letterbox," Fiona continued. "The man said they would keep the ring for thirty days and if it's not collected, they'll sell it."

"And you went shopping with the money?" I wasn't as shocked as I should have been. Fiona has a ruthless streak.

"Oh, not just that money!" she exclaimed. "Gosh, this dress on its own cost more than that. No, Niall gave me some credit cards on his accounts when we were engaged, so I used them."

"How much did you spend?" Rob eyed Fiona's dress as if trying to work out how approximately one metre of velvet and a few sequins could possibly equate to one diamond ring from Tiffany's.

"I'm not sure. I maxed them all out, though."

Mummy patted Fi's hand in reassurance before picking up her knife again to slash at a potato. "Well, I do think Niall has behaved very badly," she said.

I couldn't believe my Mother had taken all this so coolly, but then again, this was the woman who'd scored herself a nice bundle of alimony from my father when he went off with the secretary from his golf club.

Marco's shoulders shook with laughter and I knew he had enjoyed the story of Fiona's revenge on Niall's pockets. Mr. G applied himself to his dinner with renewed vigor, while Rob shook his head and moved the wine bottle out of Fiona's reach.

"Sister-in-law, you got class." Marco raised his glass in a mock salute.

Fiona giggled and lifted her own glass to chink it noisily against his. Envy stabbed me in the ribs like a knife. All my life, I've been a bit jealous of Fiona.

Marco doesn't like me to be possessive. One of his favorite phrases is "trust me, babe." And I used to, once, but now I'm not so sure. The mystery packages I'd found in his travel bag popped back into my memory and an uneasy feeling surfaced in my stomach.

As soon as dinner was finished and the last of the pudding dishes cleared from the table, Mother collared Marco and led him away for further interrogation, and, I suspected, to show him my baby pictures.

Rob talked to Fiona while he poured her copious cups of black coffee. I got left with Mr. G. Is it just me or is there something a bit creepy about your boss fancying your mum?

"Your sister seems to have taken her disappointment well," he said, and nodded over to where Fiona sat giggling and draping herself against Rob.

"Yes," I said. "Though I don't know what Niall will do when he gets his credit card statement. Or when he realizes he has to go and pay for the ring all over again if he wants it back from the hock shop."

We both took sips of our coffees.

"How is Mrs. Grebe? Have you heard from her lately?" Intent on his hot pursuit of my mother, I wondered if Mr. G had forgotten Esme's existence.

"Ah, Emma. Sadly, Mrs. Grebe and I seem to have reached a parting of the ways. She has decided to remain in Scotland for the foreseeable future." He cleared his throat and assumed a wounded puppy expression—never an attractive look for a man of his age, especially one who resembled a toad.

An awkward silence fell and I felt mean. Where on earth was Marco? I needed someone to come and rescue me. I looked over to Fiona who had persuaded Rob to try a party trick that involved sticking a teaspoon on the end of his nose. Marco was my only hope.

After what seemed like an eternity of making small talk with Mr. G, my husband reappeared.

"Time we were going, babe." Unusually for Marco, he looked flustered. I wondered what Mummy had said to him. I didn't think my baby pictures were so awful, although one of me with no teeth taken on a bad hair day wasn't very attractive.

"The cab will be here in a minute. Better get your coat." Marco bundled me out of the lounge door into the hall.

Mummy met us as she came down the stairs. "Leaving so soon?"

A car horn sounded outside. "That'll be the taxi." Marco flung open the front door.

Mummy embraced me in a fierce hug. "Goodnight darling. Give me a call." She turned to Marco who'd already gone outside. "Goodnight, Marco. Remember now we've got to know one another, you mustn't be a stranger."

Marco frogmarched me to the taxi and hustled me inside before he jumped in next to me. I didn't even have time to say goodnight to Fi or Rob.

"Is everything okay?" I asked.

There were little beads of sweat along his top lip and I wondered if he felt unwell.

"Yeah, babe. No worries."

I wasn't convinced but figured it was probably a consequence of having left a nice warm climate to arrive in England in the middle of winter. "Did you get on alright with Mummy?"

I hadn't expected my mother to be thrilled at my choice of husband and forgetting to tell her I'd got married hadn't been one of my best ideas. Mummy had gone through a bad time when Daddy ran off with his secretary and it had left her rather wary of men. Even so, I hoped that once she got to know Marco, they would like one another.

"Yeah, we got on okay. We just chatted a bit. You know."

Marco seemed preoccupied. I wondered if he might be headed for flu.

"What did you say your mum did for a living, Emma?"

"She works in an office. Something to do with government administration, I think." Perhaps Mummy had offered to help Marco find a job; though what skills Marco could bring to a Whitehall office I had no idea.

Going back to work, albeit part-time, had been another bone of contention after Daddy had left. Mummy had not been pleased when she'd found out that he'd salted away his retirement fund to some tax haven in the Bahamas and had somehow wangled it so she couldn't touch it.

She still did okay, but Fi and I don't ever tell her when we speak to Daddy because it only causes trouble. That reminded me…

Things to do:

Tell Daddy I'm married.

Find out what's in Marco's bag.

Get Fiona to teach me that teaspoon-on-the-nose trick.

By the time we were home and I was snuggled up in bed next to Marco, it felt too late to badger him about the contents of his bag. It didn't look good that I'd snooped inside it in the first place. I decided to leave it until morning. Maybe then he'd tell me more about the plans he'd hinted at in the cab when we'd been on our way to Mummy's.

I overslept the next morning. I'd been so tired after the dinner party that I'd forgotten to set the alarm. As I hopped around the flat on one foot, trying to pull my tights on, I figured any questions about Marco's plans would have to wait until I got home from work.

He was still fast asleep in bed with only his hair visible over the top of the duvet as I swallowed my coffee and headed out the door.

Luckily, I made it into work about five minutes ahead of Mr. G. Even if he did fancy my mother, he would still have had something to say about me being late for the third time in as many weeks.

Rob was already checking the emails, ready to write the Offer of the Day cards for the window. "You're cutting it fine again this morning, Emma," he said.

"Sorry, I overslept. At least I beat Greenback."

Mr. G went straight to his office after he'd grunted a good morning in our direction. Rob finished writing out the cards and I added a few artistic touches to them with felt pens. You know the kind of thing, smiley suns, bucket and spades—that sort of stuff.

"Oh, hell!" Rob stopped as he lifted the display board. I followed his gaze to where Gilly tottered along the pavement on her high heels toward the shop.

He turned to me in wide-eyed horror. "Hide me!"

"Too late," I said.

Gilly waved happily, looking far too bright, chirpy and perfectly made-up for this time in the morning. "Morning!" She breezed into the shop in a swirl of Burberry and Karen Millen. Her ratty little dog's head poked out of the top of her handbag.

"Hello, Gilly." Rob did a good impression of a rabbit trapped in headlights.

I carried on adding swirly lines to the cards and pretended not to listen.

"I had to come right over. I am *sooo* excited about our date and when I got the letter from the Foundation this morning, I thought I'd better come and see you straight away." Gilly beamed at him.

"What letter?" Rob asked.

I underlined *Costa del Sol* in blue, and tried to look inconspicuous.

Gilly placed her bag on top of my artistic handiwork and started to scrabble about under her Chihuahua. Triumphantly, she retrieved an envelope with the Crystal Foundation's gold and blue crest on it.

"This letter. The one with all the details about our trip. Oh, it sounds so romantic." She offered it to Rob.

He took it with all the enthusiasm of a man being asked to handle a scorpion. After he'd read the contents his normal, healthy-looking olive complexion had a pasty tone.

"It sounds great, Gilly." He looked as if she'd handed him a death sentence.

"What is it, Rob?"

I shouldn't have spoken. Gilly, who had been gazing misty-eyed at her reluctant date, suddenly noticed I was there.

"Aren't you Fiona Morgan's sister?" She gave me a quick top-to-toe assessing look. "You don't look much alike. I heard her fiancé dumped her for his secretary."

I hadn't liked Gilly much before, but now I decided I didn't like her at all.

"Actually, she dumped him. He cheated on her." News in Fi's circle travelled fast.

"Whatever." Gilly clearly wasn't interested in anything that didn't involve herself. "We can meet up tonight then, Rob, to discuss our plans for the date."

"I'm a bit tied up tonight, Gilly."

"Oh?" She picked her bag up and petted the miserable dog.

"I…erm…have to…um…fix something on the car."

It sounded a lame excuse even to my ears. Mind you, I've always been better liar than Rob and I'm rubbish at it.

"I could come over to you. It's been ages since I've been to your place," Gilly suggested.

"Er, no, I don't think that would be a good idea. I mean…" He looked at me in desperation.

"Rob needs to take the car to a friend's garage tonight. It's about an hour's drive away." I made a point of picking up the cards that Gilly had flattened and slotted them noisily into the plastic holders.

Gilly looked discomfited for a split second, and then recovered her composure. "Oh, but surely that isn't going to take all night! Meet me at Toscini's at half nine." She hitched her bag further onto her shoulder, causing her dog to yap in protest, and without giving Rob another chance to get out of it, marched from the shop.

"Terrific, I'm doomed," Rob muttered. He banged the display board back into the window so hard that three of the cards jumped out of the holders.

I leaned over and popped them back in again. "You could just not go," I suggested.

"Huh! You haven't seen the contract the Foundation makes you sign. If I back out of this date thing or if Gilly backs out because of something I do, then I become liable to pay the Foundation for the money Gilly pledged."

"You're joking! That's mercenary!"

"I wish I was."

Poor Rob. He looked so dejected and no wonder—Gilly would eat him for breakfast. Don't get me wrong, Rob's a pretty tough guy. I mean, he tackled Marco when he thought he was a burglar. But when it comes to women, he's too much of a gentleman.

"What did the letter say exactly?"

"The date is set for March thirtieth and the yacht's moored at Puerto Banus on the Costa del Sol. Gilly and I are to be flown first class to Malaga where we'll be met by a stretch limousine and taken to the boat. There, we'll be served with a champagne lunch. We then spend the evening having dinner in a five star restaurant before returning home the next day." He looked wretched. "I have to spend the whole day with Gilly."

The telephone rang and I went to answer it before Greenback could stick his head out of the office and remind us we were meant to be working.

"Hey, babe, what time do you get to go for lunch today?" Marco's voice—dangerously sexy—tickled my ear.

"Twelve. I've got the first hour."

"Cool. I've got a little surprise for you."

"What kind of surprise?"

"You'll see. Meet you at twelve." He hung up.

I wondered if the surprise had anything to do with the contents of his flight bag. But the phone rang again before I had too much time to think about it. By the time I'd dealt with what felt like a million inquiries and bookings, it was lunchtime.

Rob made himself scarce when Marco came in to see me. Fortunately, I'd just finished with my last customer as he arrived.

I grabbed my bag and coat and told Mr. G I was off to lunch. Marco looked really pleased with himself.

"Well babe, what do you think?" He pointed to the silver BMW parked at the curb.

I blinked in stunned surprise. "You've bought that car?"

"Come on, I'll take you for a ride."

We pulled away with the stereo player thumping out hip hop.

"Where are we going?" I asked.

"That's the second part of the surprise." Marco grinned.

The interior of the car smelt like a mix of new leather and pine. A little green cardboard tree dangling from the rear view mirror was responsible for the pine but the leather was pure new-car smell. I tried to figure out how Marco could have acquired a new car.

"Did you get a job?" It had to be a pretty cool gig if it came with a brand new, top-of-the-range BMW.

"Here we are." Marco bagged a space at the curb, beating an elderly lady in a red Ford to the punch.

"And where exactly is here?" I didn't recognize the road.

"We've an appointment with the bank. Come on."

Baffled, I followed Marco inside. It wasn't my bank, so what on earth was he up to?

When we emerged some forty minutes later, I was joint signatory on a bank account which held a seriously scary amount of money.

"Where did you get all that money?" Marco had never had any money before—let's face it, he'd "borrowed" all my savings when we got married. He'd been so broke, I'd even bought my own wedding ring and paid for the service.

"I told you, I made some good investments. I'm paying you back with interest, okay? Then, when a good opportunity for a business comes up, you and me will be sweet, babe."

Marco dropped me off back at the shop. I should have felt really excited; I mean Marco had made a big effort. And with the car and everything, I should have been buzzing. I don't know why I wasn't. Maybe I needed to adjust to having Marco back in my life again. Or maybe it was my conscience worrying about the contents of his bag.

I covered the shop for Rob while he went for lunch, which wasn't long. I think he was worried Gilly might still be lurking about.

When lunch had finished and the rush had died down, I rang Sara and told her about Marco's car and the money in the bank account.

"And you don't know where he got the money?" Her voice was instantly suspicious.

"From a business investment, he said. He used the money he had from me for his stake and now he says he's paying me back. He hadn't stolen my money, after all." I waited for her to probe deeper.

"Guess I'll know where to come for a loan then." Sara's voice sounded forced. Was she jealous or something?

"So, how are things with you and Shay?"

"Oh, the usual." She brushed me off. "Listen, Emma, have you met any of Marco's so-called business associates yet?"

Her question threw me. "No, not really. I think they're just some people he's networking with. He seems keen to suss out some kind of investment for us to get into."

"Oh, I just wondered. Shay thought he recognized a couple of guys talking to Marco the other day. They were outside the club where Shay's been gigging."

She had held something back, I could tell by her tone. "And? Spit it out, Sara."

"Look, Em, Shay didn't say too much, just that they were bad news, that's all."

"Fine." I knew I was abrupt. What was it with my friends these days? Why couldn't they just be happy for me?

"Emma, it's probably okay. I thought I should tell you, that's all," Sara said, back-pedalling.

The shop had filled up with customers again and Rob signalled me to get off the phone.

"Well, thanks," I said. "I'm sorry I snapped. I have to go, I'll call you later."

I hung up on Sara and plunged straight into helping a harassed mother of twins plan her Disneyland break. But all the time I nattered on about Mickey Mouse and the Magic Kingdom, my mind went over what Sara had said.

Perhaps Marco had been right when he said I didn't trust him. I'd accused my friends of having no faith in him when I had behaved the same way. After my customer left, I doodled a new list on the edge of a Thomas Cook brochure.

Things to Do:
Be more positive.
Stop being so suspicious of my husband.
Find out what was in his travel bag.

Mr. G left early, so Rob and I locked up.

"Are you going to meet Gilly tonight?" I asked.

"If I don't, she could cause a lot of trouble. I guess I'll be okay in a public place." Rob locked the traveller's cheques and deposits in the safe. He didn't sound as if he thought he would be okay.

"Couldn't you take someone with you?"

"Yeah, I'll ring Madonna and ask to borrow her bodyguards." He switched off the office light and locked the door.

"That's not what I meant and you know it." We did a last check of the workstations and put our coats on.

"Normally I'd ask any of you guys, but if Fiona goes, Gilly will either cut her dead or pump her for gory details about Niall all night. Shay is gigging and Sara has to stay with Jess. Meantime, you're all loved up with Marco." We walked outside together and Rob locked the front door.

"But you're going to Toscini's, so Marco and I could call in for a drink or something. We wouldn't be with you as such, but if Gilly got difficult you could sort of accidentally bump into us and we could rescue you."

Rob finished setting the shop alarm and we waited for the shutter to descend.

"I appreciate the offer, Emma, but I don't think your husband is going to be very excited about it."

"That's my concern. We'll be there." Whether Marco likes it or not, I added to myself.

Chapter Seven

Toscini's looked packed. It wasn't a place I usually went to. The drinks were too expensive and you had to shout over the music to make yourself heard.

I had wracked my brain all the way home for a way to persuade Marco that spending an evening there was a good idea. In the end, I needn't have worried. Marco had suggested it himself to celebrate buying the new car.

I couldn't see Rob or Gilly anywhere in the crowd. Marco left me by the doors while he braved the crush at the bar to get us both drinks.

"Emma!" Rob appeared from nowhere and made his way through the crowd toward me.

"Where's Gilly?" I expected her to follow him, hot on his heels. I wondered if she would bring her dog.

"No idea. I don't think she's here yet. Where's Marco? Or have you left him at home?" He scanned the crowd.

"He's gone to get the drinks. Look, there's Gilly."

I didn't bother to explain to Rob that coming here had been Marco's idea and that I hadn't told my husband that Rob would be at Toscini's, as well.

Rob followed the direction of my gaze. Gilly had squeezed into the shortest skirt and the strappiest vest top I think I'd ever seen.

"At least she hasn't got the dog with her," Rob said, watching Gilly wobble on her spiky heels.

"You'd better go and get it over with, Dangermouse."

"Wish me luck then, Penfold. I'm going in."

I squeezed his arm in sympathy and watched him walk reluctantly away into the crowd. My feet had already started to ache—not a good sign. Maybe it had been a mistake to wear my bargain shoes that night. There was a serious shortage of chairs in Toscini's; either that or we should have arrived much earlier in the evening to claim the few that were there.

Marco must have gone to France to fetch my wine. Being a lone female without a drink in a wine bar frequented by lots of single men is not a good idea. In the timeframe between Marco going to the bar and Rob turning up, I got propositioned twice.

I decided if Marco didn't come back with my drink soon, then I would go home. Rob could fight Gilly off all by himself.

"Sorry, babe, I got talking to a guy I know at the bar." Marco handed me a drink that smelled like a vodka and Coke. God, he'd been at the bar so long he'd forgotten what drink I'd asked for. And how come he'd managed to find someone he knew to talk to? I swear if he went to the moon, he'd bump into some friendly Martian who just happened to be passing.

"Listen babe, I'll be right back. There are some people he wants to introduce me to." Marco pressed the glass into my hand and disappeared before I had chance to wail "But what about me?"

I took a gulp of vodka and glowered at the melting ice-cubes that floated forlornly on the surface of my drink. After five minutes and almost half the glass, I decided to go and find Marco.

Perhaps I should find out a bit more about these mysterious friends of my husband. He didn't seem to be in any hurry to introduce me, as usual, so I might as well go and introduce myself.

As I made my way through the crowded room, I wished, not for the first time, that I was taller. Even with my heels on I still couldn't see more than a couple of feet in front of me. By the time I'd bumped into and apologized to half a dozen people, I was disgruntled, grumpy and my feet were definitely not happy, either.

"Oops, sorry." I knocked into someone else.

"Emma Morgan?" Gilly looked at me as if I was something nasty stuck to the bottom of her shoe.

"Hello, Gilly." Uh-oh, major booboo. She was not supposed to know I was here. Guess Rescue Plan A, the casual interception, had been blown.

"What a surprise, you being here tonight."

I didn't like the emphasis she put on the word 'surprise.'

"Hi, Rob," I said weakly, and hoped he wouldn't give away that this was a put-up job.

"Emma! Are you here on your own?"

Rob would never win an Oscar for his acting. Gilly, meanwhile, folded her arms and tapped the toe of a Jimmy Choo-clad foot on the polished laminate floor.

"Um, I was looking for Marco. We're out celebrating tonight."

An "I don't believe you" expression settled on Gilly's perfectly made-up face. "What a coincidence," she said sweetly. "And here I was thinking you might have followed us. Where is this mythical man of yours, Emma? You must have come up with him mighty quickly; after all, you were single and dateless on Valentine's Night."

Ouch, Gilly didn't pull her punches. I consoled myself with the thought that I wasn't as dateless and desperate as she was, seeing as this was the woman who'd bid thousands of pounds for a single date with my best friend.

"Well, where is this husband of yours? If he exists at all…" Gilly added in a nasty tone.

If it wasn't so difficult to get drinks in this place, I'd be tempted to toss what was left of my watery vodka and coke right into her smug face.

"Oh, he exists all right." Rob winced. I think he still carried some of the bruises from his first meeting with Marco.

The crowd parted and I caught a fleeting glimpse of my errant husband talking with a small group of people. I was about to point him out to Gilly and wipe the smirk off her supercilious face, when I realized he had his arm around the waist of the beautiful girl who was stood next to him.

I had an immediate flashback to Antigua, where day in and day out I'd watched Marco flirt with the tourists, working the crowd until they were putty in his hands while tropical rum cocktails whizzed over the bar as if prohibition was imminent.

"Well, don't let us keep you, Emma." Gilly slipped her arm through Rob's and started to pull him away.

"See you later, Emma." Rob noticed Marco and the girl. I could tell by the way his jaw tightened and the pitying look in his eyes.

I took a big swallow of my drink and headed in Marco's direction. Up close, it became clear that he was the main man in the small group of people. A roar of laughter went up at one of his jokes and he was slapped on the back by one of the men. The pretty girl remained glued to his side, simpering and fluttering her fake lashes.

As soon as Marco noticed me, he took on a contrite expression and let go of the girl. He reached out a hand to pull me into his circle. "This is my lovely Emma."

"Yo, Emma." They greeted me with disinterest, then ignored me as Marco continued to entertain. The girl looked daggers at me and carried on eyelash-batting at my husband. The group laughed at another one of Marco's bar stories; I'd heard them all before.

I finished my vodka and debated interrupting Marco to ask him to get me another drink. The people in the group were all complete strangers to me, although they seemed very well dressed and both the men and the women wore plenty of gold jewelry.

Every now and then, the crowd would part and I'd catch a glimpse of Rob and Gilly. Rob looked thoroughly miserable while Gilly laughed a lot and gestured with her hands. At least somebody had enjoyed the evening.

Rob caught my eye to semaphore desperation signals at me with his eyebrows.

"Isn't that your friend, Rob?" Marco said.

"He's meeting his ex-girlfriend," I replied. "The one who bid on him at the auction the night you came home. She got the letter about their date today. It's in the Costa del Sol and she wanted to finalize all the details."

"Spain, huh?"

One of the men in the group interrupted our conversation, then murmured something to Marco I didn't quite catch.

"So when is this date?" Marco asked me.

"Thirtieth of March. They fly to Malaga and then get taken by car to Puerto Banus to spend the day on a private yacht."

Marco exchanged a glance with his friend, who in turn gave him a short nod, then he said, "Rob doesn't look very comfortable with his lady." There was an understatement if ever there was one. "Maybe you should go over there," he suggested.

If I'd had anything left in my glass to drink I probably would have sprayed it everywhere. Okay, so where was my husband and who was this stranger in his place?

"Come with me, then, and I'll introduce you to Gilly," I said, tugging on his arm to dislodge him from his friends. At least now I'd get one-up on her. Petty, I know, but so satisfying.

"Emma, I see you found Marco," Rob said as we approached. His face brightened at the sight of us, which, considering he and Marco didn't like one another much, showed how desperate he must be for a distraction.

"Gilly, this is my husband Marco. Marco, Gilly." I was tempted to add, *What do you say to that then, you silly cow?* but that would have been childish.

"Gilly, Emma told me how generous you were with your winning bid at the auction." Marco took Gilly's hand and raised it to his lips to kiss it. "The Foundation must be very close to your heart for someone as lovely as you to give up their time and money for such a worthy cause."

Rob and I stood there like two spare parts while Gilly blushed and giggled like a teenager.

"Well, I always think you should do what you can to help these things," she said.

Oh please, I thought. Pass me the sick bucket.

"Is he taking the piss?" Rob whispered in my ear.

"You won a date on a yacht?" Marco still held her hand.

"Yes, in Spain. Have you ever been to Puerto Banus?" Gilly gazed into Marco's eyes.

"It's somewhere I've always wanted to see."

This was going too far. I shivered as if someone had walked on my grave. I saw Marco's friend watch us from a few feet away and wondered what his interest was.

A big chunk of conversation must have whizzed over my head while I'd gazed around the bar, because the next thing I heard was Marco say, "That would be great, wouldn't it, Emma?"

I blinked at him like an owl. "Sorry?"

"I said to Gilly, we could go over to Spain with her and Rob. They could have their time on the yacht then maybe we could all meet up. Perhaps stay an extra day and make a weekend of it."

Okay, this is definitely not my husband. Alien abduction! Call up Mulder and Scully! What the hell was going on?

"I…I'm not sure," I stammered. "I mean, Gilly's trip is all organized." A weekend with Gilly? Oh, my God, I think I'd rather get my nipples pierced.

Rob looked like a drowning man who'd been thrown a lifebelt. "It'd be fun, Emma!" he urged.

Fun for whom? Rob clearly wanted me to agree. Marco, for some reason, seemed to think he'd had the greatest idea since sliced bread. Even Gilly nodded her approval. Although, if she held my husband's hand for much longer I might have to remind her of whom exactly her date was with.

"Well, if Mr. G will okay it, I suppose a holiday would be nice." There isn't much point working in a travel agency if you don't travel anywhere. Even if one of your traveling companions was a fully paid-up member of Stalkers

Anonymous. It would be nice too, I supposed, to spend some quality time with Marco.

The last-orders bell sounded and Rob offered to get us all a final drink. I went with him to help carry the glasses.

"Thanks for agreeing to come to Spain, Em," he said. "I can't tell you the relief of knowing I'm not going to spend all that time on my own with Gilly."

The laminate floor near the bar glistened wet from a spilled drink and my new shoes slipped on the surface. Rob popped his arm around me and scooped me upright. He held me close until we got near enough for me to lean on the bar.

"Is everything okay, Em, with you and Mr. Smooth Talker?" he asked. "I know I'm butting in again but earlier, when you were with those other people, you looked almost as miserable as me."

I took my wine glass straight from the bartender's hand and swallowed a gulp. "Everything's fine," I said. "Marco can't help flirting with anything in a skirt. It's like breathing; he doesn't mean anything by it. I mean, we still have a lot of issues to work through. Our marriage didn't get off to a great start but I suppose all this kind of stuff takes time."

Rob gave me a sympathetic hug. "Remember I'm here for you if you need me." He looked at me as if he was about to say something else, but then turned around. We picked up the other drinks and headed back to our respective partners.

Gilly and Marco stood chatting away like old friends. I'm not even sure they'd noticed that we'd been gone. Marco's other friends appeared to have left and the crowd inside the bar had gradually dispersed into the frosty night.

"Do you want to go on to somewhere else?" Marco asked, and quickly finished the rest of his drink. I thought he had asked me, but he looked at Gilly instead.

"Rob and I have to work tomorrow," I said. Christ, I sounded like my mother. Why didn't I invite everyone back for a nice mug of Horlicks?

Gilly pouted. "That's such a shame. It's early yet. Come on, Rob, don't be a spoilsport."

Marco looked at me and I knew he wanted to go.

"Okay, just for a while then," I mumbled. Maybe I'd be able to sit down. My feet seriously hurt.

"Oh, goody, we'll go clubbing!" Gilly announced, and off we went.

Two hours later in a rather dim place called Eclipse, my head thumped along with the music. Marco and Gilly were somewhere out on the dance floor and Rob sat on the chair opposite me, a hyper-expensive bottle of Japanese lager cradled in his hands.

I watched a girl walk past wearing what looked like a tinfoil bikini and I felt conspicuously overdressed. Gilly, it transpired on our arrival, was on first-name terms with half the doormen in London. We got waved up to the head of the queue and inside before you could say 'stringfellows.'

It had been a long time since I'd gone out clubbing. Living abroad and then Sara having baby Jessie meant my night outs now tended to be a Chinese or Indian dinner with the gang from work. Except when Fiona press-ganged me into taking part in one of her charity events.

I stood up to try to see Marco and Gilly. But they were nowhere in sight, lost among the sea of people on the dance floor. I wanted to go home. I suspected Rob, too, would have slipped off ages ago if he'd had the chance.

"I can't see them anywhere." I flopped back down on my seat.

"Gilly can party for England." Rob yawned and stretched out as much as he could on his chair.

"I'm going to feel crap in the morning," I said.

Rob glanced at his watch. "It is morning."

"We're a couple of miserable old farts, aren't we?"

Rob grinned. "No, it's just we have to get up early for work. If they don't come back in the next five minutes, I'll take you home."

"You're on." I wriggled around in my seat in an attempt to get comfy. "Hey, there's that bloke I saw talking to Marco in Toscini's earlier."

Rob turned his head to see. "The big guy? The one wearing all the gold necklaces who's standing by the pillar?"

It was definitely the same man. He had been the one who'd nodded at Marco when we'd been talking about Spain. Rob and I watched as he met up with two other men. Although they were all smartly dressed, they all had the same thick-set appearance, as if their heads had been joined directly to their shoulders without the benefit of necks.

Marco's friend seemed to give them some kind of instructions, because they nodded in agreement then dispersed in different directions.

"Interesting fellow," Rob remarked.

Something about the man made me uneasy and I didn't know why. He'd been pleasant enough when he'd been in the group at Toscini's. True, he had a face only his mother could love, but that wasn't his fault. It was late and I felt tired. I suppose if I was honest, I was jealous of Gilly's monopolization of Marco and it had made me paranoid.

"Five minutes is up," Rob said. "Stay here, Em, and I'll go and see if I can prise the dancing queen off the dance floor. Then maybe we can get at least a couple of hours' sleep." Rob put his empty bottle down on the table and walked off to find his date and my husband.

From my chair, I watched the bullet-headed man scan the crowd. He must have spotted whoever he'd been searching for, because he raised his hand and beckoned them over. A massive swathe of dancers meant I couldn't see who it was. Perhaps it was his henchmen, or maybe a girlfriend. I tried to be charitable with the second guess.

Rob came back with Gilly in tow.

"Where's Marco?"

Gilly looked vague. "I'm not sure. We were dancing, and then he said he needed to speak to someone." She flopped down on Rob's chair.

"We'll give him a few minutes to show. If he doesn't appear I'll see if I can find him." Rob gave my shoulder a friendly squeeze.

Gilly fidgeted about on the seat. Her cheeks were flushed with patches of red and her eyes looked glassy. "I don't see why we have to go now. There's ages 'til the club shuts."

"Some of us have to work, Gilly." My patience had worn thin and my bed called me.

Gilly scowled and looked petulant. Fortunately, Marco strolled toward us from the direction of the dance floor.

"I need to go home, Marco."

He glanced at Gilly and Rob. "Sure, babe. We'll go find a cab."

He'd left the precious new set of wheels at home. He'd only had the car for one day and had already discovered how difficult it was to park in town.

We stood shivering in the doorway of the club while Gilly collected her jacket. Tiny flakes of snow whirled down from the night sky, the light from inside the club making them appear yellow in the darkness.

How come Gilly's legs hadn't taken on the same unbecoming mottled blue tinge that mine had? Life wasn't fair, especially as she had a lot more leg on show than I did.

The taxi rank was empty, so it appeared as if we'd have to freeze and dither for a while longer until a black cab came back. Gilly had looked as if she would have a stroke when I mentioned the word, 'mini-cab" as a suggestion.

"Marco, can I offer you and your friends a ride?" Bullet-head's voice made me jump. He emerged from the shadows inside the club doorway and stood behind us.

"I…that's very kind of you," I began. Riding anywhere in a car with this man sounded decidedly unappealing to me. "But I…I'm sure—"

He cut short my protest with a raise of his leather-gloved hand. "I insist. I'll have my driver bring the car around. I have some business to attend to here. He'll drop you wherever you need to go."

Gilly's face lit up at the mention of a personal driver and a few seconds after Bullet-head had spoken into his mobile, a sleek black Mercedes pulled up at the curb.

"Thank you very much." Gilly beamed.

Bullet-head opened the rear door for us, while Marco got in the front next to the driver.

"Not at all. For my friend Marco, it is a pleasure. You, too, Emma."

Bullet-head smiled at me as I climbed in and I wondered why his remembrance of my name sent a shiver down my spine.

Chapter Eight

The car glided off into the traffic and Rob gave the chauffeur (also without a neck) Gilly's address. The plan was to drop Gilly off first, then Rob, and finally me and Marco.

It took me a few minutes to work out why the back seat of such a large car felt so cramped. Gilly had tried to cozy up to Rob, who sat in the middle, and he in turn had attempted to put some space between them. I ended up squished against the door.

"This is very kind of your friend, Marco." Gilly didn't seem to have any qualms about accepting a lift from a complete stranger. Not even one who looked like a budget version of a Bond villain. She snuggled in closer to Rob.

Luckily for him, Gilly's home wasn't far from the club. We watched from the car as she tottered up the stone steps to her front door, clinging on to the wrought iron handrail as she went.

"I'll call you!" She opened the front door and waved us off, blowing exaggerated kisses in Rob's direction.

The car moved off again. Rob sank back against the luxurious leather upholstery with a sigh of relief. I gave him a sharp dig in the ribs to encourage him to move over now that Gilly had gone.

"Sorry, Em." He shifted across a fraction and, at last, I could ease my cramped leg away from the door.

"Thanks for the rescue tonight," he murmured in my ear, his breath warm on my face. His arm brushed against mine and the length of his thigh pressed against me.

"That's okay." His proximity had a sensually disturbing quality and I felt a bit guilty, as if I'd done something naughty. Tiredness does strange things to the brain, I guess.

The car stopped again, this time outside the large, modern block of flats where Rob lived.

"Well, this is me. Thanks again, Em" He kissed my cheek and jumped out.

I expected Marco to get out ready to come and sit in the back with me, but he didn't. Instead he stayed in the front passenger seat next to the driver. Their heads were together as they talked in low voices and I couldn't quite hear properly. The chauffeur's eyes met mine in the rear view mirror and he turned the radio on.

By the time he dropped us off outside the flat I could hardly keep my eyes open. There were a lot of things I wanted to say to Marco—none of them very complimentary—but sleep had to be my priority.

I set the alarm on my mobile and fell into bed without removing my make-up. The mattress dipped as Marco slid in next to me and began to snore.

Things to do:
Wake up in time for work.
Find out who Mr. Bullet head is.
Work out why I feel like I've come home with the wrong man.

No, scrap the last one, that couldn't be right. I loved Marco. Didn't I?

By the time the alarm sounded, all too soon, my head buzzed. I couldn't figure out where I was at first as my mascara had welded my eyes shut. My reflection in the bathroom mirror wasn't a pretty sight. I resembled Morticia Addams' twin sister on a bad hair day.

Marco didn't stir; I don't think he even heard the alarm. Car or no car, it looked as if I still had to get the tube into work every day.

I met Toby as he collected his bike from the shared hallway on my way out of the flat.

"Ooh, you look a bit rough today, Emma. We heard you come back last night…or should I say this morning." He gave me a wink.

"Yeah, we went clubbing. Got back later than we'd planned." I didn't feel in the mood to launch into a big explanation.

Toby opened the front door and wheeled his bike outside. "I like the new car, very flashy. It looks as if things might look up for you now that Marco's here."

I pulled the door shut behind us. Toby straddled his bike and began to fasten the helmet buckle under his chin. He fancied himself in his cycling clothes, always wearing tight Lycra shorts and a nifty little black helmet. He changed into a suit when he got to work.

"Maybe," I said.

Toby stopped fiddling with his chinstrap and looked at me. "Trouble in paradise already?"

"No, not really. I'm tired this morning, that's all. I'll be fine once I've had some more coffee."

I shouldn't have said anything. Toby would be bound to tell Steven and they would want to spend hours discussing my problems. They'd come up with more and more outrageous solutions until I chucked them both out of my flat.

"Well, we're here for you, Em. Although I wouldn't kick Marco out of my bed in a hurry." He grinned and wriggled his eyebrows suggestively.

"Thank you for that note of support, Dear Deirdre. I'll bear it in mind." I gave him a gentle push and he wobbled off down the path, laughing.

I arrived late at work. Fortunately, so did Rob, and there was no sign of Mr. G. It was a good thing, because we were fifteen minutes late lifting the shutters. I heard the phone before we finished switching off the alarm and opened the door.

"Hello, Pack and Go. This is Emma."

"Emma, thank goodness. You haven't seen Fiona, have you?" Mummy sounded panicky.

"Not since we were all at yours. I spoke to her yesterday though, and she sounded fine. Why? What's the matter?" It wasn't like Mummy to flap, so something had to be wrong.

"I'm probably being silly, but she went out last night and didn't come home. I thought she might have gone back to her own place but her housemates haven't seen her."

"Have you tried her mobile?" My brain didn't function well enough to deal with a crisis first thing in the morning, and we ought to try the obvious things first.

"It was the first thing I did, but it's switched off. I called Sara in case Fiona had gone there, but they haven't seen her either."

"What's the matter?" Rob mouthed at me from across the shop.

I covered the mouthpiece with my hand. "Mummy says Fiona didn't come home last night."

It wasn't like Fiona not to let anyone know where she was.

"You don't think she's done anything silly, do you?" my mother fretted.

"Oh, Mummy! She seemed fine yesterday at teatime." At least, I thought Fiona had sounded okay. "Did she say where she was going when she left?"

"All she said was that she had to pop out and not to wait up for her."

"Well, then, I expect she's gone to see a friend somewhere, stayed later than she thought and slept over. She'll phone soon or come home." That must be the most likely explanation.

"You don't think I should ring around to the hospitals?" I re-evaluated my opinion of Mummy not being a flapper. Now I knew where I'd inherited my talent for melodrama.

"Give her until lunch time. We'd feel silly if she strolled in this afternoon and we'd reported her missing." I managed to reassure Mummy a bit more until she rang off.

As I put the phone back down, I wondered if I'd done the right thing. Suppose Fi was lost or missing. Visions of me and Mummy appearing on Crimewatch clutching a picture of Fiona flashed through my mind.

"Where do you think she's gone?" Rob looked worried.

"I don't know. I can see why Mummy's upset though. It's odd, Fi's phone being off."

The shop door opened and some customers walked in, so we didn't get a chance to talk any more. Every time the phone rang, I expected it to be Fiona. Or Mummy to say she'd heard from Fiona.

By the time twelve o'clock rolled around, I had begun to contemplate phoning the hospitals myself when the shop door opened again and my prodigal sister meandered in.

"Where have you been? Mummy's been worried about you." I kept my voice low to avoid scaring off a prospective customer who had filled her arms with skiing brochures from the rack.

Irritatingly, Fiona looked her usual, immaculate self which was pretty bloody annoying considering I'd tortured myself all morning with images of her floating Ophelia-like down the Thames.

"Oh, honestly, I only went out for a drink with a friend," she said. "You know what it's like when you get talking. It got late, so I stayed over."

"Mm-hm." I knew there was something she wasn't telling me. "You could have phoned."

Fiona tossed her shiny blonde hair. "You're turning into Mummy! The battery's down on my phone and I forgot."

"What do you want, anyway? You never usually come to see me at work."

"A little bird told me that you and Marco intend to go to Spain with Rob and Gilly on the Foundation trip."

It must be a little bird with a flipping big beak if Fi had heard that, especially as Mummy had posted her missing to all and sundry since before nine o'clock this morning.

"Who told you?"

Fiona looked smug. "Let's say I have my sources. Anyway, I want to go, too. I've got all the details in my bag about the flight and hotel."

"You'd better give them to Rob. He's organizing our booking."

Rob had finished sorting out the ski customer, so Fi tootled across the shop to see him.

I rang Mummy to let her know she could call off the search. Fi made herself at home in front of Rob's console and pointed out something on the wad of papers she'd pulled from her handbag.

There wasn't time to go over and see what she intended to arrange as more customers started to arrive thick and fast. The rush didn't die down until it was time to lock up and then we virtually had to turn the lights off on the last customer in the shop to get him to go home.

I decided to pop in to see Sara and baby Jessie on my way home. I'd felt a bit mean ever since I'd snapped at Sara on the phone the other day. Sara's been one of my closest friends since we were at junior school together and I never liked it when we argued.

I heard Jessie crying even before the front door opened. Sara looked tired. Dark circles were under her eyes and she looked skinnier than ever.

"Are you okay, Sar?" I asked.

"Jessie's teething again. She's got five now and I'm not getting much sleep," she said dully and led the way into the lounge.

Jessie sat in her high chair drawing yogurt patterns on the plastic tray with her podgy little fingers.

"Hello, Jessie bear. It's Auntie Em."

Jessie peered at me and flashed me a smile before resuming her yogurt art.

"That's all she'll eat at the moment, yogurt." Sara sighed and extracted the empty pot from Jessie's fingers before she cleaned them with a wipe and lifted the baby out of the chair.

"Where's Shay?"

"God knows."

It wasn't like Sara to be so down, even when she was tired.

She handed Jessie over for me to cuddle while she put a kettle on. Jessie grinned toothily at me and dribbled on my jacket.

"Is everything alright between you and Shay?" I disentangled Jessie from her attempts to strangle me with my necklace.

"Yes, fine. Why wouldn't it be?" Sara bumped the mugs of tea down onto the mantelpiece out of Jessie's reach.

"Nothing, it's just that you don't seem very happy." Talk about walking on eggshells.

Sara slumped into an armchair and burst into tears. "Oh, Em, it's Shay. I think he's got someone else." She fished around in the pocket of her cardigan for a tissue and blew her nose.

"Sar, he wouldn't. Shay loves you. What makes you think there's someone else?"

Sara sniffed and grabbed the tissue box off the shelf. "He's being so secretive and a couple of times he's lied to me about where he's been."

"But that doesn't have to mean there's someone else. What did he say when you asked him about it?"

"Nothing." She blew her nose hard on a tissue.

"What do you mean nothing? He must have said something."

Jessie gurgled happily on my lap and tried to bite the leather strap on my handbag.

"I didn't ask him," Sara said.

"But…"

"I saw him with her. Mum had Jessie for me so I decided to treat myself to a Starbucks. I was sitting in the window when they walked past together."

"And you're sure of what you saw?" I couldn't believe it. Of all the couples I knew, Sara and Shay were the last two people in the world I could envisage as having problems.

"Of course, I'm sure!" Sara snapped, and then let out a despondent wail. "Emma, what am I going to do?"

I rescued my handbag from Jessie and gave her one of the squeaky toys littering the laminate floor of Sara's lounge.

"Talk to him. What else can you do?"

"Suppose he wants to leave me. What about Jessie?" Sara pulled a fresh handful of tissues from the box.

"Don't jump to conclusions, Sar. First you need to know where you stand." I'd want to know, if it was me.

"I could ignore it and wait for it to blow over." Sara hiccupped and dabbed at the remains of mascara on her cheeks.

"If Shay has got someone else, you can't just ignore it."

Sara rounded on me, causing Jessie to look up from her game, a pout on her little lips. "Why not? It's probably my fault. I mean look at me, he probably doesn't fancy me anymore."

Since Sara is incredibly slim, blonde and, when not completely knackered from lack of sleep, drop dead pretty, I found this a hard line to swallow. "That's ridiculous."

"No, it's not. You should have seen her, Em. She had a gorgeous suit on and her hair was all done. I look like a charity shop reject compared to her."

I didn't answer for a minute. In a way, she was right. Money has been tight for her since Jessie'd been born and I couldn't remember the last time we'd shopped for something for Sara. All her money went on Jessie.

Then it hit me—Marco had put oodles of money in our new joint account. I could use some of it to treat Sara. After all, he'd said it was to pay me back for the money he'd taken from me when we got married, so really, it was my money too.

"I still think you should talk to him."

"Like you did with Marco before you left him in Antigua and came back to England?"

Maybe she had a point. I'd made a proper hash of that. Although things seemed to have worked out now, if I'd adopted Sara's head-in-the-sand ostrich attitude, who knew what would have happened.

"It's my day off tomorrow," I said, "Ask your mum if she'll have Jessie and we'll go shopping, my treat."

Sara looked doubtful.

"It'll be fun! You'll feel better if nothing else. Marco's paid me back with interest on the money he borrowed so why can't I treat my best friend if I want too?"

"Okay, I'll ask Mum to watch Jessie."

Jessie beamed up at us while dribble ran down her chin and onto her bib. How could Shay even think of seeing another woman when he had a beautiful baby and a great girlfriend at home?

Marco was out when I got back. He'd left the bed unmade and a heap of wet towels lay dumped in the bathroom. I wondered how long he would be. The fridge was almost empty and I'm not one of those people who can create the perfect fluffy omelette from a nub of stale cheese and an egg.

At least now that Fiona's wedding had been called off, I didn't have to watch the calories. Although, if we did go to Spain in a few weeks maybe I should try to lose a few pounds. With Fiona and Gilly strutting around all slim and glamorous in little micro bikinis I would feel like Miss Piggy.

Things to Do:

Start an immediate diet.

Buy a new bikini.

Pray that Gilly and Fi retain five pounds in water from the flight while I miraculously lose five.

I abandoned my half-formed plan to dial for a pizza and poured myself a bowl of cornflakes. I added a note to pick up a weeks supply of SlimFast when I went shopping tomorrow.

I clicked the telly on as I changed into my pajamas. I only half-paid attention to the news program that had started. By the time I'd stuck the dirty towels in the washing machine and sat down with my cornflakes, I'd missed the weather.

Things To Do

I heard Marco's key in the front door just as I shovelled an extra large spoonful of cornflakes into my mouth. Intent on catching up on the soaps, I was completely unprepared for Marco to walk in followed by Mr. Bullet-head.

To his credit, Mr. Bullet-head appeared unfazed by the state of the flat and the sight of me in my pink Minnie Mouse pj's. Which was a damn sight more than I was at seeing him; I shot off the sofa and into the bedroom, grabbing my dressing gown. I made a mental vow to kill Marco as I went.

I peered through the crack of the open bedroom door into the lounge and shrugged my robe on as fast as I could.

Mr. Bullet-head appeared to be in high good humor. He slapped Marco on the shoulder and shook his hand. He stowed something in his jacket pocket and I caught murmurs of "a good deal" and "plan can go right ahead."

"Emma, delightful to meet you again." Mr. Bullet-head smiled at me, revealing a gold tooth, as I rejoined them.

"Excuse the state of the flat. Marco didn't tell me we expected company."

"No problem, Emma. I'm sorry I disturbed your supper."

My cheeks burnt as I tried to nudge my bowl of soggy cornflakes out of sight with my foot. Marco steered Mr. Bullet-head towards the door. This must be intended as a flying visit.

"Goodbye, Emma." Mr. Bullet-head smiled at me again. He nodded at Marco, "I'll be in touch about the shipping."

He walked off down the path to the Mercedes which waited for him at the curb, the engine running. I bided my time until Marco had closed the door.

"Right, who exactly is that man?" I demanded, planting my hands on my hips. "And what kind of business is he in?"

Chapter Nine

"Everton is an old friend from home," Marco said. "He dabbles in all kinds of business, import and export. He owns a couple of bars and some nightclubs." He shrugged as if it was no big deal.

I tried to get my head around the idea Mr. Bullet-head's first name was Everton.

Marco strolled back into the hall and headed for the kitchen. "Everton was very taken with you last night, babe."

Ordinarily I'd be flattered, but the thought of Everton Bullet-head finding me attractive gave me the creeps. Marco reached into the fridge for one of his cans of iced tea.

"Marco, you'd tell me if you were involved in anything really dodgy, wouldn't you?" I asked.

Marco took a swig from his can. "Babe, everything's cool."

Should I ask about the contents of the bag? Oh, hell, I had to know. "You wouldn't get involved with drugs or anything?"

Marco's eyes narrowed. "Hey, what's with the questions? You know I do some Ganja." He stroked my cheek with his finger. "You worry too much, babe. Maybe you should try some."

I gritted my teeth. "Are you doing any work for Everton?"

Marco put down his drink and took me in his arms. "He's an old friend, babe. Trust me."

And as he slid his hand under my dressing gown to stroke my breast, I did. It was later when Marco lay peacefully asleep beside me that I realized he hadn't answered my question about working for Everton.

✔ ✔ ✔

I had arranged to meet Sara at her flat quite early so we could go shopping. Marco sat up in bed, propped against the headboard with his hands behind his head and watched me as I dressed.

"I hate it when you stare at me while I'm dressing." It made me aware of all the things that were wrong with my figure.

"You're sexy, babe. Have a good time shopping," he said, as I put on my lipstick.

"We will."

I saw his reflection smile at me in the mirror. "Do you fancy going out for dinner tonight?"

"Okay, it would be nice to go out."

The diet could wait one more day, and anyway, sex is supposed to burn lots of calories so I must have lost loads of weight last night.

I left Marco in bed, dodging out of his reach when he tried to entice me back under the covers for a quickie. He said he planned to visit some premises which might offer some scope for a business. I would have pressed him for details but I'd promised Sara I'd be on time.

In the end, I was only fifteen minutes late, quite good for me. Sara had her coat on ready and waiting to go. Her mum sat in the kitchen feeding Jessie her breakfast.

"Shay's in bed. He did a gig last night." Sara whispered and picked up her handbag.

"Humph! It's about time he packed that nonsense in and got a proper job," Sara's mum remarked as she spooned cereal into Jessie's open mouth.

"It was all very well before you had the baby but he needs to realize he's got responsibilities now."

Normally Sara would leap in to defend Shay, but this time she bit her lip and said nothing. I thought it best if we left as quickly as possible. Sara and her mum have a very volatile relationship; if Sara said something was black, then her mum would immediately argue it was white.

"Thank God you turned up when you did." Sara banged the front door shut behind us with considerable force. I didn't comment. I wasn't sure who Sara felt most angry with, her mum or Shay.

By the time we stopped for a slice of Sara's favorite Rocky Road cake and a latte at Starbucks, we'd acquired several carrier bags and Sara looked more like her old self. I had to admit it was really enjoyable spending Marco's money. I suppose in reality, it was my money with lots of interest, but it still felt more like a lottery win.

"How's married life shaping up?" Sara took a contented bite out of her cake.

"Okay, I think. It's strange having Marco in the flat. It's strange Marco being here." I told her about Everton and the trip to Spain.

Sara nodded and her ponytail bounced up and down as she dropped crumbs onto the tabletop. "I never thought you'd have Marco back after the way he treated you. I guess now the shoe's on the other foot." She put down her cake as if her appetite had disappeared.

"Have you thought about what you're going to do?" I hoped she'd changed her mind and planned to talk to Shay.

"I've thought about nothing else." She frowned. "I don't know what to do."

I tried to think of something helpful to say, but before I had a chance to speak, Sara leant forward with a glint in her eye.

"Emma, there's Fiona! Who's she with?" She nudged me and pointed toward a table on the far side of the coffee shop.

I didn't have as good a good view as Sara, so I shuffled around on my chair. By leaning backwards as if reaching for something from my bag, I managed to get a glimpse.

Fiona had her best coat on, one I longed to be slim enough to borrow. I didn't recognize the man with her. Smartly dressed with a strong and distinguished face, he looked at least twenty years older. Since his hand was on hers and stroking her fingers, it certainly wasn't a business meeting.

"Well, who is he?" Sara asked, gawking for all she was worth.

"I don't know. He does look familiar though." The longer I looked, the more certain I became that I'd seen him before, though I couldn't think where.

"Let's go over." Sara picked up her mug and swallowed the last of her latte. "Come on!" She gathered up the bags and grabbed my arm to hurry me along.

Fiona's eyes widened with dismay when she spotted us heading toward her. She untwined her fingers from those of her companion. "Sara, Emma, what are you doing here?"

Her man friend broke off from whatever he'd been saying to stand up politely. He was very good looking, just a little, well…old.

"We've been shopping. It's Emma's day off." Sara gave Fiona's friend a pointed look.

"Won't you join us?" The man pulled out the chair next to him. Sara flashed him a beaming smile and sat down.

Fiona's face took on a sucked lemon expression as I took the other vacant seat.

"I'm Sara and this is Fiona's sister, Emma. And you are…?"

"Paul Goddard." He shook Sara's hand then turned to shake hands with me. "I'm delighted to meet you, Emma."

Paul Goddard. I'd heard his name before. I trawled through my memory banks of Fiona's friends and acquaintances, but couldn't find anything certain.

"Paul, would you go and get the girls coffees, please?" Fiona smiled at him and he moved off to obey after he'd asked us what we'd like.

As soon as he'd gone to the counter to get more lattes, Fiona pounced.

"What are you two doing here? You can't stay."

"Oh, really, and why not? What are you up to?" Sara asked and settled onto her seat as if she planned a long visit.

"Got it!" I exclaimed. "I know who he is!"

Fiona and Sara ignored my outburst and carried on bickering. I finally remembered where I knew him from—Paul Goddard was the big cheese of the Crystal Foundation. He'd started it in memory of his wife, after she'd died of cancer ten years ago.

"I'm not up to anything, as you so elegantly put it. Paul and I have a lot to discuss. In private." Fiona glowered at us.

"You look very friendly for people who aren't up to anything. If it's all above board, why are you skulking around in a coffee bar?" Sara challenged.

"Because until a short while ago, I was engaged, and there are people out there who might see Paul and I together and make more of it than there really is," Fiona huffed.

If Sara and I hadn't seen the two of them hold hands, we might have believed her. Paul came back with our coffees. He seemed really nice, but age-wise he's more of a match for Mummy than for Fi. It would be like me dating Mr. G! Urgh, scrub my skull out with carbolic at the thought.

"Have you two known each other long?" Sara was immune to the look Fiona shot her. Years of living with her own mother had helped to give her an incredibly thick skin; so Fi didn't make any headway with her glares.

"We've worked together for a few years now, haven't we Fiona?" Paul smiled at Fi. From the look on his face, he was besotted. *Uh-oh*, I thought. *Rebound romance!*

"Oh, you work together." Sara sipped her latte and tried to look innocent.

"Charity work." Fiona struggled to talk through her gritted teeth.

"You're connected with the Crystal Foundation, aren't you?" I felt certain I knew who he was now.

"Yes, Fiona helps us with our fundraising. I'm trying to persuade her to carry on helping us. It would be terrible if we lost her expertise due to the unfortunate business with Niall."

Sara choked on a mouthful of coffee and coughed hard to clear her throat. "Oh, yes, that would be terrible."

"Well, I expect you two have lots more shopping to do." Fiona whisked my mug away and shoved it on an empty table behind us before I'd finished my drink.

"We're not in any…" Sara began.

I kicked her ankle.

"…hurry but then again, there are quite a few more shops we want to go to." Sara glared at me and rubbed her ankle surreptitiously under the table.

It would be better to let Fiona carry on with whatever it was she was up to. No doubt I'd find out all about it in due course when Mummy got wind of it. We gathered up our carrier bags, said goodbye to Fiona and Paul and headed back to the high street.

"Spoilsport," Sara muttered as I dragged her past the display of tiny jeans in Baby Gap's window. Sara had perked right up after running into Fiona. Speculating about my sister's love life had distracted her from thinking about her own.

We finished off our spree with a visit to the nail-bar for a manicure. It felt like the old days before Shay and Marco and Jessie, as I sat alongside Sara, singing to the radio and giggling with the manicurists.

It started to get dark so I said goodbye to Sara and headed for home. I imagined sitting down to a nice cozy dinner with Marco. I wondered where he planned to take me. He'd found his way around the city pretty fast considering he hadn't been in the country long.

It would be nice to spend some quality time alone together. Since he'd arrived, we hadn't had much chance, and when we had, we hadn't bothered to use the time to talk.

I heard Marco on the phone when I let myself into the flat.

"Yeah, it's all cool. Everything's set to go. No probs, man. Yeah, you can trust me."

I dumped my bags down on the sofa and went into the kitchen to get a drink. Marco finished off his conversation and then hung up. "You and Sara have a good time?" he asked me.

"Yes, it was really nice. It's been ages since we went out and had some fun together." I flashed my nails at him. "What do you think?"

"Nice."

I guess nails aren't a man thing. I poured some Coke from the bottle on the worktop. It tasted flat and warm. "So, where are we eating tonight? Do I need to glam up?" Maybe I could wear the nice new top I'd got the other day from Monsoon.

"How does the new Mexican restaurant near Toscini's sound?" Marco grinned and waited for my reaction.

It was rumoured to be wildly expensive and to get a table meant you either had to sleep with the maitre'd or be a blood relative of the cook.

"Have you got a table?" If he had, it called for the new top. Hell, for dinner at the Mexican, I might even wear the torturous shoes again.

"No problem."

I put my glass down so I could give him a hug.

"How long have I got to get ready?"

"Couple of hours. I thought we would go for drinks first." He slipped his arms around my waist. "Everton's sending the car for us at eight."

"Everton? I thought it would just be you and me?" I was glad my face was buried against his chest so he couldn't see my expression. My heart sank—so much for a cosy, romantic evening for two.

"He got us the table. It's just you and me, Everton, and a few of his friends. These are important people, babe. We're with the in-crowd."

If Everton and company were the in-crowd, then God only knows what the out-crowd looked like. I suspect me, Sara, and Rob were part of the on-the-edge-of-the-planet-we-were–so-far-out-crowd.

All the prospective pleasure in the evening fizzled out of me. I felt as flat as the fortnight-old Coke I'd just sipped. Marco continued to talk, oblivious to the sudden rigidity in my spine.

"Tonight is going to be so cool, babe. Everton is really taken with you. He's the kind of guy who, if he likes you, will really help you business-wise." He hugged me again, unable to hide the jubilation in his voice. "You and me are going places, babe. You'll be able to wave good-bye to that travel agent job and we'll be sitting pretty."

Okay, so I'm not the world's greatest travel agent. It certainly isn't top of the great jobs list and Mr. G isn't the best boss. But it's my job and I like working with Rob and the others.

A pile of estate agent leaflets casually dropped in a heap by the phone caught my eye.

"What are those?"

Marco kissed me on the lips and broke off the embrace to snatch up the details. He waved them under my nose.

"I got these today. I thought we could look at some of them tomorrow."

I looked at the leaflets. "These are flat details!" Then I spotted the prices and the locations. "These are expensive flat details!"

"We need to start looking, babe. This place was fine when you were here on your own, but we need somewhere with a bit more space."

I followed his gaze around my lounge, seeing it through his eyes. The old-fashioned, wall-mounted gas fire that popped when you turned it on. The peeling bit of wallpaper in the top left-hand corner by the bay window. The stain on the carpet I'd covered with my Ikea rug.

"It's not that bad." I felt compelled to defend my home.

"You deserve somewhere better than this. Wait until you see some of these places."

107

He led me to the sofa and started to enthuse about Jacuzzis and kitchens with clean lines. It was hard not to be swept along by Marco's excitement.

Maybe we should look for a new place, I thought. He had a point about space being in short supply since he'd moved in. Not to mention hot water. I swear Marco must have been a cat in a previous life, he spent so much time and care preening himself.

I left him to gloat over the details while I soaked in a blissfully hot bath with a Lush bath bomb and an illicit Galaxy bar. I'd hidden the chocolate in my dressing-gown pocket and forgotten all about it until now. A huge, white penthouse apartment and the life of a lady of leisure had a certain appeal.

But something wasn't right with this picture. Though I didn't like or trust Everton and his cronies, the explanations Marco gave me for the money and his business plans were plausible I suppose. But…

And that was exactly it. But what? Marco had asked me to trust him and I didn't have a definite reason not to. Chocolate crumbs had melted on my boobs, so I popped the remains of the Galaxy bar in my mouth and washed away the evidence with my Hello Kitty wash mitt. Perhaps I could find out more during dinner. If I had to spend time with Everton, I might as well get to know him better. Perhaps his company might grow on me. Then again, so might a wart.

Marco took even longer to get ready than I did. I have to say, though, my husband is a very handsome guy. Six-foot-two of mocha-latte hunk with dark soulful eyes a girl could drown in. I could never figure out what he saw in me. Don't get me wrong. I'm not ugly, but Marco is like Fiona; one of life's golden people, blessed with good looks, personality and charm by the bucketful.

Everton's chauffeur was very prompt. He knocked on the door as I deliberated over whether I should wear the cute shoes with the kitten heels, or the funky lime-coloured wedges I got in the January sales. I went with the kitten heels; for once I put comfort before fashion. My feet were puffy from all the shopping I'd done with Sara.

We followed the chauffeur with no neck down the garden path. I was pretty sure Toby and Steven had seen us leave from upstairs. Everton had remained seated in the back of the car waiting for us, which felt a touch disconcerting. For some reason, I'd imagined he would meet us at the wine bar before we went on to the restaurant.

"Emma, you look lovely, as usual." Everton's gold tooth gleamed in the car's interior light.

"Thank you." I was sandwiched between Marco and our generous host as the car pulled away.

"Marco tells me you and your friends have made arrangements to go to Spain for the weekend."

"Um, yes, there'll be quite a crowd of us. My sister's decided to come too."

"Your friend will be staying on a yacht, Marco said?"

"Only for a day. It was a prize in a charity auction." I wasn't quite sure what Everton found so riveting about all this, unless he had a secret yearning to join the sailing fraternity.

"Who does the yacht belong to?" Marco joined in with the questions.

"I'm not sure. Fiona knows. It's someone who supports the Crystal Foundation. Apparently he's due to sail back to England a few days after the charity date."

Everton and Marco exchanged glances. Maybe Everton had thought of buying a yacht after all. "I've always had an interest in sailing."

Ha ha, I was right!

"Where is the yacht moored normally in England?" Everton asked.

"Salcombe, I think. I only know because Fiona was faffing on about possibly using it to get some extra publicity for the Foundation."

The car slowed to a halt outside Toscini's and the chauffeur jumped out to come around and open the door. Everton climbed out first then extended his hand to help me.

Mother would approve of his manners. He tucked my arm through his while Marco climbed out of the other side of the car. I noticed Everton had a small spider's web tattoo on the back of his hand near the gold strap of his Rolex watch. Marco had a similar design in the same place. He told me once that he'd had it done years ago when he was still at school. Weird coincidence.

Chapter Ten

Marco stayed to talk to the chauffeur as Everton swept me across the road and into Toscini's as if we were minor Hollywood celebrities on a night out.

Everton smelled of Armani. Actually, once I took a closer look, I felt pretty sure the suit was Armani, as well. Toscini's looked just as busy as the last time we'd been there. My escort stood in the doorway with me on his arm as if he was the lord of all he surveyed. I wished Marco would get in and rescue me.

"What do you think of this place, Emma?"

Everton's question caught me off-guard. "It's always very busy." That sounded lame.

"No, I meant what do you think of the setting, the ambience?"

Ambience, not a word I would have thought of from Everton. "Um, well, it's very nice, I suppose. People must like it or it wouldn't be so popular. I wish there were more seats, though."

Everton smiled and displayed his gold tooth more prominently. "People drink faster—and therefore drink more—if they're standing up."

I wasn't sure why he'd asked me about Toscini's, but thankfully Marco came in to join us.

"The others will be at the bar," Everton announced, as if he had x-ray vision and could see right through the densely-packed throng. Marco took my hand and we followed Everton as he cut a path through the crowd.

"What were you saying to Everton?" Marco whispered in my ear.

"He asked me what I thought of Toscini's."

"What did you say?" His tone sharpened.

"I said it needed more chairs." I felt a touch irritated. "Why all the fuss?"

"He owns it." Marco's expression was speculative.

I blinked, stumbling momentarily in surprise. Well, I suppose that explained a lot. I knew some of the business ideas Marco had involved bars or restaurants.

"The club we went to with Rob and Gilly—does he own that too?" Time I found out more about our new friend, Everton.

"Uh-huh, and a whole load of others."

The bartender must have seen us coming, because a bottle of champagne stood freshly-opened in a bucket of ice and a tray full of glasses was at hand.

Three people stood waiting for us, two women and a man. They might have been introduced to me the other night, but I wasn't sure. I didn't recognize any of them.

The man appeared older than Everton and Marco, probably in his early forties, and one of the women looked as if she might be his wife or girlfriend. Gilly would have loved her Jane Birkin handbag. The other woman must have been Everton's date for the evening. She attached herself to his arm as soon as he approached the bar.

The bartender appeared as if by magic He ignored the crowd waiting to be served (which was three deep by now) and poured out the champagne and produced Tapas platters from under the bar.

Everton handed me a glass of champagne as I nibbled at a slice of spicy sausage from the Tapas plate. The two stick-thin women exchanged supercilious glances and just accepted a glass of champagne.

The men were busy chatting so I thought I'd try to talk to the stick insects.

"So, what did you say you did?" I asked Everton's date. I was well aware she hadn't said. But, since I hadn't even caught her name during the introductions, I had to start somewhere.

"I'm a model." She looked very bored.

It explained the anorexic expression, I suppose.

"What about you?" I thought I'd better ask the other one in case she felt left out.

"Sorry?" A vacant look flitted across her face.

"What kind of work do you do?" God, this was hard.

"Oh." She brightened slightly. "Work?" She thought for a minute. "I'm a personal assistant."

Right, and I belong to Mensa. I abandoned my attempts to talk to Dumb and Dumber and carried on tasting different Tapas while half-listening to Marco and Everton's conversation.

"Those are very high in calories. Are you doing Atkins?" Stick Insect stared accusingly at the umpteenth slice of Chorizo, which I was about to pop in my mouth.

Cheeky cow! I stuffed the sausage into my mouth and chewed it quickly. "What diet do you recommend?" The Stick Insect's face lit up and even Einstein looked interested. I'd found their level.

By the time we rolled out of Toscini's and on to the Mexican restaurant, I'd eaten nearly all the Tapas, drunk several glasses of champagne, and knew the pros and cons of every diet on the planet.

I also knew far more than I ever wanted to about colonic irrigation, detox therapy and illegal appetite suppressants. Eating dinner would be fun.

The cold air outside made me feel a bit woozy. Maybe I'd drunk more of the champagne than I thought.

"Hey, careful babe." Marco caught hold of my elbow to steady me as we stepped inside the door.

Stick Insect and Einstein had begun to discuss dress designers by the time we were seated at the table. It felt like being at home with Fiona and Mummy.

The restaurant looked really cool. The interior designer had done a good job. The table area was a cross between minimal industrialist and Aztec temple, while the bar area reminded me of old spaghetti westerns. I half-expected Clint Eastwood to come striding through the service door.

The waiters bought us a tray of margaritas along with the menus. Marco sat on my left and Stick Insect on my right. Marco and Everton continued to talk. Einstein speculated with the Stick Insect on the number of calories in her margarita. I took a swig of my drink and tried to focus on the menu. Putting my glass down, I picked up some bread from the wooden platter in the centre of the table and nibbled it. I needed to soak some alcohol up fast or I would be in trouble later.

"Really, Emma!" Stick Insect frowned at me. She fished in her clutch purse for her mobile phone. "I'll give you my therapist's number. She's marvelous at sorting out eating problems. I mean, I was a size twelve until she took me in hand." She whispered the last remark conspiratorially at me as if she'd confessed something really shameful.

She found the number from her list of contacts, scribbled it down on a napkin and tucked it inside my handbag. Great! I'll add it to my list.

Things to Do:

See a diet therapist. (Not!)

Have a colonic washout. (Yeah, right!)

Never, ever, under any circumstances agree to see these lunatics again.

The food tasted great, which was a good job really. It helped to make up for the company. The scary thing was that, listening to Stick Insect and Einstein swap tips on diets, brands of bottled water and manicurists, I had the feeling that this might be the kind of future Marco envisioned for me.

I know being a travel agent isn't my first choice of career, but at least it's something. Einstein and Stick Insect seemed to be there only to bolster their partners' egos.

I tried to listen in on the men's conversation but it consisted of a lengthy discussion of numbers and figures—boring. Marco and Everton glanced at me occasionally and took turns asking, "Enjoying yourself, Emma?"

I didn't want to upset Everton. I guessed he wasn't the kind of man it would be wise to upset, so I smiled a lot and said, "lovely, thank you" and "great" in the appropriate spaces.

At last, the evening drew to a close. Thankfully, Everton ordered taxis for us so at least we didn't have to take another ride in his car.

"My baby will want his bit of sugar on the way home," Einstein confided with a wink while we were in the loo. Argh, too much information. The thought of Everton Bullet-head getting his leg over with Einstein in the back of the car on his way home made me feel sick. Or maybe it was because margaritas and champagne aren't a good mix. Either way, I felt queasy.

"Don't forget to call my therapist!" Stick Insect called after me as I escaped into the back of the taxi. Since I'd flushed the napkin with the phone number on it down the restaurant loo, the chances of me getting a colonic irrigation or having my poo examined by an 'expert' wasn't great. SlimFast suddenly seemed like an attractive proposition.

"What did I tell you, babe?" Marco said, grinning. "Wasn't that a great night? I'm glad you and the other girls hit it off so well."

"Oh, yeah, they were a bundle of laughs." The sarcastic inflection in my voice appeared to escape him, as he carried on talking at a rate of knots.

"Everton plans to open a new club soon," Marco burbled on, full of enthusiasm.

"Really." Perhaps Einstein and Stick Insect would pole-dance for him. Then again maybe not—you need boobs to be a pole-dancer, or so I'm told.

"…so it's going to be a fantastic opportunity for me," Marco concluded.

I'd missed something. That'll teach me to go off into a daydream when I'm being told something important. I don't think I'd have made much of a career as an international spy. (Which, incidentally, had been one of my top three career choices when I was at school.)

The taxi drew to a halt outside the flat just as Toby and Steven were dropped off by some friends.

"Out late again, Emma? You are such a dirty stop-out!" Steven helped me out of the taxi while Marco sorted out our fare.

"Where was it tonight?" Toby asked as he slipped his arm through Steven's.

"The new Mexican restaurant near Toscini's."

"Oh, my God! It's so hard to get a seat in there." Steven looked envious.

"Isn't that the place owned by that gangster?" Toby asked.

Marco joined us.

"A friend of Marco's owns it." I wasn't surprised people thought Everton must be a gangster; he certainly looked the part.

"Everton's a wealthy and influential man. He has enemies, that's how these crazy rumors start. He's really a kind and generous person, isn't he Emma?" Marco looked to me for confirmation. His eyes flashed with irritation and I sensed the guys had hit a nerve.

"He's very kind to you." I meant to say "to us" but I still felt uneasy about Everton, even if he was an old friend of Marco's.

Marco grinned. "It's best to stamp on these rumors as soon as they start. Everton would be very hurt if he thought people misunderstood him. It wouldn't be wise to hurt his feelings." He opened the door into the communal hall.

Steven and Toby glanced at each other uneasily and started up the stairs.

"Night!" I called after them, but they'd let themselves into their flat and didn't hear me.

"Funny how rumors start, isn't it?" My imagination ran away with me again. Everton couldn't really be a gangster. Could he? Oh, God, all my doubts about Marco's involvement with him bubbled back up.

"Yeah, funny." Marco disappeared into the bathroom.

Well, thank you, Mr. Reassurance I thought. I dropped my bag on the sofa and went to get a drink of water from the kitchen. My head had already started to ache from the drinks.

"Marco, have you seen the aspirin?" I opened the kitchen drawers and started to rummage through them. Heaven only knows where I'd left the spare headache tablets; Toby had borrowed the last of the ones I kept in the bathroom when he'd accidentally bumped his head walking into a cupboard door that Steven had left open.

Marco's passport lay at the back of the junk drawer. I had a quick peek for a giggle; passport photos are always good for a laugh. As was typical, Marco still managed to look good even on his passport. Ratbag! I look like Ozzy Osbourne on mine.

I was about to close it to put it back in the drawer when I noticed they'd made a mistake with Marco's name.

"What are you doing with that?" Marco snapped, as he reached over and snatched the passport from my hand. I hadn't heard him come back in from the bathroom.

"I was looking for the aspirin."

"Well, don't mess with my stuff." He looked cross and a shiver ran up my spine.

"It's only your passport. It's not as if I was going to lose it. Anyway, how come your name's wrong?"

Marco paused for a second. "It's not wrong. It's just how they printed it; they put my middle name first, that's all." He stuffed the passport back in the drawer. "Come on, babe, let's go to bed."

He clicked off the lights and led the way to the bedroom. Too tired to debate any further, I followed him. I wasn't happy with his answer, but if I didn't get to bed, I'd fall asleep in the kitchen.

My eyes didn't feel as if they'd been shut for more than a few minutes when I heard the phone ring. I tucked the duvet over my head and shuffled further down the bed to bury my head in the pillows.

Through the wadding, I heard Marco answer the phone and start talking to somebody. A minute later he snapped on the bedside lamp. I screwed up my eyes against the light flooding the room.

"What are you doing?" Ugh, my voice wasn't working properly and my tongue felt fuzzy.

"Its okay. Go back to sleep, babe." He scribbled notes onto a little pad as I disentangled myself from the quilt to peer blearily in his direction.

"What time is it?"

Marco ignored me and carried on scribbling. I groped around on the bedside cabinet until I found my wrist watch. Squinting at the dial, I realized it was five-thirty. Who knew there were two five-thirty's in a day?

Marco jumped out of bed and shrugged into his jeans.

"What are you doing?" I asked. "Where are you going?"

He tucked the phone under his chin, still listening to whoever was on the other end. "It's okay, go back to sleep."

By now of course, sleep was a distant memory. "Who are you talking to?"

Exasperated, he glared at me before throwing on his shirt. "It's Everton." He resumed his phone conversation while he hunted for his shoes. "Yeah, it's cool. I've got it covered." Finally he hung up.

"Well?" I wasn't very pleased at being woken up at the crack of dawn. Didn't Everton ever sleep like a normal person?

"I've got to go out babe; Everton wants me to do a favor for him." He slipped his shoes on and grabbed his jacket from the chair at the end of the bed.

"What kind of favor? Where are you going?" God, Everton only has to say "jump" and Marco says "how high?"

He leaned over to kiss me on the lips. "I'll only be an hour, then later this morning, we'll go and look at some of those flats."

With that, he went. I heard the door of the flat close and the communal door bang shut. Then the BMW engine started up and roared away.

Frustrated, I gave the pillows a thump and settled back to sulk. What had Princess Diana once said? Something about there being three people in her marriage? I knew how she felt.

I was thoroughly awake by now, so the chance of a nice, long, lazy lie-in had gone. Marco's flight bag, the one that had held the mysterious packages lay empty and bundled up in the corner. I never had found out what was inside.

I hesitated for a good ten seconds before I jumped out of bed to start rummaging in the wardrobe and chest of drawers. Okay, I did feel a little twinge of guilt. After all, Marco had asked me to trust him yet here I was ferreting around in his possessions. What on earth I thought I would find, I really couldn't say. Not that it made any difference, because I didn't find anything other than Marco's clothes. No mystery parcels, no secret stash of anything more interesting than several new pairs of Armani briefs.

I decided to give up and treat myself to a big bowl of Coco Pops. Feeling better for a sugar boost, I snuggled into the corner of the sofa and flicked through the T.V. channels. Kid's cartoon, stock market update, a political discussion, and breakfast news talking about a gangland shooting. I turned it off, not interested by any of it.

I leafed through the flat details Marco had left out. If any of them involved living near Everton, Einstein or Stick Insect, they were a no.

The phone rang and I dived on it, expecting it to be Marco telling me he was on his way back. Instead it was Mummy.

"Hello darling, are you alright?" This was odd; my mother never rings me this early in the morning when she knows it's my day off, especially not to ask me about my health.

"Fine, Mummy. Why wouldn't I be?"

"No reason, I was just asking. How's Marco?"

"He's fine, too."

"You're up early."

Blimey, what was this? Twenty questions? "Marco had to go out; his friend needed a favour."

"Is everything okay between you two, Emma?"

Uh, oh, now what was coming? "Fine, Mum."

"You would tell me, wouldn't you if anything was wrong?" She sounded anxious.

"Mummy, everything is great. We're going out later to look at some flats together because we need somewhere a bit bigger now we're back together." I tried to make my voice sound as reassuring as possible. Mummy would be the last person I'd ever tell if it all did go pear-shaped with me and Marco.

Normally I wouldn't have said anything about the flat hunting, either, because knowing Mummy, she might insist on coming with us.

"Oh, well, that's nice." She didn't sound very convinced. "You will make sure it's a nice neighborhood darling, won't you? I mean, it's on the news about that terrible shooting near Toscini's early this morning."

"Near Toscini's? We were only there last night." I hadn't realized the news footage I'd flicked through earlier had been of Toscini's.

"See what I mean? And that place always looks so respectable. Some quite nice people go there."

I had to admit, an icy chill ran through me when I thought about it. Although by the time the evening news came on tonight it would probably turn out to be some kind of domestic incident or a nutter with a firearm fetish. Not a thought that gave me much comfort, but better than the other thoughts I had.

"How's Fiona?" I changed the subject to do some fishing of my own. I wondered if Mummy had got wind of Fi's new man yet.

"She's gone back to her own flat. Niall's been phoning after her, and I told him where to get off." Mummy sounded quite indignant.

"I don't suppose he's very pleased about having to pay a pawnbroker to reclaim Fi's ring." Not that I had much sympathy for Niall. He'd made his bed and all that.

Mummy snorted. "That man treated your sister very badly. I don't know if she'll ever get over it."

Hmm. So Mummy didn't know about Fiona's new sugar daddy. That wasn't like Fi at all. I mean, she might keep a thing or two from me, but from Mummy? Never, or so I would have thought, and yet apparently she had. *Why?* I wondered.

Chapter Eleven

After Mummy rang off, I decided to dress up ready for the great flat hunt. I mean, if I did go with Marco to look around all these posh apartments, I'd better try to look the part.

I almost weighed myself while I was still in my bra and knickers but after the conversation last night, thought better of it. If it wasn't for the fact that I loved food so much, I'd be tempted to become anorexic after listening to Stick Insect and Einstein.

By the time I finished my third cup of coffee, my head had begun to buzz and there was still no sign of Marco. Half of my precious day off had gone, and I still sat there like a lemon, all dressed up with no place to go.

I had decided to give up and go out to get some groceries and SlimFast when Marco rang. It was difficult to hear him; the reception was dreadful and his voice kept breaking up.

"Emma, I won't be back until late."

At least, I thought he said until late; he might have said until eight.

"Where are you?"

"…hospital…accident, Everton asked me to take someone over…" The phone went dead.

Great, now I would spend the rest of the day worrying. Who'd been in an accident? I wondered uneasily if this was connected in some way with the shooting Mummy had mentioned, but Marco had definitely said an accident.

My breakfast of Coco Pops had worn off and my stomach rumbled. I couldn't put off the grocery shopping any longer, so I trolled off down the road to the local shop.

Mr. Vassilanas's shop used to be your bog-standard newsagent-corner store, but last year his sons had persuaded him to buy and extend into the old cake shop next door. The whole place is now called Value Shoppe and the prices have gone up.

It's not much different otherwise, except it plays canned muzak instead of Radio Two and Mr. Vassilanas has his daughter-in-law, Vera, in a blue apron as his assistant.

I shoved a loaf and some Pot Noodles into a basket, as Value Shoppe didn't appear to carry SlimFast. Turning the corner by the bottles of Diet Coke and the Pringle tubs, I walked slap bang into Rob.

"Emma!"

"What are you doing here?" Value Shoppe was a bit out of Rob's way and he looked shifty.

He raked his hand through his hair so it stuck up in cute little tufts along the front. "I was on my way to your house. Your mum rang me early this morning. She sounded worried about you. I promised her I'd look in on you."

I wish my mother would remember sometimes that I'm a twenty-four-year-old married woman.

"You're a bit dressed up for Value Shoppe," Rob observed. "Are you off somewhere?"

I'd forgotten I had on my best designer jeans and suede jacket. "I was supposed to go out with Marco to look at flats but he got a phone call to run an errand for Everton."

"Well, it seems a shame to waste a good outfit." He grinned. "Fancy going out for lunch?"

It had been ages since Rob and I had spent any time together, just the two of us messing about. I knew that since Marco's arrival, Rob had felt a bit awkward. Which was silly really, because Rob's been my friend for years and you'd think he'd know better.

I paid for my groceries and Rob put them in the back of his car.

"Where are we going?"

Rob didn't reply for a second. His attention was focussed on the traffic behind us. "That's weird, I could have sworn..." He shook his head. "Never mind. How about that pub down by the river where we went last year?"

"Fine, it's nice there."

We drove along in a companionable silence for a while. The car roof appeared to be fixed, so even though the heater didn't work, I wasn't as cold as I'd been the last time I'd had a ride in Rob's pride and joy.

"Your mum was worried in case you'd been in Toscini's—you know, when the shooting happened." Rob threw me a quick sideways glance.

"We were there earlier last night but then we went on to the Mexican. We must have been at home for a while when it happened. Why would she think I'd be mixed up in that?"

Rob pulled into the pub car park. "I'm not sure. I think she's concerned about you. And Marco's friend, the one that gave us a ride home the other night, he's got quite a reputation." Rob switched off the engine. "The last news bulletin on the radio said they thought the shooting was drug-related."

"You think Everton's a drug dealer?" Oh, my God! A gangster and a drug dealer, and Marco's out there somewhere doing favors for him! Is Marco involved? Oh, my God, the packages in the hold-all!

Rob looked concerned. "I don't know, Em. You know how rumors start and he does look the part..."

I think he realized he'd scared me, because he changed the subject and opened his door.

"Come on, let's go and get something to eat."

I climbed out of Rob's car with my mind whirring over the implications of what he'd said. Rob halted mid-stride to look around the car park.

"What's wrong?" I looked around too; though God knows what or who it was I was supposed to be looking for.

"I don't know. Paranoia. I keep feeling as if we're being followed."

"Probably Mummy, making sure I don't get kidnapped by the white slave trade."

Rob smiled and slipped his arm around my shoulders to walk me into the pub. I needed a hug. I would usually crack a joke, but I didn't feel much like laughing as we went inside.

The lunchtime rush had died down so we managed to grab a good table. We'd been here a few times before with Sara and Shay. Usually, in the middle of the week, it was full of pensioners, but we didn't mind as the place was pretty and the food good.

I waited until the waitress cleared away the dirty plates from the people who'd sat there before us. Once she'd gone to the bar to fetch our drink order, I asked Rob the question niggling away in my mind.

"Do you and Mummy think Marco is involved in something shady?"

Rob fiddled with his knife, turning it over and over on the table. "I don't know. You know him better than anybody, Em. You've met his friends." He looked up, his eyes serious. "Have you talked to him about them?"

It was like my conversation with Sara bounced right back at me. The waitress returned with our drinks and menus. As soon as she headed back to the kitchen with our orders, we resumed our conversation.

I felt disloyal, talking about Marco like this, but all the talk of gangsters and drug dealers had unnerved me. "Marco doesn't tend to say much about his connections with Everton. They've been friends for years, though."

"Really?" Rob sounded surprised.

I nodded. "It's quite cute. They were friends together at school. They have the same tattoo on their hand by their wrist."

"Tattoo?"

"I think they had them done when they were young. It's a little spider's web near their watch straps. Marco has an empty web but Everton's has a creepy black spider on it."

Rob shuffled on his seat.

"Are you alright?"

"Emma, you do know what those kind of tattoos usually mean, don't you?"

Um, well, apparently not. Color me clueless but I didn't know what he meant. A tattoo's a tattoo; all the celebs have them.

"Tattoos like that usually mean the person wearing them belongs to a gang," Rob said.

I didn't think he meant the Bash Street kids. Okay, so my husband was in, or had been in a gang. I took a deep breath. It wasn't that unusual, so it didn't have to mean anything bad.

"Look, forget I said anything," Rob said. "I'm sure you're right. It may have been something from when they were kids. Everton's probably perfectly respectable. He might just be trading on the past." Rob still looked uncomfortable and I don't think he believed a word of what he'd just said.

I didn't want to think too much about it. I was sick of thinking and second guessing what Marco might or might not be doing. The implications of Marco being in a gang were too scary to think about. I needed to talk about something else.

I fished around for a change of subject. Some friend I was to Rob; I'd been so busy with my own concerns, I hadn't once asked him about his life. I wondered if Fiona had told him she had found someone new.

"Enough about me," I said. "I can't think about all that now. What about you? How are things?"

"I'm fine. I still can't shake Gilly, though. She keeps popping up everywhere I go. It's beginning to freak me out. I know I have to keep her sweet until we've been to Spain, but I don't know if I can do it. I'm so glad you guys are coming with us."

The waitress returned with our meals and we stopped talking for a few minutes while we dug into our lasagne and chips.

"Did Greenback make much fuss about us both being off on the same weekend?" It shouldn't make any difference. We overlapped one day off a week anyway and Rob was deputy manager. I, on the other hand, was

Things To Do

definitely never likely to make it any higher than my current lowly position of agency junior.

"No more than usual. He's still seeing your mum. Esme has decided she's found her true vocation in the Scottish Highlands and wants him to divorce her as soon as possible." Rob grinned at the sour expression on my face.

"I emailed Dad to tell him about Marco. I tried phoning, but there's a message on the machine saying he's on vacation. I expect he'll be in touch when he gets back."

Rob didn't say anything. He didn't need to. We both knew my dad was only interested in anything Fi or I did if he thought it would cost him money.

"Mummy hasn't said much about seeing Mr. G. Do you think it's serious?"

Rob had emptied his plate and stole some chips off mine. "Don't know. If he does divorce Esme, it might affect our jobs, though."

"How?" I couldn't think of any way it would affect me unless he proposed to Mummy. What a thought: Mr. G as my boss and my step-dad. I bet even then, I still wouldn't be promoted.

"He'd have to give Esme half the agencies as part of a settlement. I doubt if he could afford to buy her out." Rob stole another chip.

I smacked his hand away from my plate. "Leave me some chips! Esme wouldn't want the shops anyway."

"I'm doing you a favor—you keep saying you want to lose weight! And she wouldn't want the shops, but she would want the money." He leaned back in his chair and grinned, having just speared my last three chips with his fork.

"Rob! I said—!"

"Oh, shit!" The grin evaporated from his face. He sat bolt upright in his chair, ready to run at any moment as Gilly's voice rang out across the pub.

Sure enough, she headed toward us on her trademark high heels with her little dog peeking out of her handbag. Reaching our table, she sat down uninvited on the empty seat next to Rob and beamed at us.

"I drove past and saw your car in the lot," she said. "Wasn't that lucky?"

"Quite a coincidence," Rob muttered into the remains of his lager.

"I'm glad I've seen you, Emma," Gilly said, turning to me.

I almost fell off my seat.

"Rob tells me everything is booked for Spain. We're looking forward to having you and Marco join us for a short while. But you will remember the date on the yacht is just for two, won't you?" She slid her hand along Rob's arm and he moved it out of her reach.

"Oh, of course," I replied. "But there'll be a photographer and a chaperone with you. Apparently it's to protect the Foundation from any litigation risks should one of the auctioned bachelors turn out to be a secret axe murderer or something." I'd only found this out from Fi a few days ago. Personally, having seen the women at the auction (who were all like Gilly), I think the bachelors were more likely to be the ones in danger.

Gilly's eyes narrowed. "Well, I'm sure Rob and I will still find a little space for a romantic moment."

Somehow, I feel Gilly is destined for disappointment. Rob's tried everything to shake her off but she still clings on to the idea that if she can get him alone in a romantic setting, he'll change his mind.

"I think we're only on the yacht for a short time, Gilly." Rob edged away from where she had leaned into him.

I unhooked my bag from the back of the chair. Gilly mentioning Marco's name reminded me I needed to check my messages in case he'd tried to ring me during lunch.

Nothing. Disappointed, I switched the ring tone back on. Gilly continued to witter on and Rob looked increasingly desperate to escape.

When my phone rang as I was about to put it back in my bag, I almost dropped it in surprise. A quick glance at the name flashing on the front before I pressed the connect button told me it wasn't Marco calling, but Toby.

"Emma, where are you? You've got to come home now! The police are here and I can't tell them what's been taken or anything."

Things To Do

"What's the matter? What police?" Oh, my God, it must be Marco.

"You've been burgled! I called back at lunchtime to pick up Steven's dry cleaning and your door was open." Toby's voice was shrill with adrenaline. My pulse slowed down a little once it hit me that Marco wasn't dead or arrested.

"What's wrong?" Rob leaned across the table and took the phone to speak to Toby.

"I've been burgled." Nausea washed over me. Someone had been in my flat, in my things. I'd only cleaned it a few hours ago, too, damn it.

"Oh, my God, that's ghastly. I mean, I know you live in a high crime area but really!" Gilly's face was a mask of disapproval. It was a good thing the waitress had already cleared away our plates or I'd have been compelled to stab her with my fork.

Rob finished talking to Toby, then handed the phone back. "Toby says they've made quite a mess. He can't tell what they've taken. The police want some details from you."

I felt numb; it's not as if I have anything very valuable, except a few pieces of jewelry.

"I'll take you home. Do you want me to call Fi or your mum?" Rob got to his feet and shrugged his coat on.

"No, I'll see what's happened first." My legs felt as if the stuffing had leaked out of them and I was glad of Rob slipping his arm around me for support.

"I'll follow you. You might want some help," Gilly announced and gathered up her doggy-in-a-bag.

I wasn't sure what kind of help Gilly had in mind, but I was too worried about what I might find waiting for me when I got home to argue with her.

Rob said very little as he drove to the flat. I hoped Marco would ring so I could tell him what had happened, but of course he didn't. I could have kicked myself for getting rid of Einstein and the Stick Insect's phone numbers. At least then I could have rung Everton and asked him to try and get hold of

Marco for me. I suspected he would be able to find him much more easily than I could. Which made me even more pissed off with my missing husband.

Toby and Steven were outside by the front gate talking to a policewoman as we pulled to a halt. Gilly's pink car skidded to a stop behind us, inches from Rob's back bumper.

"Miss Morgan?" The policewoman looked at her notebook.

"Yes," I said.

Toby and Steven glanced at each other and I knew why. I'd never bothered to use my married name. I'd fully intended to when I first got married, but then it had all gone wrong and I'd flown back to England without Marco. Since then I hadn't thought about using anything other than my maiden name.

The policewoman asked me lots of questions about who lived in the flat, what time I'd gone out, and all that kind of stuff.

"The forensic team is in your flat at the moment, Miss Morgan. Fortunately they were just about to leave another job nearby when we got the call." She spoke in a tone which suggested I should be honored they'd consented to take fingerprints at my lowly burglary. I suppose it had been lucky; when Mummy got burgled a few years ago, no one came and she had to go to the police station to get a crime number.

Gilly stood next to me, her ears flapping as the policewoman explained the procedures. I wanted to get inside my flat to see what had happened.

Two men came out of the front door carrying little bags and boxes. "Okay, love, you can go in now," one of them called as he loaded the boxes into his car.

I wasn't sure what to expect. Years of watching *The Bill* and *Crimewatch* left me a bit disappointed that there was no incident tape or crime scene notice by my front door.

The inside of my flat was a complete mess. Everything was everywhere, the contents of my kitchen canisters not that there had been much in them were emptied onto the floor. The seat cushions of my sofa and chairs were slashed open and the foam fillings left to hang out. In the bedroom the pillows had been slashed and feathers lay like grey snow all over the floor.

"What were they looking for?" Gilly asked. She'd wandered in uninvited behind me while Rob, Toby and Steven were still outside with the WPC.

I wanted to cry. Everything I owned had been destroyed. Every drawer and cupboard had been tipped out, all my underwear, Marco's CDs, everything. And where was bloody Marco? I don't know why I was angry with him apart from the fact that he'd gone missing.

"I appreciate things are a mess, Miss Morgan, but can you tell if anything has been taken?" The policewoman joined us in the bedroom.

I spotted my jewelry box lying on the floor with the lid broken off. I'd had it since I was little; Daddy gave it to me for my birthday when I was seven. It was white with a picture of Cinderella on the lid and it had one of those little ballerinas inside that turns to the music that plays when you open it.

All my jewelry lay spilled out in a tangled heap of gold chains and earrings amongst the feathers on the floor. "I don't think anything's missing."

"Are you sure, Emma?" Rob picked up the lid of my box. He looked angry.

"It's hard to tell. There's so much mess, but I don't think anything's actually gone." I picked up my wedding ring. I'd only ever worn it for a few brief blissful hours after the ceremony. I tried to slide it on my finger and it wouldn't fit. Maybe it was an omen.

The policewoman's radio crackled into life and she went back outside to answer it.

"What are you going to do, Emma? You can't stay here." Gilly cradled her dog closer to her and stepped over a pile of my knickers to stand next to Rob.

"I don't know." I hadn't thought about it, but I didn't want to stay in the flat tonight. I didn't feel safe. Marco had been right about moving.

"You could sleep on our couch," Steven offered. "But there wouldn't be room for two."

"Thanks guys, but its fine, I can go to Mummy's." And I wasn't going anywhere until Marco came home.

The policewoman popped back in to say she'd had another call and would be in touch in a few days to get us to sign statements. We followed her to the front door, where the lads inspected the locks that had been jemmied.

"You need to call a locksmith," Rob pronounced.

"And the insurance company," Gilly added.

I didn't feel up to doing anything.

"Come up to our flat, Em. I'll make you a cup of tea while you phone." Toby patted my arm.

"I'll wait down here for the locksmith and try to straighten a few things up for you," Steven offered.

I felt really touched by their kindness. Rob gave me a hug and Gilly glowered at me.

"Well, as you seem to be getting sorted out, Rob and I ought to go and leave you to it." Gilly smiled meaningfully at Rob.

"You go, Gilly. I'll stay and help Emma clear up until Marco gets back," Rob dismissed her suggestion.

"Where is Marco?" Gilly asked and peered around as if she expected him to materialize out of the woodwork at any moment.

Toby and Steven looked uncomfortable and Rob developed an interest in the jemmied door.

"I can't get hold of him at the moment. He'll probably get back soon." I wished Gilly and her stupid dog would take themselves back to the land of the Sloanes and leave me alone.

A noise from outside made us all turn just Marco's BMW pulled up in front of Rob's car.

Chapter Twelve

Toby and Steven melted away faster than butter on hot toast. Rob took on a defensive stance, while Gilly and the pooch were alive with interest as Marco made his way up the path toward us.

One of the things that had attracted me to Marco when we first met was the way he walked. He prowled like a large, lazy cat, king of all he surveyed. It still made my pulse move up a notch.

"What's going on?" He examined the splintered wood around the lock on our front door.

"We've been burgled," I said.

Marco didn't wait for me to say anything else, but instead pushed past Gilly and into the flat. "Emma, come in here!"

I followed the direction of Marco's shout and found him in our bedroom, scowling at the feathers lying in little grey drifts all over the floor.

"Have the police been?"

"They were here when we got back. They've taken all the details and fingerprinted," Rob answered for me.

"I don't think anything's missing." I felt sick of the whole thing, and for some reason, my teeth had started to chatter. I felt nauseous.

"Good." Marco eyed the wreckage.

"It's as if they were looking for something special," Gilly remarked brightly, as she stroked her dog's head.

Marco's lip curled. "What would anyone expect to find here? Emma doesn't even keep groceries in."

Gilly gave a false little laugh, stopping when Rob glared at her.

"Emma's had a nasty shock. We were about to go upstairs to Toby and Steven's," Rob said.

Marco put his arm around me and gave me a quick hug. "Of course. I'm sorry, Emma, go on up and we'll get the locks fixed."

I left Marco, Gilly and Rob downstairs and went with Toby and Steven. I heard Rob try to persuade Gilly to go home as I climbed the top step.

Toby and Steven's flat had everything mine didn't. Toby had decorated in shades of coffee and parchment; all the contents were coordinated and elegant.

"I've made you some tea, Emma." Steven carried a tray of Clarice Cliff-inspired mugs into the lounge and placed them carefully down on the coffee table.

"You look awful, darling." Toby fussed around, puffing up cushions behind my back.

"I'll have to phone Mummy and see if Marco and I can stay there tonight." The thought of having to tell Mummy about the burglary on top of the talk earlier about gangs and shootings made the nausea come back. I put my mug back down on the tray.

"Emma..." Toby began to speak, but Steven stopped him from continuing with a warning shake of his head.

"What did Marco say?" Steven offered me a biscuit from an art deco plate that matched the mugs.

"Not much. He asked if anything had been stolen." It occurred to me then that he hadn't seemed very shocked by the robbery actually—more annoyed by the mess, and I still didn't know where he'd been all day.

"Em, you don't think that..." Toby began, but his voice faded.

"Don't think what?" I asked, glancing toward him in time to see Steven make throat-cutting gestures.

"What is the matter with you two?" I began to feel ratty with them. Talk about making a drama out of a crisis.

"Darling, I hate to say this, but you don't think this burglary has anything to do with you-know-who?" Steven whispered the last three words.

Maybe I'd strayed into a Harry Potter movie by mistake.

I must have looked blank because Toby added, "Marco's friend the gangster."

"Why would Everton have anything to do with me being burgled?"

"Oh, Emma, honestly!" Toby threw his hands up dramatically. "Not Everton himself, silly, but if Marco is known to be a friend of his…" He leaned back on the cushions, looking very pleased with himself.

"They could have been searching for something hidden in your flat," Steven agreed with Toby, his expression equally smug. His earlier reluctance to say anything had been overcome by his ambition to play detective.

"Well, thank you, Holmes and Watson. You've been in my flat; you couldn't hide anything larger than a cornflake."

"Mmm." Steven didn't appear convinced.

"You don't even know Everton really is a gangster. It's probably one of those urban myths because he looks so sinister," I persisted, ignoring my conscience's mutterings about tattoos and gang memberships.

Steven flashed Toby a told-you-she-wouldn't-believe-us look.

There was a rap on the lounge door and Rob peered in.

"Gilly's gone home and the locksmith's arrived to do the door. So I'll leave you and Marco to it."

I walked over to him. "Thank you for everything today, Rob. I don't know what I'd have done without you." His cheek felt rough beneath my lips and I smelt the lovely, familiar scent of his aftershave.

"Well…erm…I'll be off then. Hang on in there, Penfold." He disappeared downstairs and I sat back down on the sofa.

"Can I use your phone?" I asked.

Toby handed it over. I got the number from Yellow Pages and called the insurance people. Then I rang Mummy. I'd braced myself for the conversation, so it threw me for a curve when Mr. G answered the phone. I'd forgotten today was half-day closing.

"Um, is Mummy there?" My carefully prepared non-alarmist spiel deserted me completely.

"I'll call her for you. Is this Emma? Is everything all right?"

I heard him shout, "Charlotte, its Emma!" I caught a snatch of brief muffled conversation, and then Mummy came on the line.

"Is everything all right, Emma? Ian said he thought you sounded distressed. It's nothing to do with the shooting is it?"

I hurried to reassure her. "No, Mummy, it's not that. I wondered if Marco and I could come and stay tonight. The flat's been broken into and it's a bit of a mess." I waited for the fall-out.

"Oh, Emma, my poor girl! Do you want us to come and get you? We'll come straight away. What's been stolen? Have the police been? You weren't there when they broke in, were you? Have you called the insurance? How did they get inside?"

I waited until she paused for breath and dived in with answers. "Don't come to get me, nothing's been taken, the police have been. I've told the insurance company and the locksmith's here now to mend the doors. The flat will be fine once I've cleaned up, but I don't want to stay there tonight." To my dismay, I started to cry. I suppose it must have been delayed shock or something.

"Oh, darling, of course you must come. Are you sure you don't want us to fetch you?"

I managed to stop sniffing long enough to decline the offer of a lift. It was only after I'd put the phone down that I realized she'd said *we* and not *I* throughout our conversation. Her relationship with Mr. G must be serious.

Toby and Steven still hovered. Toby passed me some tissues.

"Sorry, guys."

Things To Do

"Don't even think about apologising." Steven patted my shoulder awkwardly.

"I'm going to go back downstairs. I need to pack a few things and tell Marco we're staying at Mummy's."

"Of course." Toby hugged me and I thanked them both for the tea.

The locksmith had packed up his tools, ready to leave and Marco was busy on his mobile when I got back to the flat.

"No man, nothing gone. Yeah, everything's still cool." He finished the call when he saw me. I guessed from the tone of the conversation, he'd probably been talking to Everton.

The locksmith handed me the bill to pass on to the insurance company.

Marco didn't make a move to tip him, so I delved into my bag and gave the man a fiver for coming out so promptly. Thanking me, he handed over the new keys and left.

"I've told Mummy we'll stay there tonight."

"You frightened, babe?"

"No, but I don't want to stay here tonight, everywhere is such a mess." Okay, so logically I knew the burglars weren't likely to return, but even so, I didn't want to be in the flat.

"Okay." Marco didn't argue. He draped his arm over my shoulders. I wished I knew what his thoughts really were about the break-in.

"Where were you today?" I asked. "I wanted to get hold of you earlier."

Marco's arm stiffened and he removed it from my shoulders. "I told you, I've been doing a favor for Everton, okay? Somebody got sick and I had to take them to hospital. You aren't allowed to have phones on in the emergency room." He sounded impatient.

"I'll pack a bag." I didn't feel in the mood for an argument; I might start to cry again.

I grabbed some of our clothes from the piles on the floor and got the toothbrushes from the bathroom. Even in there had been trashed, with my talcum powder lying in white heaps all over the floor. It flew up into my face and over my hair when the scent made me sneeze.

Marco made no move to get out of the car when we arrived outside Mummy's house.

"You go in, babe. I'll be back later. I've got some business to take care of first." He roared away and left me standing on the pavement with my mouth open, clutching a bag of clothes.

"Emma, darling! Where's Marco going?" Mummy peered down the street after the disappearing BMW.

"He'll be along soon." At least I hoped he would.

Mr. G lurked in the hall. We were about to close the front door behind us when another car skidded up to the curb: Niall's bright red Porsche.

"Oh, dear," Mummy said.

We all turned to see what would happen next. Niall jumped out.

"Good grief, he's got that woman with him!" Mummy muttered, a frown of displeasure creasing her brow.

Niall paused to tug Glenda free from the low-slung passenger seat of the sports car. She shot free like a fat cork from a bottle.

"What do they want?" Mummy murmured, as I stifled a giggle.

"Ah, Mrs. Morgan." Niall hurried towards us, Glenda puffed along behind him. I was shocked to see how pregnant she already looked.

"Niall, to what do I owe the pleasure of this visit?" Even someone as thick-skinned and self important as Niall couldn't fail to notice the frosty tone in Mummy's voice.

Glenda caught up with him and attached herself to his arm like a human leech, which was ironically befitting. "We need to speak to Fiona," she panted.

Mummy ignored her. "Niall?"

Niall turned red; he was clearly there under Glenda's orders.

"Fiona is refusing to talk to me and I need to speak with her as a matter of urgency." His lips pursed and he looked like a toddler about to throw a tantrum.

Things To Do

Pompous twit. Why would Fi want to waste her breath on him?

"Can you blame her for not wanting to speak to you?" Mummy glared at Niall.

"I don't think you realize how badly your daughter has treated poor Niall," Glenda piped up.

I've often read in books about people "bristling with rage" and wondered what it meant, but as I watched Mummy look at Glenda, I knew.

"I suggest you and your tart remove yourselves from my doorstep immediately," she said. "I have nothing to say to either of you and neither does Fiona."

Mummy slammed the door in their faces and we heard Glenda wail, "Fiona owes Niall one hundred and eighty thousand pounds!"

A frantic hammering sounded on the front door as the letterbox was pushed open. "Tell her we'll sue!" Glenda screeched, and then they were gone.

"Well, really!" Mummy shepherded us along the hall and into the kitchen. Mr. G toddled along with us, trying to appear unconcerned by the ruckus which had just taken place.

I wondered what on earth Fi could have spent one hundred and eighty thousand pounds on. I know she loves to shop, but even she would draw the line at blowing that much in one spree, wouldn't she?

I escaped upstairs to my old bedroom. Mummy called Fi and left her a message to tell her about Niall's visit.

Mr. G gave me a day off so I could get the flat sorted out and all the paperwork done for the insurance and the police. I still felt uncomfortable with the whole idea of him and Mummy dating. It disturbed the natural order of things.

Two hours later, and there was still no sign of Marco. I toyed with the thought of calling him on his mobile, but it didn't seem worth it. He never answered, at least not for me. He'd ignored it when I'd tried to contact him about the break-in. No doubt he'd show up eventually. I only hoped it would be before Mummy went to bed and put the chain on the front door.

After I'd had a nice soak in the bath with some of Fi's Chanel bath stuff, I called Sara. She sounded suitably shocked and sympathetic about the break-in and offered to meet me at the flat the next day to help clean up. We chatted for over an hour and I felt much better by the time I hung up.

At least Sara hadn't gone on about gangsters and shootings or implied that Marco was caught up in something murky like Steven, Toby and Rob had done. I snuggled down under the Laura Ashley duvet cover and tried to work out how I felt about Marco.

It wasn't easy; Marco still had the power to make my heart beat faster and my whole being ache to be with him. But then there was the down side—I couldn't trust him and I never knew where he was or what his plans for us actually involved.

Sex with him was good—no, it was better than that. It was fantastic. But was that enough to build a future on? Especially when he might be a gangster? I had never envisioned myself as a gangster's moll and the idea of prison visiting didn't appeal.

I heard the front door open and my sister giggle in the hall. I tried to make out who she had with her. Surely she hadn't brought Paul home. There were footsteps on the stairs and more laughter, then my bedroom door opened and Marco came in.

"Hey, babe, thought you might be asleep. Fiona just came in. She is one cool chick, your sister." He sat down on the side of the bed and the mattress dipped under his weight.

"I've been waiting for you," I said. "I thought Mummy might lock you out if you weren't back soon."

He slid a long brown finger down the side of my cheek. "You look tired. I'm sorry we didn't get to look at those apartments today."

I wasn't sure if I felt sorry or not. The break-in had upset me, but I wasn't sure if I wanted to move to the kind of place Marco had in mind for us. I wasn't sure if I wanted to move with Marco anywhere anymore.

He seemed to pick up on my mood and stood to peel off his shirt in one fluid movement. Normally my pulse would race and I would long for him to hurry his undressing. Instead I just felt weary.

He paused for a fraction of a second as if assessing my lack of response before he finished his preparations and slipped into bed beside me.

"Are you okay, babe?"

I turned out the light. "Fine. Tired, I think, like you said."

Marco must have been satisfied with my answer as within minutes he fell fast asleep, leaving me to lie awake in the dark. I stared at the ceiling and tried to think.

Things to Do:

Clean up my flat.

Clean up my life.

Investigate whether Calvin Klein made a line of prison garb.

I didn't sleep very well. After waking up every hour on the hour, I gave up at six o'clock and crept past a still-snoring Marco to go downstairs and make a cup of tea.

The last thing I expected to find when I reached the kitchen was Mr. G in a stripy toweling dressing gown. He held a tray set with two mugs ready to carry back upstairs.

"Ah, Emma. Good morning."

Oh, my God, how embarrassing. Thank heavens I had on my pj's and not one of my shortie night shirts.

"I couldn't sleep so I came down to make some tea," I said.

"Splendid, I've just made Charlotte a drink." He didn't turn a hair as he reached an extra mug down for me.

My toes curled with embarrassment as I turned away to get a teaspoon from the drawer. My brain wasn't up to making small talk with my boss in my mother's kitchen at this hour of the morning.

Besides which, I didn't know where to look. If I looked down I could see his lily-white, hairy legs and if I looked up, his dressing gown had gaped open to reveal an equally pale hairy chest. It was not attractive.

The kitchen door opened again and Fiona drifted in, yawning her head off. "Any tea?"

"I'm making some more now." Mr. G pulled another mug from the cupboard.

Fiona didn't seem at all phased to see Mr. G make himself so at home. Instead she settled down onto one of the kitchen stools and started to leaf through a copy of *Vogue* that lay on the breakfast counter.

"That's a nice color. What do you think, Em?" She pointed to a lipstick in a cosmetics advert.

"You've got that one." I think she had every shade they made.

"Mmm, maybe."

Mr. G finished making our drinks and picked up his tray again, ready to leave. "Your mother said to tell you there were some croissants if you were hungry."

The door closed behind him and I sat down on a stool next to Fi.

"Is it serious between him and Mummy?"

Fiona didn't lift her eyes from a fashion spread of skinny girls in sarongs. "Dunno. He's here a lot though."

"You heard Niall and Glenda came looking for you, didn't you? Glenda claims you owe Niall one hundred and eighty thousand pounds."

Fiona continued to placidly flip the pages of the magazine. "She never was any good at maths. I make it nearer two hundred and fifteen thousand. He's probably trying to fob her off with a cheap ring."

I almost choked on my tea. "What are you going to do?"

Fiona looked at me as if I was deranged. "Do? I'm not going to do anything. He owed me big time. It's compensation. Glenda can sing for the money." She slid gracefully from her stool. "Do you want a croissant? There's some cherry jam."

I watched her pad across the kitchen in her ice blue satin pajamas.

"Where does Paul fit in?" I asked.

She tipped the croissants onto the plates and got out the jam. "Paul is a really sweet guy. I'm very fond of him."

I passed her the knives. "How fond?"

"What is this? The Inquisition?" She passed a plate over and came to sit back down, licking a smear of jam from her thumb as she did so.

"Well?" I asked.

"If you must know I'm meeting him in Spain. You know it's his yacht the Foundation is using? Well, I'm going to be Rob and Gilly's chaperone and handle all the publicity. Afterwards, I'm staying on in Spain and then sailing back to England with Paul." She took a large self-satisfied bite of her croissant.

"I see."

"Are you sure I've got this lipstick?" Fi turned her attention back to the magazine and the subject was closed.

I couldn't wait to meet Sara at the flat to fill her in on this latest gossip.

Chapter Thirteen

Mummy gave me a lift over to the flat on her way into work. Marco was still in bed, Mr. G had left earlier, and Fiona had retreated to her room with *Vogue* and the last of the croissants and jam.

"Oh Emma, I didn't realize they'd done this much damage. You'll need new furniture and bedding, everything." Mummy gazed around at the wreckage of my flat.

"Sara will be here soon to help me clean up and the insurance assessor is due this morning too, so hopefully I'll be straightened up in no time." I tried to sound optimistic, but I felt more like crying all over again. The flat looked worse than I remembered and even when it had been all cleaned up, I wasn't certain I would ever feel happy living there again.

"Do you want me to call my office? I can stay and help you."

"No, Mummy, really, it'll be fine." I know it was kind of Mummy to offer but she would take over when the assessor came and be full of the Dunkirk spirit while she cleaned. I couldn't cope with a morning of stories of how Granny had survived the blitz.

"Well, if you're really sure, darling." She sounded doubtful.

"Really Mummy, I'm fine. It looks worse than it is because of the feathers and stuff." I patted one of the slashed sofa cushions to make my point and sent a cloud of bits flying up into the air.

"Promise me you'll call me if you change your mind." She kissed me on the cheek and I managed to ease her out of the flat.

Things To Do

Left on my own, I surveyed the carnage. Gilly had been right when she'd said it looked as if they'd been searching for something. Maybe all burglars left houses like this; I'd never had anything stolen before so I couldn't make a comparison. I still couldn't shake the idea that the break-in was somehow connected to Marco and his activities, though.

I picked up the roll of bags I'd brought with me and headed for the bedroom. My poor broken jewelry box stood on the dresser where Rob had placed it. At least they hadn't stolen any of my jewelry, not that I had much of any value. Some gold earrings, a necklace with my initial on it, and a gold dolphin bangle I'd bought for myself when I'd visited Rhodes with Fiona and Mummy after Mummy and Daddy's divorce.

Perhaps they'd been after money or credit cards. Whoever had broken in must have been sadly disappointed with what they'd found in my home.

I'd hardly begun to scoop the free-floating feathers and bits of foam into a bag when the front door bell rang. Sara stood outside with a big plastic bucket full of cleaning products.

"Sorry I'm a bit late. Shay's taken Jessie to Gymbabes. He dropped me off at the corner. I bought some coffee and milk as you said they'd tipped all your stuff out." She walked past me into the hall. "Gosh, Emma, you weren't kidding. Put the kettle on. I'll get the vacuum cleaner and we'll make a start."

Sara shifted the ransacked contents of the hall cupboard. She unearthed the vacuum cleaner from underneath a pile of old coats and the ironing board Mummy had given me as a flat-warming present but which I'd never used. I had always been too lazy to get it out. I used a folded towel on the kitchen worktop instead.

Obediently, I crunched my way across the carpet of spilled teabags, coffee, sugar and flour that lay across my kitchen floor, and plugged in the kettle.

The sound of vacuuming came from the hall and Sara began to sing. She's one of those strange people who likes to clean. Even before she had Jessie, she was never happier than when she had an excuse to pull on her rubber gloves and get stuck in.

I made two mugs of coffee with Sara's supplies and took one to her.

"Do you want to keep all these old coats, Em?" She switched off the vacuum cleaner and started to pick through the contents of the cupboard.

"I suppose now would be a good time to have a clearout." One of the coats was my old school blazer. It didn't fasten across my bust any more and the last time I'd worn it had been at a St Trinian's-themed charity do of Fiona's.

Sara shook open a black bag and stuffed the blazer inside. We disposed of four other jackets the same way—one my mother had bought me (yuck), one that didn't fit, one that had paint on it, and one that Sara said made me look like the "before" advert for Weight Watchers.

Marco's cases lay on the floor under the coats. The burglars had slashed the linings inside them along with those of my best imitation Louis Vuitton case.

"You should make a list of these, Em, for the assessor when he comes." Sara helped me stack them back inside the cupboard and we made notes on a piece of paper.

With the hall restored to some kind of order, we drank a fresh cup of coffee. I longed to ask Sara about Shay and I knew she wanted to talk.

"I read Shay's text messages last night on his phone. He'd left it on the kitchen counter while he was in the shower." She said it as if she thought I would lecture her on respecting his privacy. Not bloody likely. I'd do exactly the same thing if I was in her position.

"Did you find anything?" I asked.

She shook her head. "Nothing definite, just one text which hinted at some secret he didn't want to tell me."

"You should talk to him." I took another slurp of coffee and felt a fraud because I was as guilty of not confronting Marco as Sara was of avoiding Shay.

"I can't say I've read his texts, can I?"

I didn't reply. I'd been awake all night thinking about my issues with Marco. I could hardly give Sara advice when I couldn't get my own problems sorted out.

Sara switched the vacuum cleaner back on and we carried on through into the lounge. I attempted to reassemble the sofa and between us, we wrestled the most badly damaged things into more bags. The list of items that had been ruined or that needed to be replaced grew longer.

"The trouble is, I'm too scared to ask Shay about this woman," Sara said suddenly.

We were in the kitchen. I held the dustpan while Sara swept the mess into it with a broom. I considered what she'd said. "Scared it's true?" I asked. "Scared he'll leave you? What kind of scared?"

Sara tucked an escaping piece of hair back into her ponytail before continuing. "Scared he doesn't love me anymore." Her voice wobbled and she brushed a heap of flour up into the air and all over my sweatshirt.

"But you could be worrying about something that just isn't true." I wondered what held me back from confronting Marco. Maybe I was scared of something that might be nothing, too. I had to stop watching so much television. It only added fire to my already vivid imagination.

"I can cope with him being unfaithful," Sara said. "Kind of. I mean, since we had Jessie, we haven't had much the chance to have sex as often." She flushed up to the roots of her hair. "But if he didn't love me anymore, then that would be different."

Poor Sara. She loved Shay, really loved him. He and Jessie were her life. I remembered when he'd come to the flat the day after the bachelor auction, he'd been so worried about Sara and Jessie. Surely he hadn't changed so much in such a short time?

"I don't know, Sar, I always thought you and Shay were ideal together. He seems to adore you and Jessie." I tipped the dustpan into the trash bag, releasing another plume of dust which made us both cough.

"But I saw them, Em. I saw how she looked at him and I saw them kiss." Sara grabbed the mop and plunged it into a bucket of soapy water, making suds slosh over the sides onto the vinyl floor of the kitchen.

"But you'll never know if you don't ask him. Is anything different at home?"

"He's not so grouchy, and he gave me flowers." She swished the mop vigorously across the floor and I skipped backwards out of her way.

I wasn't sure if this was a good sign, but for Sara's sake I decided it was best to be positive. "Is that since we went out shopping and you decided you were going to try to change things?"

Sara stopped mid-swipe and considered. "Could be. I don't know any more. I try to read something into every little thing he does. Even him taking Jessie to Gymbabes."

The doorbell rang and I left Sara to the mopping while I answered it. I thought it would be the insurance man, but instead it was Rob in his work suit. He had my groceries from yesterday and takeout Starbucks coffee and cake. "Thought you might need a break," he said.

I took the brown bag with the food from him and he followed me down the hall. "Sara, Rob's here. With cake!"

I put the bag down on the newly-cleared worktop and got the cups and cakes out.

"Looks better in here," Rob said.

"Don't come in here yet. The floor's wet," Sara ordered, shooing me and Rob back into the lounge. We perched on the tattered remnants of the sofa and slurped our drinks.

"Thank you for this. I am so hungry." I took a bite of cake.

Rob rolled his eyes in mock despair. "Emma, you're always hungry. I remembered your shopping was still in the boot when I got home last night, so I thought I'd bring it over."

"How did you get rid of Gilly?"

Rob groaned. "Please don't talk to me about Gilly. She's driving me crazy. When I got to the shop this morning, she was waiting outside."

"Sounds serious," Sara said.

"She's bonkers." Rob slumped down on his seat, spilling more foam pieces from the cushion onto the carpet.

"Will you be careful? We're done in here." I tutted and smacked his leg.

"So how long until you guys go to Spain and Rob can get an injunction against Gilly?" Sara giggled as Rob grabbed a handful of foam and tried to shove it down the back of my top.

"Next weekend. Apart from Gilly being there, I'm looking forward to it. A spot of sunshine and sangria will be lovely." Rob answered her as he pinned me against he cushions while I tried to pick the foam from under my sweater.

"And *senoritas*?" Sara added with a grin.

Rob grimaced. "After Gilly, I'm sworn off women for a while."

I wriggled free. "I thought originally there was supposed to be a romantic dinner out as well as time on the yacht?" Glaring at Rob, I tried to smooth my hair down and refasten my hairclips.

"There is. The Foundation has booked a top place in Marbella." He picked up his coffee and scowled into the cup.

"At least it'll all be over soon plus you'll have Emma and Fi for company," Sara soothed. She didn't mention Marco and I didn't correct her. After all, knowing Marco, if Everton asked him not to go, then he wouldn't. So it could just be me and Fiona anyway. Oh, and Paul of course.

I wished Sara could come too, but there was no way she'd be prepared to leave Jessie. I had hinted at it but she'd ignored any suggestion that a break might do her good.

"I'd better get back to the shop before Greenback notices how long I've been gone." Rob stood up with a yawn and gave a lazy stretch. "If I sit here much longer I'll go to sleep. All the Gilly dodging is making me tired."

I followed him to the door. "Do I need to smuggle you out under a blanket?"

Rob laughed, but he still glanced around nervously as if he expected her to pop up at any moment. "Are you okay, Penfold?"

I knew he meant more than the burglary. Marco was conspicuously absent and Rob, being Rob, had noticed. "Yeah, Dangermouse," I said. "I'm fine."

He bent and kissed my cheek. "Take care. I'll catch you later."

I watched him walk out to his beloved wreck with a funny feeling in my tummy. This was crazy. I was not about to fall for Rob. I'd been there and done that and was so not going there again. Besides which, I was a married woman now and wasn't going to get sidetracked. Even if the man I'd married was a gangster.

"Come on, Em, we still have the bathroom and your bedroom to do!" Sara called over the sound of the vacuum cleaner.

I closed the communal front door and caught a glimpse of a familiar pink VW Beetle driving past. Gilly was still in full stalker mode. Poor Rob.

Two hours later, Sara and I collapsed on the chairs in the lounge with the flat finally looking presentable, but still no sign of the insurance assessor.

The phone rang and I picked it up, hoping it wasn't the assessor calling to cancel. Mr. G had given me one day off, but anything more would probably be stretching it.

"Hey, babe, how's it going?" Marco's familiar lazy drawl.

"Where are you and why aren't you here helping us?" I was not a happy bunny.

"Chill, babe, I've been busy. I found a really nice apartment I think you should take a look at." He didn't sound phased by my grumpiness.

"Marco, I really don't feel like looking for a new flat right now."

"Honey, a place like the one I've found won't stay empty for long. Everton's already got two or three other people who are interested." Marco sounded hurt.

"What's Everton got to do with it?" I forced the words out through gritted teeth.

"He has a few apartments which he lets out in his property portfolio. He's given us first refusal on this one. It's in the same block as his."

Terrific. Why didn't we just move in with bloody Everton and have done with it? "No, Marco." I put the phone down with a bang.

Sara raised her eyebrows. "What's up?"

"Marco wants us to move into a flat in Everton's block. Owned by Everton."

A silent "o" formed on Sara's lips. "I take it you're not too thrilled."

"Would you be?"

The phone rang again and I ignored it, letting the machine take the message.

"Emma, pick the phone up, babe." Marco tried pleading for a few more minutes before giving up.

A loud rap on the front door made me and Sara leap out of our skin. I'd been so busy being annoyed with Marco I'd forgotten about the assessor.

The insurance man looked about sixteen and didn't seem very sure of himself. We presented him with the list of damaged items and showed him around the flat. He offered to send in a team of cleaners, which pissed Sara off royally considering how hard we'd worked to tidy up.

Eventually he tucked our list into his briefcase and, after a flurry of phone calls with his office, agreed to us getting prices to replace most of my stuff.

Shay arrived with Jessie as the insurance man left, so I got a chance to cuddle the baby while Sara collected her things.

"Do you want a lift back to your mum's?" Sara buttoned her coat and lifted Jessie from my arms.

"No, it's okay. Fiona said she'd stop by on her way home and we'd go back together." I didn't fancy squashing into Shay's van. It was always full of bits of musical equipment and baby gear. Plus, I felt uncomfortable around Shay, knowing what Sara had told me.

"Well, if you're sure." Sara hoisted Jessie further up her hip and handed Shay her bag and bucket.

"I'll give you a call, and thanks for everything." I waved them off. Shay fussed over Jessie, making sure her little pink woolly hat was on straight. They looked the picture of a perfect little family.

I shut the communal door and hoped Fiona wouldn't be too long. The locksmith had replaced the lock on the communal door as well as the one on my own front door. Whoever had been responsible for the break-in must have been really determined to have forced their way through two locked doors.

The phone rang again as I got back into the lounge. I let the machine take it as I guessed it would be Marco again. I was right.

"Emma, pick up the phone. We need to talk about this, babe. It's not every day you get a chance like this. Come on, Em, pick up."

I was certainly not going to, and I'd already turned my mobile off. If I listened to him, I knew I'd end up with Everton as my landlord and Einstein and Stick Insect as my neighbors. Welcome to Gangsterville.

The telly drowned the answering machine out and I concentrated on the late afternoon news bulletin. The shooting outside Toscini's had remained topical. The newsreader described it as a drive-by gangland shooting. A police chief came on and spoke about a flourishing underworld culture ensnaring young people. I was glad when they changed the subject to redundancies in Scotland, not that I wanted anybody Scottish to be out of work.

Fiona was late, as usual. It was one of the few things we had in common, a genetic inability, inherited from Daddy that prevents us arriving anywhere on time. It's something that always infuriates Mummy, who has a thing about punctuality. Knowing Fiona, I guessed she was probably out shopping or avoiding Niall and Glenda.

I turned the television off and played Marco's message again. He sounded as if he was more concerned about upsetting Everton than about me and what I might want.

Fiona arrived three quarters of an hour late, which was quite good for her. I felt glad to see her. It had started to get dark and every time I heard a noise, I jumped, even though I knew Toby and Steven had come home and were only a shout away upstairs.

"I had to call in at Harvey Nick's and get some more face cream. There's a really good offer on perfumes. Oh, and I got that lipstick, the one I showed you this morning." Fiona's arms were loaded with carriers. "I thought I'd better bring these in as you live in a high-crime area."

"I thought you'd spent out on Niall's credit cards the other week? You're never buying more stuff." I didn't think there could possibly be anything left in the shops that Fiona hadn't already got. I ignored the jibe about the high-crime area.

Fiona whipped out a bottle of perfume and sprayed her wrist. "You can never have too much perfume. Here, smell this—it's lovely. I got the body lotion, too." She held out her arm for me to sniff.

"Nice," I agreed. "But what are you going to do about Niall?"

Fi tucked the perfume back inside the carrier bag. "You worry too much. I told you already, I'm not going to do anything. As far as I'm concerned, he owed me and if he wants his money back, he can sue." She flicked her hair with her hand and smiled. "And we both know he's not likely to do that."

I wished I had as much confidence in that belief as Fiona. I didn't think Niall would sue. He was too chicken to do anything on his own and he'd worry about his reputation, but Glenda would have no hesitation.

"We'd better go or Mummy will have a search party out for us," I said, as Fiona gathered her bags together and I turned out the light.

"Dunno about a full-blown search party. Probably just Ian Grebe in his Volvo." Fiona laughed and gave me a nudge.

"Ha-de-ha-ha, very funny." I locked the front door and ignored the sound of the phone beginning to ring yet again inside my flat.

Chapter Fourteen

Marco's car had gone when we arrived home. He'd probably gone off somewhere to sulk. Mummy bustled around the kitchen and a lovely smell of garlic and tomato filled the air.

"Marco's been trying to call you, dear." Mummy lifted the lid of a saucepan to peer in at the contents.

"Yes, I know. He wanted me to go and look at a new flat." I dumped my bag on the breakfast bar and sat down on a stool.

"He's had to go out, said to tell you he might be away for a couple of days. Something to do with that friend of his." Mummy glared at my handbag so I lifted it off the worktop and onto my lap.

"You know, Emma, I'm not sure this Everton is a good influence," she continued.

"Tell me about it." I wondered if Marco would bother to come back. More worrisome, I wasn't sure that I wanted him back. I waited for the old "marry-in-haste-repent-at-leisure" comment from my mother, but it didn't come.

"Marco isn't in some kind of trouble is he, Emma?"

"No. At least, not as far as I know." Answering Mummy's question made me realize I didn't know very much at all. I'd guessed at a lot of things. "Everton is an old childhood friend of Marco's, and he's been very generous to Marco since he arrived here." I might as well stick to the party line as I hadn't any proof to the contrary.

Things To Do

"I see." Mummy stirred the contents of the saucepan.

Fiona strolled into the kitchen. "Mmm, smells nice. I'm starving." She picked up an apple from the fruit bowl and took a bite.

Mummy frowned at her. "Fiona, your supper is nearly ready!"

"Sorry." Fi walked off into the lounge and after a few seconds we heard the sound of the shopping channel.

"I'm glad she's gone." Mummy closed the door. "I wanted to talk to you about your sister. I'm very worried about her. Since she and Niall broke up, she's seemed very depressed. I'd like you to keep an eye on her, see if you can get her to talk. I thought while you were together in Spain it might be a good time." She looked at me hopefully.

"Mum, I'm sure she's fine. I think she might even have met someone new." I felt a bit of a snitch dobbing Fi in to Mummy but I figured I needn't give her all the details. Just a few vague hints might be enough.

"Who is he?"

Uh-oh. "I think it's someone she's met through the Foundation. I don't think it's serious but it shows she's not depressed." I'm not good at lying to Mummy.

"Mmm." Hawk-like eyes watched me as I fiddled with my handbag and tried to slide off the stool to escape. "So, what's he like?"

I sidled along the breakfast bar. "Um, he seemed nice, very polite." Almost at the door.

"What's his name?"

"Paul." I slipped out of the door and up the stairs to my room before she could wheedle any more information out of me. I guess I'd been right. MI5 wouldn't have been a good career move. I'd never have been able to withstand enemy interrogation.

Marco had left the top of the dressing table in a mess: socks, aftershave and tubes of hair gel were scattered everywhere. None of the containers had their lids on. Exasperated, I began to tidy up the mess before Mummy could see it.

155

Under a bag containing brand new toiletries, I found an old envelope with writing on the back. I picked it up ready to put it in the bin.

It looked like a list. I smiled, thinking about my own lists.

Marco's writing was hard to read. It looked like a spider had fallen into a jar of ink and scuttled over the paper. The words I could make out looked like, *passport, money, yacht, holiday, Emma*.

Maybe it was for the holiday. Typical Marco, he hadn't included clothes anywhere on the list. Still, if my name was there, perhaps it meant he planned to buy me a present. Either that, or to remember to take me, and although that wasn't flattering, the way things were between us, it was a strong possibility.

I stacked the envelope up with his things and went to take a bath. All the cleaning with Sara earlier had made me feel grubby as well as hungry. I pinched some more of Fi's Chanel bath stuff and had a nice soak in the tub, though not for as long as I'd intended as Fiona banged on the door.

"How long are you going to be? I want a bath, too."

"Can't you use the shower in Mummy's bathroom?" My toes had begun to turn shrivelled and pink in the warm water.

"No. I want a bath. I've got a date with Paul. You're not using my Chanel are you?"

I sat up quickly with a guilty splash. "No. Look, I'll be out in a minute. Is supper ready?" I dried myself off and hoped Fi wouldn't notice that the bathroom smelt of Chanel.

"Yes, Mummy's done spag bog. Hurry up! You know the steam makes your hair frizzy if you stay in there too long." Fi thumped on the door again.

With the water drained out of the bath, I opened the door to let her in. She pushed past me, re-inserted the plug and started to run the taps.

"Bloody hell, Emma! You have been using my Chanel!" Fi peered at the jar trying to gauge how much had gone since she'd last used it.

"I only used a bit. Anyway, Sara says it goes off if you keep it too long." I crossed my fingers behind my back to off-set the fib, though I supposed it might be true.

"What did you tell Mummy about Paul for?" Fiona demanded. She straightened up and began to examine her complexion in the bathroom mirror while the tub filled up.

"I didn't say much. She thought you were depressed. I think she had visions of me keeping a suicide watch on you when we were in Spain."

Fiona looked exasperated. "Oh, for Heaven's sake! I'll be glad to go out tonight to get some sane conversation. Between Mummy thinking I'm about to top myself and you twittering on like blooming Jiminy Cricket, it's like being trapped with the cast of *Eastenders*." She dipped an elbow in the bathwater then turned off the taps.

"We're concerned about you," I said.

She slipped off her robe and stepped into the bath. "Well, don't be. And close the door on the way out, it's drafty in here."

I left her to it. When Fiona was in one of her Prima Donna moods there was no talking to her. The smell of Mummy's spaghetti bolognaise wafted its way upstairs so I hurried up and changed for supper.

I wasn't too surprised to find Mr. G already at the table and tucking in when I got back downstairs.

"Ah, Emma. Your mother tells me the tidying up has gone well?" He looked up from stuffing himself full of spag bog.

"Yes, Sara gave me a hand. The insurance people have agreed to replace most of the damaged stuff so I'll need to go shopping soon." I hoped he'd take the hint and tell me to have the rest of the week off.

"Plenty of time for that when you and your friends come back from Spain." He beamed at me, sauce moustache and all.

Mummy bustled in with two plates of spaghetti. "Yes, you don't want to be too hasty, Emma. I don't mind you and Marco staying here for a while longer. It's like old times having you and Fiona at home again." She slid the plates onto the tablemats and flapped an oven glove at me to indicate I should sit down.

"That's nice of you, Mummy, but I want to get back into the flat as soon as I can." I remembered only too well what it was like before living under the same roof as Mummy and Fiona.

Mummy looked hurt. "But you won't move back until after your holiday, surely? It'll take time to get your furniture replaced."

I knew she was probably right, but I had already decided to call into Ikea and pick up the latest catalogue after work tomorrow. I'd seen a really nice sofa the last time I'd gone there with Sara.

Fiona appeared at the door in her satin dressing gown. "Mummy, have you seen my green top?"

"I ironed it yesterday. Look in the utility room."

Fiona vanished and we heard her stomping about. I suppose living back at home had some advantages: cooked meals and laundry service for one thing. I know that's really two things, but there would be a price to pay—dealing with Mummy every day—so it evened out.

"Where are you going tonight, Fiona?" Mummy called.

"Not sure, just out." Fiona's voice was muffled.

"Is this with your new man?"

What sounded like an expletive came from the direction of the utility room. Fi arrived back in the dining room clutching her green top and looking cross.

"He's just a friend, Mummy."

Mummy patted her lips with her napkin. "If he's just a friend, why do you want your best top?"

Fiona glared at me. "This is all your fault!" she flounced out.

I carried on eating my spaghetti. I had got to get that catalogue tomorrow.

Things To Do

Marco called after I'd gone to bed. Admittedly I'd gone upstairs early; concentrating on the telly had proved far too hard with Mr. G and Mummy acting like a pair of lovesick teenagers on the settee.

Oh, and Greenback prefers less lightweight programmes, so we watched some really dull thing on politics in the developing world before Mummy insisted she watch something about cleaning your house instead.

Marco and I didn't talk for long. He was his usual evasive self when I tried to find out where he was and what he was doing. He insisted he'd be back in time for our holiday to Spain and that he loved me.

I wished he wouldn't do that. I know he's up to no good and I should cut loose, but every time I build myself up to talk to him about our marriage he plays the "I love you" card and I fall apart all over again.

> *Things to Do:*
> *Buy chocolate*
> *Apply fake tan*
> *Get a straight answer from Marco*

That's another problem with living back at Mummy's—a chocolate shortage. It's not that there isn't any, it's just that she hides hers and it's more than my life's worth to touch the box of Guylian seashell chocolates belonging to Fiona.

✔ ✔ ✔

Mr. G gave me a lift into work the next morning so for once I wasn't late. I even got there before Rob. It meant I had to listen to Classical Gold all the way to work, but it had to be better than taking the tube.

I spent most of the morning on the phone, ringing people to say their tickets were in or sorting out booking problems. By the time it got to half past eleven, my stomach thought my throat had been cut. I wondered if Rob had a Kit-Kat left in his desk drawer.

159

The phone rang again. I glanced around the shop, hoping someone else might pick it up but they were all busy with customers.

"Hello, Pack and Go. This is Emma." I hoped it wasn't another complaint; the last man who'd called seemed to feel it was entirely my fault that his flight home had been delayed for four hours.

"Oh, Emma, thank goodness it's you! I don't know what to do! I've called the police but they don't want to know and it's been two hours…"

"Gilly?" It was hard to be certain amongst the sobs.

"What should I do? Oh, Emma, my precious little Robbie's gone!"

I glanced across the shop to where Rob sat, hale and hearty, selling a holiday in Portugal to a woman with a moustache. I wondered if Gilly had finally flipped.

"What do you mean, gone?" I thought it best to humor her till I could find out what she was on about.

"He's been dog-napped!"

I moved the receiver a little way from my ear. Gilly can shatter glass when she's upset. Only she would name her dog after an ex-boyfriend. I wondered if Rob knew he had a doggy namesake.

"How do you know he's been dog-napped?" Perhaps he'd simply got fed up of being hauled about inside Gilly's handbag and made a break for it.

"He's missing, and my little snookums would never wander off and leave his Mummy!"

"So, you haven't had a ransom note or anything?"

Bad move. This sparked a fresh wail of despair from the other end of the line.

"My poor baby! He could be in the hands of terrorists. They'll mistreat him and he needs his special diet!"

"Gilly, will you calm down? You don't know anyone has taken him. When did you last see him?"

Things To Do

There was a pause and then some sniffing. "This morning, when I let him out into the garden." She dropped her voice to a conspiratorial whisper. "He needed to go, you know, outside."

I wanted to bang my head off the desk. "Then he could have escaped from the garden."

"He wouldn't do that. Oh Emma, can't you come and help me?"

Rob finished with his customer and made inquiring signs at me with his eyebrows. I mouthed back, "Gilly," and a terrified expression crossed his face before he made a dash for the back offices.

"Gilly, you know I'm at work."

"I came and helped you when you were burgled," she said reproachfully.

I'm not sure I would describe Gilly's presence at my flat in the aftermath of the robbery as being helpful, but she clearly felt it was. I looked at the clock. It was nearly twelve now and Gilly didn't live too far away.

"Listen, I'll try for an early lunch hour and come over." I didn't really want to spend my lunchtime with Gilly. I really wanted to go to Ikea, but I had a horrible feeling that if I didn't agree, then she might turn up at the shop.

"Is Rob there?"

Well, I couldn't see him, so I felt safe in saying, "Actually, Gilly, I think he's popped out."

"Oh. Well, will you tell him what's happened? I know he'll be worried. Rob is so fond of my little coochie-pie."

I think Gilly hoped Rob would drop everything and rush to her aid. I was second-best in the doggie squad stakes.

"I'll let him know."

"Thank you, Emma."

Rob reappeared by my desk the instant I put the phone down.

"What did she want?" He lowered his voice and leaned in toward me so no customers could hear.

"She says her pooch has been dog-napped."

There was an expression of complete bewilderment on Rob's face. "That ratty little thing that lives in her handbag?"

"Yep, that's the one. Robbie, he's called apparently." I bit back the urge to grin as Rob struggled to digest this latest bit of information.

"Well, has she called the police or somebody?"

"She says they aren't interested. I've promised to go over in my lunch break."

Rob's look of bewilderment was replaced by alarm. "You didn't say I'd go, did you?"

"No, but it'll cost you! Can I take a longer lunch?"

Rob's shoulders slumped with relief. "Okay, it's worth it. Greenback Grebe's gone out anyway, so I can cover for you."

Poor Rob. I stifled an urge to ruffle my fingers through his hair. After he'd gone back to his own desk, I wondered where that urge had come from.

✔ ✔ ✔

Gilly was at the door when I got to her house. I'd stopped off at Burger King en-route to scoff a burger and fries. Well, a girl's got to eat.

"I've been waiting ages. The police won't come out and the RSPCA say they can't help. My poor little Robbie!"

Gilly's eyes were pink from crying and I felt really mean for not going there straight from work. She led the way inside. Her house looked like one of the interiors you see in those beautiful home magazines all pale walls and cream leather sofas. Steven and Toby would approve.

"I let him go outside here," Gilly explained as she led me through her state-of-the-art kitchen and out the back door onto a small decked patio.

Gilly's garden was what you'd describe as low maintenance. It consisted of the decked area, surrounded by huge planters full of bamboos and other frondy things I didn't recognize. Around the edge was gravel. A high fence surrounded all the sides.

Things To Do

I could see why Gilly couldn't understand how the dog had got lost. The garden might resemble a mini rainforest but it was the size of a generous handkerchief and it certainly appeared to be securely fenced.

"Have you checked the fence to make sure he didn't dig his way out?" I suggested.

Gilly put on a baleful expression. Much as she loved her dog, I don't think she wanted to risk messing up her pastel pink Juicy tracksuit.

"I'll look." I prowled around the garden under the monster greenery and hoped my work clothes wouldn't get too dirty. Mr. G had designed our uniforms, with Esme's help, before they'd split up. Let's just say if they were a crime, the fashion police would lock them up and throw away the key.

"Can you see anything?" Gilly paced up and down the deck, wringing her hands.

"Nothing! Oh, wait…" I had seen something. At the back, behind something that looked like a giant rhubarb plant, the gravel had been scuffed up and there were marks on the fence. Maybe Gilly was right. It did look as if someone might have climbed over the fence and grabbed her dog.

"What is it?" Gilly peered at me through the greenery.

"It looks like someone may have been here."

Gilly let off a wail like a fire siren.

"What's on the other side of this fence?" I scrambled my way back on to the deck, brushing loose bits of plant off my shoulders. Mr. G would kill me if he knew what I was up to in my uniform.

Gilly looked bewildered. I don't think it had occurred to her that there might be anything on the other side of her fence.

"Nothing, really. There's a narrow path, I think, which leads to another house."

"Can we get to it?" I don't know what I expected to find there but I felt quite excited. Like being one of Charlie's Angels or Nancy Drew.

"I suppose so."

163

Gilly led the way back through her house and out through the front door. She carried on past another half dozen frontages, all identical to her house, before turning the corner.

A little way along the road, we came to a narrow service passage that ran behind the backs of all the houses in Gilly's row. It looked dark, overgrown, smelly and decidedly dangerous. All at once, I wasn't sure I wanted to be Nancy Drew anymore.

Chapter Fifteen

Gilly peered into the alley. "Do you think we ought to call the police again?"

"Perhaps you're right." After all, Robbie the dog had been liberated from Gilly's garden with human help. There was no way his little doggy legs had carried him over the fence on their own.

I followed Gilly back to her house. "I really should get back to work now."

She grabbed at the sleeve of my coat. "Don't leave me! What if they come back? They might demand a ransom."

Gilly might be thin but she had a grip of iron.

"I'll stay while you phone the police," I said.

She let go of my arm and went inside the house while I tried to restore the circulation in my wrist.

"Will you talk to them?" she asked, carrying a cordless phone to me. "They weren't very nice to me when I called earlier."

I wondered what she'd said to them. Her phone call to me hadn't been very coherent. Gilly gave me the number, and after a couple of attempts I got through to a nice man who listened patiently as I explained what we thought had happened to the dog.

"Well?" Gilly demanded as I put the receiver down.

"They'll send an officer round as soon as someone is free."

"When will that be? My poor little snookums could be anywhere by then!" She dissolved into tears.

I sneaked a quick look at my watch. If I didn't get back to the shop soon, I was going to be in trouble, favor for Rob or not.

"Look, Gilly, I'm sorry, but I have to get back to work." I felt awkward. She seemed genuinely upset about her dog, but I was still baffled about why she'd called me rather than someone else. "Do you want me to call one of your friends to come over?"

She shook her head and made pathetic dabs at her eyes with a soggy tissue. "Everyone's away. They've all gone skiing. I couldn't go because I spent the money at the auction."

I guess that was one mystery solved. Personally, I'd have thought she'd have done better spending her cash on a trip to the Alps instead of stalking Rob all over town.

"Will you come back after you finish work, Emma?"

She looked so dejected that I didn't have the heart to say no. Ikea would have to wait. "Okay, I'll get back as soon as I can." I made a bid for the door where she surprised me by squashing me in a bear hug.

"Thank you for coming over. I'd have asked Rob if he'd been there but I know he has a lot of managerial responsibilities."

Great, thank you, Rob. He could give me a lift to Gilly's after work. I'd say he owed me.

My mobile rang as I was on my way back to the shop.

"How long are you going to be?" Rob complained. "I'm starving to death here and somebody's eaten all my Kit-Kats."

I didn't care for the accusatory tone of Rob's voice when he mentioned the Kit-Kats. I'd been sure there had been one left in the packet. "I'm on my way back now. I'll get you a sandwich. Has Mr. G come back yet?"

"No, but you'd better get a move on."

He hung up and I guessed he'd been interrupted by a customer.

I nipped into the sandwich bar and got him some lunch. I even splashed out on some more Kit-Kats. Not because I felt guilty you understand, I just thought it might take some sort of bribe to persuade him to give me a lift to Gilly's later.

The shop was dead by the time I got in with Rob's lunch. It was school run time and the part-time staff had already left for the day.

Rob pounced on the bag and took it through to the back office, opening it as he went. I followed him, keeping an eye on the shop floor through the glass in case anyone came in.

"You didn't ask for horseradish, did you?" Rob peered suspiciously into his roast beef and salad baguette.

"No, you don't like horseradish. Anyway, do you want to know about Gilly's dog or not?"

He took a big bite of his lunch and nodded. I told him I thought Gilly's dog had been stolen and how distressed she'd been. "I promised to go back after work to check she was okay."

Rob nodded again and carried on eating.

"I thought you could come with me. I need a lift."

He swallowed hard. "Are you mad? I spend most of my life these days avoiding Gilly, not going out of my way to visit her at her house."

"I know, but she's so upset and she doesn't seem to have any friends she can call on. Let's face it—she must have felt pretty desperate to ring me." He couldn't argue with that.

"Look, I'll give you a ride over and drop you off at the corner but I'm not going in to see her," he said.

"You're a sweetie." I gave him a quick kiss on the cheek and scuttled back onto the shop floor just as Greenback puffed his way in through the door.

"Those racks are very untidy, Emma." He pursed his lips at my apparent idleness and I went over to straighten the brochures before he found something worse for me to do.

Luckily, more customers soon arrived and I even managed to sell two holidays before closing time, which was good because my sales figures for the month didn't look very healthy compared with everyone else's.

Mr. G went a little earlier than usual, leaving me and Rob to close up. The shutter had just gone down when my mobile rang. I half expected it to be Gilly again to check what time I intended to come back, but instead it was Marco, the vanishing husband.

"Hey, babe, how's it going?"

"Where are you?" I ignored his question. What was I supposed to say?

"I'm in Birmingham. Listen, I'll be home Friday morning, ready to go to the airport. Pack my gear for me, okay?"

"Marco!"

"Love you, babe." The phone went dead.

I stuffed it back in my handbag. If Marco had been within reach, I would have hit him on top of the head with it.

"Are you okay, Emma?"

I wasn't sure how much of the conversation Rob had heard.

"Marco says he'll be home Friday morning."

"Where is he?"

"Birmingham."

Rob raised one eyebrow but didn't ask me anything else, thank God. "I've got the printouts of the itinerary for the weekend." He delved inside his suit pocket and handed me a folded piece of paper.

We reached his car and I waited while he performed his ritual check of the bodywork in case anyone had bumped it while he'd been in work. After a couple of minutes, he unlocked the door to let me in.

"The itinerary doesn't look too bad, does it?" he asked. "The worst part is the time on the yacht with Gilly and then I suppose I've got Fiona to rescue me. For the dinner at the restaurant, I thought you and Marco could sit nearby…? I feel uncomfortable if I'm on my own with her."

Things To Do

I folded the paper back up and popped it in the glove box. "No, it looks okay."

Rob swung the car into a gap in the traffic and peered into his rear view mirror.

"What's the matter?" I asked.

He looked worried. "I tell you, this business with Gilly is making me paranoid. I keep thinking I'm being followed."

"Calm down, Dangermouse. Gilly's car is easy enough to spot. It's pink, for a start."

"No, this car is a dark BMW. I noticed it first a few days ago, parked outside my flat and now I keep seeing it all over the place."

"There are loads of those. Are you sure it's the same one?" It wasn't like Rob to imagine things. He was the one who usually shot my flights of fancy down in flames.

"I think so, but whenever I try to get near enough to see who's inside or to take the number, it drives off."

"It's probably a coincidence. Who'd want to follow you? Unless Gilly's employed private detectives." I tried to look in the wing mirror and see if I could see the car he meant, but all I saw was a supermarket delivery wagon.

"Yeah, you're probably right. Sorry, Penfold."

He pulled up around the corner from Gilly's house.

"You should come in with me." I could understand why he didn't want to, but I had a feeling Gilly expected him to show his face.

"If I do, it'll give her ideas."

"But you've told her you don't want to date her, haven't you?"

"Emma, how many ways can you tell someone you don't want to go out with them before they believe you? Gilly only hears what she wants to hear. If I go in there with you, she'll read more into it."

It was selfish of me, I suppose. I wasn't sure how long Gilly wanted me to stay with her or even what I was supposed to be staying with her for.

169

"Okay, I'll let you off. Has Gilly had a copy of the itinerary?" Perhaps I could use it to cheer her up if she was still moping about her dog, always assuming he hadn't turned up, of course.

"I expect so. Listen, Emma, you know this business of Gilly's dog going missing… You don't suppose she's done it herself, do you?"

I thought back to the morning. Gilly had seemed genuinely distressed and she hadn't made the scuffle marks by the fence. She hadn't even wanted to go under the trees and risk getting her tracksuit dirty.

"No, she isn't faking. Somebody climbed over her fence and stole her dog, but for the life of me I can't think why."

I could see Rob turning it over in his mind.

"I'd better go. Gilly will be expecting me and I'd like to find out what's happened. She might have had her dog back."

"Maybe," he said. "I'll see you tomorrow."

I wriggled out of the car and watched him drive off. As he turned the corner, a black BMW pulled out from a parking bay higher up the street and followed him.

What do you call it when a shiver runs up your spine—giving you the creeps? Well, that's the feeling I got. It was probably coincidence, like I'd told Rob, but even so, it was pretty strange.

I rang Gilly's doorbell twice before she answered.

"The police are here to interview me," she announced, before installing me in a little lobby off the hall. "I'll be back in a minute." She pushed me down onto a dark green leather Chesterfield sofa and dashed off.

She left the door ajar in her haste to get back to the sitting room and from my vantage point on the sofa I could see a good-looking policeman talking to her. I edged along the sofa so I could get nearer to the door. Eavesdropping runs in our family. We have no shame over listening to other people's conversations.

"We'll be in touch, Miss Brown-Jones, should there be any developments. Please let us know if the dog returns or if you hear anything."

"I will. Thank-you so much for coming. I'm sure you'll do everything to get my poor little Robbie back."

They were in the hall now, right outside the door.

"We'll do our best, miss, but there have been a couple of these cases lately. We suspect the owners have paid the ransom to get their pets returned, but haven't admitted doing so to us. So our opportunity to catch these so-called 'dog-nappers' in action has been limited." He tucked his notebook inside his shirt pocket.

"I promise I'll be in touch immediately if I hear anything."

I tried to see Gilly's expression through the opening of the door, as it sounded very much like flirting talk to me. The door closed with a sharp click and I couldn't see. I heard some more muffled conversation as Gilly let the policeman out the front door, but I couldn't make out what they said.

I just had time to pounce on an elderly edition of *Country Life* and pretend to be engrossed in an article on rose care before Gilly returned.

"That was the police." Her cheeks were flushed and she had a look of pleasurable excitement in her eyes. "After they were so rude to me this morning, I decided to call Daddy at Val d'Isere. He rang an old friend of his who knows the Chief Constable and they sent Gavin round."

I took it Gavin was the policeman she'd been batting her eyelashes at in the hallway.

"He says there's this gang targeting wealthy pet owners. It's all the rage apparently, a bit like having your Rolex stolen." Trust Gilly—even her crimes had to be fashionable. My burglary was obviously very passé.

"Did Gavin say if he thought you'd get Robbie back?"

A shadow passed over her face. "He said to wait and see if I got a ransom note."

"What kind of ransom are they likely to ask for?" I was curious to know what the average dog-napping made.

"One lady got asked for five thousand pounds and an Arab princess was asked for twenty thousand."

"Whew!" It was a profitable industry. "What will you do if they ask you for that kind of money?"

Gilly frowned. "I suppose I'd have to ask Daddy, I blew a couple of month's allowance at the auction that's why I didn't go skiing. I couldn't tell Daddy what I'd spent the money on because he doesn't approve of Rob."

"Oh." I didn't know what to say. My mind had boggled at a couple of months of Gilly's allowance being worth more than double my annual salary.

"Anyway, take your coat off, Emma, and come and have a drink. I'll show you the dress I've bought for the restaurant date in Spain." She plucked *Country Life* from my hand and towed me off toward the kitchen.

Three hours, two bottles of wine, some pizza, salad and a tub of Haagen-Dazs ice cream later, I began to warm to Gilly. I also had the feeling that between her and Fiona, I would look like the raggedy version of Cinderella on this holiday.

Gilly had acquired five new bikinis, four dresses, God knows how many pairs of shoes and some gorgeous silk pajamas all ready for the trip. Fiona, of course, had already stocked her wardrobe up at Niall's expense.

It crossed my mind that I could go shopping with some more of the money Marco had put in the joint account but at the speed our marriage had begun to disintegrate, I felt uneasy about using any more of it.

Things to Do:

Lose my conscience.

Definitely lose some weight.

Raid Fiona's wardrobe and see if she had anything I could borrow.

Gilly's bedroom was huge. We'd taken the second bottle of wine upstairs while she showed me her clothes. Her walk-in wardrobe looked as big as the bathroom in my flat. Sitting on her massive bed surrounded by coat hangers and clothes with a glass of wine in her hand, Gilly seemed a lot more human.

"I'm really glad you're here, Emma. I know Rob would have come if he wasn't so busy but it's nice to do something girly, especially when it's been such an awful day." She topped up our glasses with what was left of the wine.

Things To Do

"Rob's a very kind person." I paused trying to think of a nice way of spelling it out to Gilly that Rob wasn't interested in her.

"I know. It's one of the things I love about him. He's always so modest, too." She sighed happily and I tried not to snigger. Modest was not one of the adjectives I'd use to describe Rob. Sweet, kind, soft-hearted—yes; bossy, irritating and pernickety—yes; but modest? No.

"I think he's losing it a bit lately. He keeps saying he thinks he's being followed." I scrutinized Gilly from under my lashes to see if she showed any sign of guilt. I knew she'd done some of the stalking; let's face it, her pink cabriolet Beetle was pretty hard to miss.

"How weird! I've had that feeling too."

I almost fell off the bed. "What do you mean?"

"Well, yesterday when I went to the gym and then the hairdressers, I felt as if someone had followed me."

I stared at her. "Did you see anyone?"

She took a sip of wine and shook her head. "Nothing definite, just this BMW, but there are a lot of those about. Do you think I ought to tell Gavin? It could be the dog-nappers." She spilt a drop of wine on her duvet in her excitement.

"I suppose it might be a possibility, but Rob doesn't have a dog, so why would they follow him?"

"Gavin gave me his phone number and told me to make sure any messages were passed directly to him."

"I don't suppose it would do any harm to let him know," I said. "Just in case."

Gilly put down her glass and picked up the phone. "It could be a really important clue."

I wondered if Gilly had ever read Nancy Drew. It ruled out my theory about her employing private detectives to follow Rob, though.

173

Gilly left the message for Gavin and put the phone down, having done her civic duty. "He's out on a case but they said they'll make sure he gets the message."

"I ought to go home, Gilly." My head wooshed a bit from the wine and I had the feeling that given half a chance, Gilly would suggest opening another bottle.

"Oh, but it's early yet!" Gilly pouted.

"I know, but I've got work tomorrow and I haven't even started packing yet." It wasn't a fib and I wanted to look in Fi's wardrobe while she was out to see if there was anything I might manage to coax her into lending me.

After some persuasion on my part, Gilly gave in and we went downstairs so I could find my coat and call a cab.

A white envelope lay on the doormat in the hall. We rushed to the front door and flung it open but there was no one in sight.

Gilly picked up the envelope and ripped it open.

"Wait! What if it's from the dog-nappers? There might be fingerprints." I stopped her just in time.

"I'll get my eyebrow tweezers." She put the envelope down on the hall table and dashed upstairs coming back a moment later with the tweezers. Carefully, she eased the slip of paper from the envelope.

It was classic stuff—letters cut from a newspaper and everything. I always thought that only happened in the movies. Attached to the bottom was a digital photo of Robbie the dog, looking more ratty and pathetic than ever.

The note was short and simple. The dog-nappers wanted three thousand pounds in used notes by a week from Friday or Robbie the dog would chew his last bone.

There was also a dire warning about not involving the police. It said Gilly was to expect delivery details of where to drop the money next week.

"You'd better ring Gavin again." I picked the phone up and passed it to her but she burst into tears and sat down hard on the bottom stair.

Chapter Sixteen

In the end I called Gavin, though against Gilly's wishes. She didn't want to risk Robbie the dog being dispatched to meet the great butcher in the sky if the dog-nappers found out she'd told the police.

Fortunately for Gilly, Gavin came over in plain clothes. His shift finished at ten, so he managed to convince Gilly it would be safe for him to come back.

Personally, I thought he could have given us more credit for using the tweezers to read the ransom note. I didn't think slipping everything into a plastic sandwich bag and making jokes about watching too much *C.S.I. Miami* was very professional.

I left him drinking coffee with Gilly. She was in a big hurry to get rid of me by then and I didn't fancy playing the third wheel. At least Rob would be pleased if Gilly opted to transfer her affections to Gavin.

I decided to get a taxi back to Mummy's house. I'd toyed with the idea of the tube, as my funds were low, but I still felt pissed off with Marco and decided I'd burn a bit more of his money from the joint account after all. Sometimes I'm more like Fiona than I give myself credit for.

There wasn't anyone in when I got home. Mummy must have gone out with Mr. G and Fi was probably out with Paul. The wine I'd drunk at Gilly's began to wear off and my mouth felt as dry as a pork scratching.

I plundered Mummy's cocktail cabinet for a shot of brandy as my mobile rang. My guilty conscience at sneaking an illicit tipple sent the contents of the crystal balloon goblet shooting into the air and all over the carpet.

"Emma, what are you doing?" For a split second I wondered if Sara had me under CCTV surveillance.

"Nothing, I just got in. Gilly's mutt was dog-napped and I was—"

Sara cut me off before I had a chance to explain. "Never mind, I'm on my way over. I need you to come with me."

"What's the matter? Is it Jessie?"

Sara sounded as if she'd been on the brandy, too. She was all sharp and decisive, not the dreary, depressed person she'd been lately.

"No, you idiot, it's Shay. Jessie's at Mum's. I'll be there in ten."

I added some more brandy to my glass and swallowed it down while I waited. Instinct told me I would need this drink before the night was out.

With any luck, Mummy wasn't secretly marking the bottles any more. She'd started to watch the contents of the bar when Fi had first split with Niall. She'd also hidden all the paracetamol and put the sharp knives in the tumble drier for safe keeping. The knives were now back in the block, so hopefully she'd stopped the bottle watch too.

I'd barely had time to wash up my glass when a car rumbled up outside: Sara and Rob. She eyed my crumpled travel agency uniform with distaste. "Hurry up and change," she told me. "We need to go."

Even in my half-cut state, I realized Sara looked good. She looked like the old, pre-baby Sara. Her blonde hair was shiny and loose. She wore a fitted jacket over a little halter top and hipster jeans teamed with killer spike-heeled boots.

Rob was in his gear, too, for a night on the town, and as he followed Sara into the hall, it occurred to me that he smelled good enough to eat.

"Where are we going? And why?" I didn't want to go out; I'd only just got in and the brandy/wine combo had made me feel deliciously sleepy.

"Shay's doing a set tonight and she's going to be there. I overheard them talking on the phone." Sara's eyes narrowed and I suddenly felt very glad she was my friend and not my enemy.

"I'm just the chauffeur." Rob held his hands up in defense.

"Will you please go and change?" Sara placed her hands on her hips and I zipped upstairs, unbuttoning my shirt as I went. I wasn't about to argue with Sara while she was in this mood. If she wanted to go for this other woman of Shay's, I'd be happy to hold her coat.

I opted for jeans, a lime green Armani top of Fiona's and my new lime wedges. I'd have to do a make-up repair job once we were in the car.

Sara climbed into the back (she's slimmer than me) and I needed the passenger mirror to re-do my lip-gloss. The cold air in the car revived me—Rob still hadn't fixed the heater—and adrenaline started to kick in.

Rob managed to park a couple of streets away from the club. It didn't look too promising an area and I was glad he was with us as we picked our way through the litter toward the club entrance.

The door was guarded by two of the largest men I'd ever seen in my life. They even made Everton's flunkies look small. One of them had *Mom* tattooed across his knuckles.

"You members?" The one with the tattoo moved to bar our access to the doorway.

"We're with the band." Sara didn't bat an eyelid. I, on the other hand, was ready to turn around and go home.

"That's what they all say." The other gorilla stepped across to join his mate, creating a six-foot-wide barrier of fat and muscle.

Sara rummaged in her handbag and flashed a band pass at the bouncers. Tattoo Boy scrutinized it, identified the photo as being Sara, and the muscle wall parted.

"Okay, Blondie. Make sure you sign for your friends."

Sara tucked the pass back in her bag and we were in.

The club looked dark, smoky and heaving with people. It was like stepping back in time to my college days. I had a feeling strobe lights would be considered an innovation in this place.

"Now what?" I asked.

Sara surveyed the club floor. "We need to find a good spot. Somewhere we won't be noticed from the stage but close enough to see what's going on."

Oh, yeah, and I was in lime green. That should render me inconspicuous.

"We'd better get drinks," Rob suggested.

Sara nodded. "Good idea. We need to blend in. I'll have vodka." She leaned nearer to me. "Emma had better have Coke. She smells like she's had enough alcohol already."

I would have protested, but Rob had already headed for the bar. Sara dragged me over to the side wall of the club.

"That's her!" she exclaimed.

I peered through the haze to try and spot Shay's other woman.

"The one in the black Levi's and the pink top."

She was easy to pick out. Long-limbed with lovely, coffee-colored skin and Jimmy Choo shoes. Gorgeous and wealthy. I hated her already.

"Shit, this place is expensive." Rob was back, he handed me a Coke and Sara a bottle of blue WKD. Sara pointed out the guilty party.

"Nice," Rob commented and whistled appreciatively. Sara and I glared at him. "Sorry."

There was movement on stage and an announcement. I knew the format from the gigs I'd been to with Sara before. Shay's band would play a sixty or ninety-minute set, then afterwards, they'd come out and have a drink in the club, see fans, and sign autographs. That was on a good night.

If it was a bad night, they'd play their set, grab the money and go. Or they'd come out, someone would accuse one of the band of eyeing up his girlfriend and then there'd be a fight.

It was hard to tell which way it would go tonight. There was the usual group of diehard fans who followed the band around from venue to venue, but there weren't many of those.

I watched Shay's other woman closely while the band played their set. She and the group of friends she was with had clearly been to Shay's gigs many times before, judging by the way they sang along.

Sara just stood and watched with a steely glint in her eyes and her bottle of WKD disappearing at a rate of knots.

Shay always dedicated the last song of the set to Sara. Even on the nights when she'd first been pregnant with Jessie and had been too busy throwing up to go along to the gigs. Sara waited for the song, to hear what Shay had to say. I knew if he dedicated it to this new woman, Sara and Shay would be over. Sara watched Shay and Rob and I watched Sara.

"This song has a special meaning for me," Shay announced, and oh, my God, he looked directly at his other woman as he said this. "This is for the two women who rock my world. They know who they are." He blew a kiss to the audience and launched into the number.

A tear trickled down Sara's cheek and I had this huge lump in my throat.

"I need another drink." Sara dashed the tear from her face, turned on her spiky heels and headed for the bar. I went to go after her but Rob stopped me.

"She'll be back in a minute. She needs some time on her own."

Rather infuriatingly, I knew he was right. I didn't know what I would say to her anyway. "What do you think she's going to do?" I couldn't help looking over to where the other girl danced and laughed with her friends. I wondered if she knew about Sara and Jessie.

"I don't know. When she called me to ask for the lift, she didn't say what she had planned."

The band finished the final song and people headed off the dance floor toward the bar.

"I can't see Sara." I looked around then, saw Shay and the rest of the band emerge from a door at the side of the stage. I ducked behind a pillar at the side of the bar, pulling Rob with me.

"You spilled my lager," Rob grumbled, shaking drops of his bottle and on to the floor. "Do you know how much this stuff cost?"

I ignored him and watched as Shay's other woman greeted him with a hug and a kiss on the cheek before she started to introduce her friends. There was no sign of Sara. I wondered if she'd gone home.

I felt sick watching Shay joking about with his glamorous new girl and her friends. I wanted to storm over and whop him one with my handbag, but Rob placed his hand warningly on my arm and indicated across the room with his bottle.

I spotted Sara. She was on the opposite side of the bar and it looked as if she was on her way over to confront Shay. He noticed her at exactly the same moment as an empty bottle of lager whizzed over our heads and an almighty free-for-all punch up began.

Rob grabbed me and propelled me toward the exit. I heard the sounds of glass smashing and girls screaming. Bouncers charged past us, heading for the melee. The last thing I saw before Rob got me out through the crowd was Shay making his way toward Sara. The girl in the Jimmy Choo shoes was nowhere in sight.

"Are you okay?" Rob held me up as people spilled out of the door of the club and into the street. I heard the sound of sirens in the distance.

My legs shook and I leaned in to Rob for support. I smelt the lovely familiar smell of his cologne as I rested my head on his chest and steadied my breath.

"Did you see what happened to Sara?" I was worried; people had begun to stagger out of the club with cuts on their heads and hands. A few feet away, a girl in a mini skirt sat on the curb with a man's jacket draped around her shoulders. Blood streamed down her left cheek.

Two police cars and an ambulance pulled up. The paramedics went over to the girl at the curb while the police all piled out of the cars and into the club.

"Sara's with Shay. She'll be okay. Come on, we need to get out of here."

We picked our way past the ambulance as a police van arrived with reinforcements. Crossing the street with Rob to get back to the car, it struck

Things To Do

me how good he was in a crisis. I couldn't help wondering what would have happened if it had been Marco with me instead of Rob.

"You're quiet, Em. Are you okay?"

We paused by the side of the car. The streetlight threw a shadow across his face, and I couldn't read his expression. My pulse felt all jumpy and my breath caught in my throat like it used to do when I saw Marco. What the hell was wrong with me?

"I'm fine, I…I just…I think I spilled something on Fi's top." I couldn't look at him. This was not supposed to happen—I'm a married woman, and Rob is my friend.

"I'd like to go home." I forced the words out. Rob still looked at me; I could feel it.

"Okay."

He opened the car door and when we were both inside, I sneaked a peep at his face. Little butterflies bounced about inside my stomach. I shouldn't have had that brandy. If Rob were to kiss me now, I wouldn't be able to resist him.

Fortunately for me, he just drove me back to Mummy's house. I didn't trust myself to say much to him, so I said goodnight and shot indoors as soon as it was polite.

My hormones must be well out of whack or I must have been drunker than I thought if I'd wanted to bonk Rob. Don't get me wrong, Rob is a very sexy guy, but he's my friend. It was crazy. It was stupid.

> *Things to do:*
> *Stop drinking brandy on top of wine again.*
> *Stop thinking about kissing or bonking Rob.*

I wasn't sure if anyone else was home, but just in case, I slipped off my wedges and tiptoed upstairs. I needed to hide Fiona's Armani top before she discovered I'd borrowed it, and especially before she noticed it had lager all down the front.

The front door opened as I made it to the top of the stairs. I didn't hang around to see who it was. If it was Mummy, she'd want to know where I'd been, and I really didn't want to bump into Fi.

I slipped in through my bedroom door, congratulating myself on my narrow escape. Someone clicked on my bedroom lamp and I stood blinking for a moment in the bright light.

"Hey, babe, where have you been?" Marco lay back against the pillows with his arms behind his head, the bare skin of his chest dark against the Laura Ashley duvet.

"I went for a drink with Sara." I didn't want to explain the whole Shay thing to him. I didn't think he'd understand. "I didn't think you were coming back yet. You frightened me half to death."

"Change of plan." He rolled onto his side, watching me as I took my make-up off and tracing one of the rosebuds on the duvet cover with a lazy fingertip.

I studied his reflection in the mirror as I slapped on my moisturiser and waited for my heart to race the way it usually did whenever I saw Marco. Marco is not the kind of man a girl would kick out of her bed and having him naked in my bed usually made all the girly bits of my body tingle with anticipation.

Except it didn't happen. I pulled the clips out of my hair and began to brush it through, not sure what to think.

"Have you packed for the weekend yet?" Marco broke the silence.

"No, I thought I'd do it tomorrow. Fiona's had her case ready since Monday, of course."

Fi wasn't the kind of girl to travel light. Her case was as big as me and that was only her essential items. Her carry-on bag usually caused a major row with the airline staff because of its weight. I nearly broke my collar bone the last time I tried to pick up Fiona's luggage.

Marco ran his finger lightly down my spine. "Make sure you pack your bikini."

Yeah, right. I'd seen the dinky designer numbers Gilly and Fiona had ready and my little Dottie P sales purchase would be staying home. I wondered if Victorian stripy neck-to-toe cozzies would ever make a comeback. If they did then I'd be first in the queue.

I slipped into bed next to Marco and for the first time ever, when I felt his hands explore under my pajamas, I pushed him away.

When I woke up, Marco had gone. I had a quick shower and put on my lovely, crumpled-up uniform before sprinting downstairs for a coffee.

Mummy was in the kitchen making toast. "You're going to be late, Emma. Marco's just left. He said he'd be back at suppertime."

I swear that man was like the Scarlet Pimpernel. Trying to keep him in one place was like *Mission: Impossible*. God knows where he'd gone this time and God knows if I cared.

Fiona drifted, in all dressed for the office in a beautiful pale grey suit, her hair in a French pleat. I felt like something the cat had dragged in. "Morning!" she said.

"You sound chirpy. What's going on?" I asked.

She had a very smug smile on her face, the way she always looks when she's up to something.

"Just looking forward to the weekend." A car horn tooted outside. She patted her hair and kissed Mummy on the cheek. "That'll be my lift. Bye."

She departed in a cloud of Chanel and I realized Mummy had been right: I was late. Really late. I bolted down some coffee and grabbed my handbag.

"You really should eat breakfast, Emma," Mummy reproved as I headed for the door.

"Okay." I pinched a piece of the toast she'd just finished buttering and shoved it in my mouth on my way along the hall.

The tube was a nightmare, as usual. By the time I got off at my stop, I'd had my toes trodden on twice, been poked in the ribs by someone's umbrella and been forced to stand virtually nose-to-nose with a man who had issues with dental hygiene.

Mr. G was in the shop when I finally arrived twenty minutes late.

"A word, Emma."

I followed him into the back office. Rob shrugged sympathetically as I went past. Mr. G closed the door behind us.

"Emma, you're twenty minutes late again today. This is not the first time I've had to speak to you about your time keeping." He paused and cleared his throat. "I know the situation vis-à-vis your mother and I is, ahem, a little delicate, but I can't allow it to be seen that you might take advantage of the situation."

It was going to be one of those days. "No, Mr. Grebe, I'm sorry."

"Please don't let it happen again."

"Yes, Mr. Grebe."

"You can go and tidy the brochures."

"Yes, Mr. Grebe."

I ducked out of the office, fighting the urge to bob a curtsey as I left, and went to straighten up the racks—which, incidentally, has to be one of the most thankless jobs in the entire universe. You can spend a whole morning getting them all perpendicular and neat. Then, after just a few browsers, you get Australia mixed with Africa, the ski trips mixed with the Caribbean… It was hopeless.

My crap morning concluded with a trip to the loo at lunchtime where I discovered I'd started my period. Great. Bang went any chance of a romantic rekindling of my marriage and by the time I stepped off the plane tomorrow, I knew I'd be retaining more fluid than Spongebob Squarepants and have an acne spot that glowed like a nuclear reactor.

I decided a day like this required special treatment, so I headed for Starbucks and managed to find a quietish corner to call Sara on my mobile.

Chapter Seventeen

Sara's mobile was switched off, so I left a message on her voicemail. I hoped she was all right. It had been frightening last night when everything had erupted.

After a slurp of latte and a nice comforting piece of cake, I felt a bit more charitable towards the world and decided to call Gilly. Initially, I thought I'd got the wrong number when I didn't recognize the voice on the other end. I repeated Gilly's name, there was a pause, and then she came on the line.

"Sorry, Emma, I'm at the manicurist's." I heard her ask the therapist to hold the phone closer. "I felt so upset about little Robbie, I thought I'd better cheer myself up and my nails were in a terrible mess."

"Does Gavin think they're any nearer catching the dog-nappers?"

"He couldn't tell me, as it's confidential information but he's been so good. I've got his personal number in case I hear anything else."

Gilly sounded much happier, so I finished the call. My nails didn't look too great, either. All the cleaning after the burglary hadn't done my hands any favors. Not that I could really afford the time or cost of a manicure. Which reminded me, I needed to go and get some money for the weekend. If I whizzed to the cashpoint now I could withdraw some money from the joint account and change it for Euros at work during the afternoon.

I finished my latte and went to find a machine. Of course, being lunchtime, there were six people already in the queue. Eventually I got to the front and popped in my card. I'd only used the joint card once before, so when the machine spat the card back out I thought I'd done something wrong. Then I realized the screen said "insufficient funds."

I must have made a mistake somehow, but looking at the time, I couldn't try again and risk being late twice in one day.

I made it back to the shop in the nick of time to find Mr. G dealing with some clients at my desk. I hoped he hadn't opened my bottom drawer and found the chocolate stash I'd hidden in there this morning.

When he finished helping the man he was with, we swapped places. He didn't mention the chocolate, so I got on with the afternoon's work. By the time the shop quietened down, Mr. G had done the banking and we were ready to close. I wondered if it might be too much to hope for that Marco had remembered we'd need Euros. I certainly wasn't going to be able to get any.

Rob offered me a lift home. I think he wanted to extract a promise in advance from Fiona that she wouldn't leave him on his own with Gilly.

I felt a bit nervous about having a lift from Rob, which was stupid because we'd driven together thousands of times. But I still felt a little odd after last night.

I'll admit when we very first met at college, I'd fancied Rob, but then I'd realized he was more interested in Fi and as time went on…well, he was just Rob. My friend. But last night, I'd wondered if he'd felt the same thing I'd felt.

"Do you and Marco want your tickets and hotel confirmations? You left them in the collection drawer in the shop." Rob felt inside the breast pocket of his jacket and handed me an envelope.

I'd forgotten all about picking them up. Some travel agent I was. "Thanks."

"I booked you both into first class, the same as Fiona, Gilly and me."

"Great! Do I owe you any more money?" I'd used some of the money from Marco to pay for the trip but presumably it would cost more to fly in style. Not that I was even sure if I'd be able to get any more money to pay Rob. I was still puzzled over the cash point incident. Unless Marco had moved the money without telling me, which was a strong possibility.

"No, I got a good deal on the hotel reservations."

I felt really self-conscious, sitting in the confined space of Rob's car. He'd promised to take me to the flat first, so I could collect some of my summer things and then over to Mummy's. Maybe these weird feelings I had for Rob were hormonal; I was on my period. Everyone said hormones were very powerful. It had to be hormones.

Toby met us at the front door of the flats.

"Emma, how are you? When are you moving back in?" He embraced me in an affectionate hug.

"Hopefully, when I get back from Spain. I need to sort out some furniture and things, and then I'll be back."

He followed us into my flat. "Steven and I have missed you. It's been eerie with your flat being empty and my nerves have been on edge ever since you were burgled. I jump at the slightest noise and there have been some odd people hanging around here lately."

Under normal circumstances, I wouldn't have taken too much notice. Toby has always had a flair for the dramatic. Now, though, with Gilly's dog-napping and the coincidences of the cars—not to mention my break-in things freaked me out more easily than usual.

I scooped up the post from the kitchen worktop; Toby and Steven had been checking it for me so I wouldn't miss anything important while I was at Mummy's. Most of it looked like junk, so I filed it in the bin. One letter, though, looked as if it might be important. It was in a thick cream envelope and had a Revenue and Excise insignia on it. It was addressed to Marco, so I tucked it in my handbag.

Rob and Toby stayed in the sitting room and chatted while I grabbed the bits and pieces I needed from the bedroom and dropped them into a hold-all. Marco already had most of his clothes at Mummy's, so all I had to get was my beach stuff and some nice clothes to wear in the evenings.

It occurred to me, as I hunted through my wardrobe looking for (a) things that actually fit me and (b) things I looked nice in, that I wasn't looking forward to this holiday very much.

Toby and Rob had been joined by Steven when I wandered through to the lounge. They were still discussing the break-in and Toby shared more about the people he'd seen hanging around by the flats.

"Have you got everything, Emma?" Rob took the hold-all from me.

"I think so." I hoped I could persuade Fi to lend me a couple of nice tops, providing that she didn't found out about the lager I'd spilled on her Armani top, of course.

"Come on, I want to check some things with Fiona before tomorrow."

Toby and Steven gave me a hug goodbye while Rob shoved my bag into the tiny boot of his wreck. I checked my mobile on the way over to Mummy's, but still no message from Sara. I hoped she was okay. I'd expected her to have called or text-messaged or something'd me by now.

Rob didn't say much while he drove. I concentrated on fiddling with my mobile and wished I could shake off these weird vibes I had about him.

Fiona was in the kitchen when we got to Mummy's. She must have been back from work for a while as she'd already changed her work clothes for a pale blue tracksuit that looked very similar to Gilly's pink one. I wondered what color would suit me, assuming they made them for anyone under five feet ten and over a size eight.

"Hi, Rob." Fi flashed him one of her thousand-watt smiles and continued to flick through yet another copy of *Vogue*.

"All set for tomorrow?" Rob loosened his collar, took off his tie and stuffed it in his pocket before leaning forward on the countertop to feign interest in the magazine.

I saw it had a bikini shoot in it. Maybe the interest wasn't feigned.

"Just a few last things to pack," Fiona replied. "I wish I could find my Armani top. I could have sworn I'd put it ready to go in the case."

Uh oh, I felt heat creep into my cheeks.

"Once the dinner is over, that's it, isn't it? The date is officially ended?"

"Yes." Fiona paused in her page-flicking to consider an advert for anti-aging cream.

"Yes!" Rob stretched and punched the air with a fist.

Fiona tore her attention away from the promise of younger-looking skin. "I know Gilly can be a little full-on, but she isn't that bad."

"Fi, she's been stalking him!" I exclaimed.

Fiona raised an immaculately-shaped eyebrow. "Niall stalks me. So what?"

"Niall is trying to serve a writ on you so he can get his money back. It's not the same thing." Honestly, sometimes my sister can be so irritating.

"It's very annoying of him. It'll be a relief not to have to go to work at the office anymore. He caused the most frightful scene the other day." She rolled her eyes.

"What do you mean, not going to work anymore?"

"I resigned. Paul didn't feel they appreciated me there. He felt they took advantage of my good nature, so he offered me a better job," she said happily.

"What kind of job?" I wondered what he could have offered that was any cushier or paid much more for doing as little as Fiona did.

"I'll be working for the Crystal Foundation full-time, in a paid capacity. Paul's very impressed by my commitment to the Foundation and all the fundraising I've done."

Fiona was good at fundraising, I'll give her that, but why do I never get those kinds of breaks? The way I'm going I'll be working for Mr. G till it's time to draw my pension.

"Congratulations, Fi!" Rob sounded impressed.

"Well done, Fi." I hope I didn't sound begrudging. I knew she would do a good job for the Foundation, although after seeing her with Paul, I wasn't sure how much of his interest was personal.

"Right," she said. "Rob, the car will pick you up first in the morning and then collect Gilly. I'll already be in the limo, so you'll both be chaperoned throughout the date." She turned to me. "Emma, you and Marco will have to make your own arrangements to get to the airport."

Terrific. I wasn't sure at the moment if Marco planned on even traveling with me. He had a better disappearing act than David Blaine.

"A champagne reception will be waiting in the first class lounge and the press will do a photo call of you and Gilly." Fi turned her attention back to Rob.

"We haven't got to be loved up or anything, have we?" Rob asked.

"No, don't be silly. But you could try to look as if you're on a proper date. It would be so much better for our publicity." Fiona looked at him thoughtfully. "I could arrange to have some red roses there for you to present to Gilly, if you like."

"No!" His alarm became transparent.

Fiona laughed. "Okay, keep your hair on. Just smile a lot and maybe put your arm around her or toast her with the champagne."

"I'll do toasting," he conceded.

"Good. Once we arrive at Malaga, another limo will take you to the hotel at Marbella to change and then I'll brief you and Gilly on the rest of the day."

It sounded more like a military campaign than the romantic experience I knew Gilly was hoping for. Rob, however, seemed relieved. I was left to wonder why I'd agreed to go along. I certainly wasn't likely to get any champagne or roses from Marco.

"Okay then, I'd better go and finish packing. I'll see you both tomorrow."

I walked with Rob to the front door.

"I'll see you at the airport, Penfold." He scrutinized my face.

"Don't worry DM, I'll be there." I tried to sound chirpy.

His eyes met mine and stayed there for what felt like forever. My heart thumped so hard I thought he'd hear it.

"See you in the morning." He kissed me on the lips and left, hurrying to his car without a backward glance in my direction. Which was a good thing, or he'd have witnessed an Emma-shaped puddle of mush on Mummy's front step. Stupid bloody hormones.

Fi was in the hall. "Have you seen my Armani top?"

"Not lately." It wasn't exactly a lie. I hadn't seen it since I'd stuffed it at the bottom of the dry cleaning pile in the utility room.

"Mmm, well, you look guilty about something."

My cheeks burned hotter. "Well, I'm not, okay?"

Fiona raised her eyebrows. "Fine. Are you sure Rob didn't make you an indecent proposal? Your face is red enough."

"Don't be stupid!" I stuck my tongue out at her just as the front door opened and Mummy walked in.

"Are you two fighting again?" Mummy tutted, and carried on past us down the hall.

"Honestly, Emma, sometimes you are so dense!" Fiona glided off upstairs.

I spent the evening packing my clothes. I didn't feel I could ask Fiona for a loan of any of her things since she was still hunting for her top. She didn't appear to be in a good mood anyway. Marco had left me a note on top of his hold-all. He'd done his own packing after all, which had to be a good thing as I didn't fancy packing for him.

By the time I'd had supper with Mummy and Mr. G, and given myself a pedicure and a mini manicure, it was late. Marco didn't appear until after the News at Ten. By then, I was ready for bed and debating whether to book a taxi to get me to the airport.

"Hey, babe." He leaned across to kiss me. "All ready to go?"

"Fine. We have to be at the airport at five in the morning." I tried to keep the terse note out of my voice. I'd decided that this weekend would be a make or break time for us. Perhaps without the sex part of our relationship to distract me, I'd be able to really talk to Marco and see if we could make a go of it. Or even if I wanted to make a go of it. Although, the sex part seemed to be wearing off, at least for me.

"Yeah, I know Fiona already ran through everything with me." He threw his car keys onto the dresser and shrugged off his coat. "Everton's driver will give us a ride to the airport. It'll be better than leaving the car in the long-stay car park." He gave me a cautious look as if to measure my reaction. I think he'd finally realized that Everton and I would never be best buddies.

Well, that was all fine and dandy then! I was too tired to argue so I let it go. "We'd better get some sleep as we've got an early flight."

He didn't disagree with me. Instead he started to unbutton his shirt cuffs. "I'm going for a shower." He picked up a towel from the pile on the chair and headed off to the bathroom. I lay back on my pillows and wondered how everything would work out.

✔ ✔ ✔

I would have missed the plane if Marco hadn't nudged me awake. I'd slept right through the alarm and it took the combined efforts of Marco shaking me and the colorful expletives from Fiona as she battled with her monster Louis Vuitton luggage on the landing to fully rouse me.

"The car will be here for us in half-an-hour." Marco was dressed and ready to go.

I'm not at my best early in the morning. Marco took one look at my bleary eyes and went to help Fi with her case. A quick shower and cup of tea later, and I began to feel more charitable.

Fiona had already sailed off in the Foundation's limo to collect Gilly and Rob. I hoped Rob was a light packer. If not, there wouldn't be room for all the stuff Fi and Gilly planned to take and Rob's case, too. If that was what they needed to survive a weekend, then a week would have required a fleet of transport.

Everton's car arrived and we set off for the airport. Marco sat up front with the no-necked driver, and I took advantage of the empty back seat to check my messages. Still nothing from Sara, so I sent another "let me know how you are" text before we arrived at the terminal.

Things To Do

The driver lifted our bags from the boot while Marco laughed and chatted with him. Once we were through the check-in, we headed straight for the first class lounge. Rob stood on his own staring gloomily out of the window at the runway. Gilly and Fi had purchased every fashion magazine going and compared notes while finishing off the champagne from the publicity shots.

A group of Spanish businessmen in striped suits sat studying the financial papers and a couple who looked as if they might be on their honeymoon canoodled on a couch. Marco went off to look at the news-stand and to claim a complimentary cup of tea.

I joined Rob at the window. "All set, then?"

He gave a small grimace and looked over to where Gilly sat with Fiona. "Fi's managed to divert her a bit and the photos are done. Thank God I persuaded Fi not to bring those bloody roses. And Gilly keeps going on about the dog. I must have seen two hundred pictures of it this morning in the back of the car."

"Well, I did tell you she was upset."

"I know, but she's even more upset that she hasn't been asked for as big a ransom as some of the others who've had their pets pinched." He shook his head. "How are things with you and Marco?"

I glanced across to see my husband chatting with the hostess who dispensed the tea. "I don't know. I'll see how this weekend goes."

Rob followed my gaze. "I'll be there for you if you need me."

Marco seemed to sense us watching him. I forced a smile and indicated I'd like a drink, too.

He brought me a cup of tea and stood next to me and Rob. It was like watching two boxers square up before a fight, seeing the two of them together. Both had the legs-apart stance, the shoulders-back and psychological staring thing going on.

Fortunately, they called our flight and we abandoned our drinks to be checked through onto the plane. Gilly grabbed Rob and hung on like a limpet while Marco placed a proprietary arm around my waist. Fi, I noticed, had

193

several of the gallant Spanish businessmen offer to help her with her carry-on bag and numerous magazines.

The flight was really boring. Marco put on his headset and didn't speak all the way to Malaga. Gilly showed me more pictures of Robbie the dog. I saw puppy pictures, pictures of him dressed up in doggy outfits, pictures of him in the town, pictures of him in the country. If I'd had a parachute, I would have jumped out over France. Only the miniature bottle of brandy I got from the drinks trolley saved my sanity.

Once we landed and cleared customs, Gilly, Rob and Fi vanished, presumably in the limo Fi had organized. I was left on my own with Marco and our luggage in a strange country.

Chapter Eighteen

"We'd better check in with the hire car people," I suggested. Rob had organized a car for me and Marco so we could drive ourselves to the hotel at Marbella.

We dutifully found the car hire desk and checked in. Marco, of course, didn't like the model of car Rob had arranged, so half an hour later, after much haggling, we drove off in a white Mercedes convertible, leaving a pile of fractured Spanish and a hefty payment on the credit card behind us.

The sight of our hotel put Marco in a better frame of mind. He'd sulked all the way on the drive down, replying to any attempts I made to start a conversation with monosyllabic grunts.

We swept in under the Moorish-style, covered archway to be greeted by a uniformed commissar who summoned a bellboy for our bags and a valet to park the car. I felt like a celebrity as we strolled into the huge, marble-floored lobby.

I could tell Marco was impressed; he relaxed enough to swap pleasantries with the receptionist, even though he kept his sunglasses on to pose behind. Rob had left a note for us saying he, Gilly and Ti had already changed and gone to Puerto Banus.

The bellboy led us to the lift and up to our room. Marco strode straight over to the window and pulled back the curtains to look at the view while I tipped the bellboy. Once he'd gone, I went to join Marco on the balcony.

The view was magnificent, looking out across the hotel's private golf course and down to the sparkling blue of the Mediterranean.

"This is nice, isn't it?" I leaned on the metal balustrade next to my husband. The warm sunshine on my face made me feel more optimistic than I had in ages.

"Not bad," he agreed. He looked around at the scenery and nodded his head slowly in agreement. He never got very excited; "not bad" counted as high praise.

"Why don't we get changed?" I said. "We can go down to the marina and have lunch. We might see some celebrities and we can take a peek at the yacht Rob and Gilly are on." My tummy rumbled, and now that I was actually on holiday, I couldn't wait to get out and see the sights.

"Okay. I want to see the boats," Marco agreed, and we stepped back inside to unpack and change.

I opted to wear a blue cotton print skirt I'd bought on Antigua when I first met Marco, with a matching halter-neck top. Marco wore cream Ralph Lauren shorts and a matching polo shirt. With his brown skin contrasting against the fabric and his Raybans firmly in place, he looked incredibly handsome and for the first time in ages, my stomach gave a little flutter of excitement.

The commissar had the car brought around for us and we set off for Puerto Banus. Parking was a pain, as we didn't have a special pass to get us on to the harbor, but we managed to find a parking spot not too far away and strolled down to the marina.

I hoped we'd see someone famous. This was supposed to be the hangout, the cool place to be seen. Sadly, all I saw were other tourists doing exactly the same as me. We found a café with an empty outdoor table under a rather natty little blue-and-white striped canopy.

The prices on the menu weren't as fierce as I expected, but I guessed they had been pitched more for the benefit of our fellow tourists than any passing celebs. As we sat sipping at our beers and posing in our sunglasses, I surveyed the yachts tied up in rows in the marina and wondered which one Rob and Gilly were on.

Things To Do

The boats varied considerably in size and ostentation. Some had crew aboard who appeared to be sweeping, scrubbing and polishing for all they were worth. I couldn't see anyone who was just sat there enjoying the whole "I've got a big boat, am mega-rich and love showing off" bit, which disappointed me a touch.

Marco leant back in his chair, his expression inscrutable since I couldn't see his eyes behind his sunglasses. I wondered if the water-front scene made him homesick for Antigua.

"What do you think of it all?" I waved a hand to indicate the general view.

"Nice. Once we've eaten, we'll go and look at the boats." He sipped his beer and the waiter appeared with our lunch.

"Do you know which one Gilly and Rob are on?" I asked.

"Fiona said it's called *The Lady Crystal*."

Funny how Marco knew more than I did. Although looking at the sheer number of boats in the marina, I suspected that spotting Rob and Gilly's yacht might be like looking for a needle in a haystack. I began to unwind a little. Marco was still inclined to stay silent.

After lunch, we left the café and joined the rest of the tourists meandering along the edge of the waterfront. We had to move out of the way to let a lovely scarlet Ferrari go past us and I thought I saw the blond-haired bloke from *Status Quo* in the distance.

"There's the yacht." Marco nudged me.

It wasn't the biggest boat there, but she still looked impressive. From our viewpoint, we saw Gilly and Rob sitting at a dining table under a canopy. A silver ice bucket stood on the linen tablecloth and a man in uniform served them food. I couldn't see Fiona anywhere.

Rob had his back to me so I couldn't see his face, but Gilly appeared to be in full flow. Which probably meant Rob was in agony.

I wondered if I'd get the chance to see what it was like on board once Gilly and Rob's date had finished. I'd never been on a yacht. When I'd been in the Caribbean, I'd been on a couple of sight-seeing boats, but not a proper posh yacht like *The Lady Crystal*.

I turned away. Rob and Gilly would be on board for a while longer and I fancied filling in some of the time by window-shopping in the boutiques which lined the walkway around the marina. Marco, however, seemed fixated by the boats.

"We'll come back later, when the date's finished." I stroked his arm to attract his attention.

He shook me off a little impatiently. "You go, if you'd like. I'd like to see some more of the yachts."

"Well, shall I meet you at the café where we had lunch in about half-an-hour?" I was a bit hurt by his reaction, but, hey, I'm a grown-up and could enjoy myself, with or without Marco.

He agreed and we split up. I suspected the prospect of looking at shoes and clothes with me all afternoon had put him off, rather than the lure of the yachts. Although he seemed very interested in *The Lady Crystal*.

I had a nice time browsing around and trying to convert Euros into pounds in my head, an exercise that made me feel giddy. By the time I remembered to look at my watch, I realized I was late. I'd also wandered off down one of the side alleys that led away from the marina.

Did I mention I have no sense of direction? When I stepped out of the shop I'd been browsing in (a little leather shop with nice handbags and belts), the street was deserted and I couldn't remember from which direction I'd come. The white-rendered walls all looked the same and I ambled along for a while before coming across the leather shop from which I'd started.

I had no idea where I was. Somehow I'd strayed from the waterfront and into a maze of tiny alleys; I couldn't even see anyone from whom to ask directions. There didn't seem any point in trying to retrace my steps, especially as I had no idea where those steps had been. I decided to keep walking until I either found someone or got somewhere I recognized. I began to panic as I speeded down the darker alleys.

Turning another corner past someone's smelly dustbin, I spotted a woman as she stepped out of a door further up the street. I hurried to try and catch her. As I got closer, I saw a man follow her out of the door and into the street. A dark, handsome man in cream shorts and shirt. A man who looked familiar. Marco.

The sound of my shoes on the cobbles alerted them to my presence; I was too out of breath from hurrying to call out. Marco turned and saw me so I waved at him with my bag. The woman stared at me and jabbered something in Spanish before walking swiftly away. Marco waited for me to catch up the last few yards.

"Emma, what are you doing here?" He frowned at me and I knew I'd interrupted something.

"I was lost. What were you doing here, and who was that?" I felt hot and cross from trying to catch up.

"You were late, so I came to look for you. I asked that woman for help but she didn't speak English." He sounded dismissive.

I walked beside him, trying to recover my breath. He was lying, I knew he was lying. I'd seen him come out of that house with my own eyes and he'd talked to that woman for a good few minutes before they'd seen me coming and she'd scuttled off.

That's when I knew, really, what I'd always known deep in my heart. My marriage was one huge, fat mistake. I'd been in lust with Marco, not love, and however hard I tried, it would never work. We turned a corner and arrived back on the marina outside the café where we'd eaten lunch. Typical.

Rob, Gilly and Fiona walked along the cobbles towards us. I've never been so glad to see anyone in my life. I even felt pleased to see Gilly. I wanted to go back to the hotel, pack my stuff and go home.

"We saw you on board the yacht. It looked like fun." Marco smiled at them.

"It's a beautiful boat," Rob agreed.

I pushed my sunglasses higher up on the bridge of my nose to hide my eyes. Rob gave me an odd look, as if he'd picked up that something was wrong. He was the only one who had.

"I'd love to look around it." Marco dropped a hint to Fiona.

Fiona shrugged apologetically. "It's all locked up now, I'm afraid, and I've given the keys back to the agent who looks after it while it's moored."

"Perhaps another time?" Marco suggested.

"I'll see what I can do," Fiona promised and linked arms with him. "If you like yachts, then you have to see this one—it's a real beauty. Apparently, it belongs to this really rich sheik!" Laughing, she led him along the walkway, teasing as they strolled.

I wasn't aware I'd relaxed until Rob joined me and murmured, "Is everything alright, Em? You look pale."

Gilly joined in. "It's probably the heat. You should wear a hat or stay in the shade."

Rob slipped his arm around my waist to give me a comforting squeeze. "Come on, we'll sit down inside here and get a drink. Fi and Marco will soon find us."

I let them draw me into the café, where Rob ordered us all glasses of fresh orange juice. Gilly went off to find the loo and Rob leaned forward as soon as she'd gone out of earshot.

"Okay, what's the matter?"

"I'm going to divorce Marco." There, I'd said it—and it felt okay. A relief, even. I wanted to cry.

"What's he done?" Rob sounded fierce.

"Nothing. Well, nothing more than usual. He's just being Marco, I suppose." And that was the part that made me want to cry. I was angry—both with Marco and myself. I was mad at Marco for being a lying, unreliable rat and mad at myself for falling for him so hard.

Rob held my hand for a moment in silent sympathy, withdrawing it as Gilly returned. Perhaps it was just as well, because I had enjoyed the feel of Rob's hand on mine a little too much.

"Those toilets aren't very nice," Gilly confided in a stage whisper as she resumed her seat.

"Are you enjoying the date?" I thought I'd better try and get a conversation started or she would produce the doggie photos again.

Gilly wrinkled her nose. "I thought we'd get a little more privacy, but the yacht was very nice. Bigger than my friend Sophie's. She keeps hers moored at Cannes."

That put me in my place. Trust Gilly. "There's the dinner tonight to look forward to," I suggested.

Rob gave me a withering look. I think he hoped to forget about the dinner.

Gilly's face brightened. "Yes, it should be lovely. The restaurant sounded wonderful when Fiona described it. Very romantic."

"Can't wait." My evening in a romantic, exclusive restaurant would be spent discussing a divorce.

"You and Marco will be seated at a separate table?" Gilly's inquiry had a sharp note. I think she'd forgotten we intended to go, too, until I'd opened my big mouth.

"Oh, yes, don't worry," I reassured her. Rob heaved a loud sigh making Gilly purse her lips.

Marco and Fiona walked back towards us and Rob shot me a quick look of concern. Surprisingly though, I felt quite calm now I'd made my decision.

"Phew, it's warm out!" Fiona said. "I gave Marco a sneak peek at *The Lady Crystal*. We couldn't go on board, but at least he got a closer look." Fiona sank down gracefully onto one of the rattan chairs and fanned her face with the drinks menu.

"It's a beautiful boat," Marco agreed. "You said Paul intended to sail her back to England the day after tomorrow?"

Fiona caught the waiter's eye and ordered an orange juice in perfect Spanish. "Yes, the crew are booked to arrive tomorrow afternoon with Paul and he's invited me to join them."

The waiter brought Fiona her juice. She took a sip and checked the time on her watch. "The car will be here to pick us up in thirty minutes, so if you want to look around the shops, now's your chance."

Gilly looked hopefully at Rob.

"Do you want to come, Em?" He tossed some Euros onto the table to pay for the drinks.

Gilly glared at me, so much as I wanted to escape from Marco's company, I thought it better to decline. At least while Fi sat with us, I wouldn't have to face him on my own. I didn't want to do that until I'd figured out exactly what I wanted to say and how best to say it.

We stayed at the café until Gilly and Rob returned, then we all walked up the small street to the limo.

"Shall we meet in the hotel bar before we go for dinner?" Fiona suggested.

"Fine by me." Rob agreed a little too hastily, I felt, for Gilly's liking.

Marco seemed keen, too. We waved them off and went to pick up our car.

"What do you want to do when we get back?" I asked. There were a few hours to fill before we were due to meet the others again, and I needed time to think.

"I thought I might try out the driving range." Marco glanced at me.

I tried not to let my relief show on my face. I didn't believe that was where he planned to go. I wouldn't have been surprised if he'd arranged to meet that woman I'd seen him with earlier. He'd never hit a golf ball in his life as far as I knew, and he'd left it a bit late in life to try and find out if he could be the next Tiger Woods.

"I might go for a dip in the pool." A swim might clear my head and allow me time to think.

We pulled up in front of the hotel and the valet came over to open the door for me.

"I'll see you later, then?" I turned to go inside.

"Sure, babe." Marco handed the car keys to the parking valet and I carried on into the lobby to collect our room key.

Marco didn't come upstairs. I hadn't expected him to. I took off my sunglasses and discovered I'd got sunburn on the end of my nose. Crap. Now not only did I feel miserable, but I looked it too. How come Gilly and Fi didn't look sunburned?

It didn't take me long to change into a bikini and sarong. I didn't plan to actually swim, but I figured I could lie on one of the sun-loungers by the poolside with a magazine and no one would bother me. Bliss.

Picking up my magazine and a towel, I was almost out of the door when the room phone rang. The voice on the other end didn't sound Spanish. The accent was soft with a bit of a lilt. Almost like Marco's. The man seemed surprised when I answered.

"Is Marco there?"

"He's out at the moment. Can I take a message?" My curiosity was piqued, although thinking about it, I figured the caller was probably one of Everton's flunkies.

There was a pause. "Tell him Tony has given the green light."

"Is that it? Will he know what that means?" More mystery.

The caller chuckled softly. It wasn't a nice sound. "He'll know."

The line went dead. I toyed with the idea of leaving Marco a note, but I figured I could tell him later when we were in the bar. If the message had been that important, I'm sure they would have called Marco on his mobile.

The pool was quiet. A large elderly woman in a green costume and a bathing hat studded with pink plastic flowers splashed around in the water and a middle-aged couple occupied a couple of the loungers. I fetched myself a Coke from the pool bar and settled myself onto a sun-bed.

Things to do:

Tell Marco we're finished.

Ask Fi if I can share her hotel room until it's time to leave.

Use a higher factor sun cream on my nose.

My mind made up, I made myself comfy on the lounger and closed my eyes. The next thing I knew, a huge splash of water as someone jumped in woke me up. I looked at my watch and realized I only had twenty minutes before I was supposed to meet the others in the bar.

I made it to the bar only fifteen minutes late and with slightly damp hair. Marco had changed and was seated with the others. I hadn't seen him since he'd said he intended to go to the driving range.

"Honestly, Emma! You'll be late for your own funeral," Fiona chided, passing me a glass of champagne.

As I took the empty seat next to Gilly, I realized Paul had joined us and held my sister's hand in his.

"Well, now that you've finally made it," Fi paused to glare meaningfully at me. "Paul and I would like to announce our engagement."

Chapter Nineteen

The thudding noise would be the sound of my chin landing on the table.

"Oh, how lovely! Congratulations!" Gilly leaned forward to examine the ring on Fiona's hand. With a solitaire diamond the size of a Jaffa Cake, it was a bit hard to miss.

I was still too stunned to say anything. Talk about a fast worker! I gulped down a big mouthful of champagne. Fiona admired the evening sun as it glinted off her diamond with a cat-who'd-got-the-cream expression, while Paul graciously accepted everyone's good wishes.

"So, when did this happen?" I managed to ask, the drink having helped me recover my senses. I wanted to ask how it had happened when only a few weeks ago Fi intended to marry Niall, but that would sound petty.

"Paul proposed this afternoon. He flew in secretly and when I got back from the marina, he was in my suite with red roses and champagne." Fiona sighed happily.

"How romantic!" Gilly breathed.

"Lovely." I took another swig of champagne.

"We're getting married next month." Fiona smiled at Paul.

Next month wasn't very far away. I hoped she didn't planning to make me wear the awful meringue bridesmaid's dress she'd picked out for her wedding to Niall…

"You will be my bridesmaid, won't you, Em?"

Oh, crap! It really did look like return of the meringue and I would never be able to lose enough weight if the wedding was only a month away.

"Of course I will, if you want me to." I did my best to look thrilled.

Paul topped up our glasses with more champagne and we drank a toast to his and Fiona's future happiness. I hoped Fi would be happy. Paul seemed like a nice bloke and Fi needed someone who'd keep her in check a little.

She had organized a stretch limo to ferry us all to and from the restaurant, so we all got to travel together for the first time since the flight. I didn't know what to do now. I'd planned to ask Fi if I could move to her room once I'd split with Marco, but I didn't think Paul would be impressed if I turned up like a gooseberry in the suite. Neither would Fi, probably, when I thought about it.

I toyed with the idea of confiding in Gilly, but I'd be subjected to more anguishing over Robbie the dog's disappearance and she'd want to know all the gossip about why we had split up.

It wouldn't be fair to camp in Rob's room and Gilly would be livid. All the way to the restaurant, my stomach churned while I tried to decide what to do.

"Emma, would you and Marco like to join us for dinner?" Paul suggested as he helped Fiona out of the limo.

"We'd be delighted, if you and Fiona are sure you wouldn't rather be alone," Marco answered, before I had a chance to reply.

There didn't seem to be any point in arguing. I might as well let things lie and have it out with Marco once we flew home. After all, there was only one more day. It would give me more time to prepare what I wanted to say.

The restaurant turned out to be one of those tiny, perfect gems you always hope you'll find for a romantic rendezvous. Built around a small courtyard with orange trees festooned with tiny white fairy lights, the intimate tables glowed in the dusky twilight.

Gilly and Rob were led away to a small alcove where a waiter hovered, ready to pander to their every whim. I trailed along with Marco, Fiona and Paul to a larger table in the main body of the restaurant.

"It'll be nice to get to know you better, Emma. Your sister has told me so much about you." Paul smiled at me as I took my seat.

Forcing a smile in return, I wondered exactly what Fiona had said.

"I gather you and Marco had a whirlwind romance, too?"

I hoped he wouldn't take that as a good omen.

"Yeah, we met when Emma worked in Antigua," Marco stepped in again.

"So, you're getting married in a month's time?" I thought I'd better change the subject away from me and Marco, especially as we were on the verge of breaking up. Or at least, I thought we were on the verge of breaking up. As for Marco, I hadn't a clue what he thought.

"Yes, Paul has the most gorgeous little chapel in the grounds of his house." Fiona gazed lovingly at Paul.

"That's handy." I said. His own chapel? Who the hell has their own chapel?

Fiona fixed me with 'the look.'

"I only meant it can be difficult to find a venue if you get married at short notice," I said. Phew, got out of that one.

It did cross my mind there might be another reason for the rapid wedding arrangements. But Fi's tummy looked as flat as ever. I looked more pregnant than she did, except my belly was due to eating too many chocolate digestives.

"We didn't see the point of a long engagement. If I learned anything from Crystal's illness, it was that you have to make the most of life while you can," Paul said.

Fiona covered his hand sympathetically with her own. I felt mean for even suspecting they might have other reasons for getting married so quickly.

"I'm sure you'll both be very happy together," I said.

Fiona beamed at me. "Thank you, Emma. We haven't told Mummy yet. I tried calling her but she must be out and you know she flatly refuses to get a mobile."

"I won't say anything until you've spoken to her." It was a good job she'd warned me or I would have dropped myself right in it, as per usual.

The waiter reappeared to take our orders, so we gave our full attention to the menu for a few minutes. Paul offered to pay for the wine as it was his and Fi's celebration. Marco didn't take much persuasion, as the prices on the wine list were nearly as high as the cost of our rental car.

I couldn't see Rob and Gilly from my seat. I hoped she'd left the doggie photos back at the hotel. The restaurant was so lovely; it seemed a shame only Fi and Paul were in the right frame of mind to properly appreciate it.

Marco asked Paul about *The Lady Crystal*, where he moored it, how often did he get a chance to sail her, how long would it take to get the boat back to England... I hoped he hadn't got ideas about buying a yacht instead of a penthouse flat. Though quite how he could afford anything at the moment was a complete mystery to me. I still hadn't broached the subject of the money that had gone missing from the joint account.

Yachting talk filled up the whole of our first course and most of the main one. I only listened with half an ear as Fi twittered on after that about invitations and guest lists for the wedding.

I debated not ordering a pudding, as it sounded like the satin horror frock was back on the agenda and a few weeks didn't give me much time to lose weight. Maybe I should have kept Stick Insect's phone number.

By the time the coffees arrived, I needed the loo, so I lifted my bag onto the table and stood up to excuse myself. I'd meant to change my handbag for the nice little evening purse I'd packed especially for this evening. But as I'd been so late getting ready, I'd forgotten.

Of course, the waiter chose that moment to reappear out of nowhere and in an effort not to fall over him, I knocked my bag over, sending the contents rolling all over the restaurant floor.

I dived down, trying to retrieve my Tampax, chewing gum packets and old bus tickets from under the table, while Paul and Fiona retrieved pens, loose change and dead lipsticks. Marco picked up the cream envelope with the Revenue and Excise mark I'd collected from the flat before we'd left home.

"Where did you get this?" Marco's voice was sharp. I banged my head on the table as I tried to scramble out from under it.

"Oh, I picked it up from the flat on Thursday. I forgot all about it. I'm sorry, is it important?" I struggled back onto my chair and smoothed my hair down.

Marco scowled before he folded it in half and tucked it inside his breast pocket. "Nothing really, but I wish you'd leave my mail alone, Emma."

Fiona raised her eyebrows at me. Paul said nothing, but I could tell by his face he was taken aback by Marco's behavior.

"Well, this has been a very pleasant evening." Paul reached inside his jacket for his wallet.

I waited for Marco to offer to pay for our half as I stuffed the last of my belongings into my bag. When I realized he wasn't about to, I wished the ground would swallow me up and prayed my credit card had enough credit.

The faint strains of a guitar floated across from the alcove where Rob and Gilly sat.

"Oh, good. The singer's arrived," Fi said.

"What singer?" The bad feeling in the pit of my stomach worsened and it wasn't down to the food.

"As part of the date, I booked a man with a guitar. He does a strolling minstrel act, going around the tables and singing love songs for the couples sitting there." Fiona slipped her arm through Paul's. "It's so romantic. I thought it would finish the evening off nicely."

It might finish Rob off, full stop. The waiter came over, ignored my feebly waved credit card and accepted a large bundle of Euros from Paul.

"Allow me, Emma." Paul gently steered my card back towards my purse. "Fiona and I are celebrating. Tonight is our treat."

"If you're sure, that's very kind of you." I felt relieved but awful at the same time. Marco didn't seem to share my scruples and returned to being Mr. Affability himself when he realized he didn't have to dip into his wallet.

"It's a beautiful night—why don't we call in at one of the cafés at the marina for a nightcap?" Paul suggested.

"We should wait for Rob and Gilly." I'd promised Rob I would be around while the date was on. At least his ordeal must be almost over, unlike mine.

"I think they're coming," Marco remarked.

Gilly had a face like thunder as they crossed the restaurant to join us. Rob, on the other hand, had the look of a man who had survived an ordeal and lived to tell the tale.

"We're going to the marina for a nightcap. Do you want to come?" Fiona asked.

"Great." Rob didn't hesitate.

"Oh, alright," Gilly muttered huffily. I think she only agreed because she thought she might miss out on something if she didn't go.

We piled back into the limo and headed back down to the waterfront. "I would invite you on board *The Lady Crystal*, but my crew isn't due in until tomorrow afternoon and my agent holds the key," Paul apologized.

"Aren't you staying on board tonight?" Marco asked.

"No. The crew have some maintenance work to do before we can sail." Paul smiled at Fiona. "And besides, tonight is for celebrating with my beautiful fiancée."

Gilly sighed wistfully and gazed at Paul all puppy-eyed, before scowling at Rob.

The marina was packed with people; all the cafes and bars were full. The waterfront twinkled with fairy lights. And all the shops were still open and their window displays tastefully illuminated Hermes scarves and Gucci handbags. Exotically-dressed call girls stood on the street corners wearing the same designer clothes that were on display in the windows.

We strolled along, enjoying the nightlife. Paul had his arm around Fiona's waist. Rob meandered along next to me and Marco, while Gilly paused every few feet to gaze in the windows of the boutiques.

She was the first to spot an empty table outside one of the bars, so we sat down quickly before someone else took it. At the table next to us, a group of Danes seemed to be holding some kind of drinking contest which only stopped when one of them paused to answer his mobile phone—the outcome which cracked their whole group up into a chorus of raucous laughter and what sounded like smutty jokes.

"You had a phone call while you were out this afternoon." The sound of the phone reminded me I hadn't given Marco his cryptic message. He'd been so cross about the letter, I thought I'd better give him the phone message while I could still remember it. And with the quantity of booze I'd shifted tonight, my memory had already become a little hazy.

"Who was it?" His face was instantly wary.

"They didn't say. They said it was to let you know that Tony had given you a green light, whatever that means." I watched him closely to see how he reacted. When I gave him the message, his body stiffened and his knuckles whitened as he tightened his grip on the stem of his glass.

"Was that all?" His eyes bored into mine.

"Yes. Why, is it important?"

"Not really, just some business."

He had lied again, I knew it. "Business is such a bore." Gilly yawned.

I decided that whatever Marco was mixed up in, I didn't want to know too much about it. He's always sailed a bit close to the wind—his friendship with Everton is definitely suspect, and the man on the phone hadn't sounded very pleasant at all.

The brandy and coffee kept us nice and warm as the evening turned cooler.

"Shall we head back?" Paul suggested once our cups were empty, and draped his jacket around Fiona's shoulders.

Gilly had a pale pink Pashmina shawl wrapped around her so she wasn't cold. In my haste to meet the others, I'd forgotten to bring anything with me.

Rob noticed me shiver and slipped his coat off to wrap it around me. Marco walked on in front, his head down and his hands in his pockets, moodily kicking at any small stones lying on the footpath. He didn't even notice me.

"Thanks, Rob," I said.

Gilly glowered at me and quickened her pace to walk alongside Marco.

"Have you told him yet?" Rob kept his voice low so the others wouldn't overhear us.

"About wanting a divorce? No. I intended to talk to him over dinner, but with Fiona's engagement and everything, it didn't seem like a good time. Things aren't good between us, so it's not going to come as a surprise." Despite the warmth from Rob's jacket, a cold feeling crept across my back and I shivered again.

"Are you scared of him?" Rob flicked a glance further along the path to where Gilly and Marco strolled along together. "He's never hurt you?"

"No, never," I answered instantly. It was quite true. Marco had never hurt me but, if I were to be honest, lately he had begun to scare me.

Rob seemed reassured and we walked along in silence for a minute.

"Gilly doesn't seem very happy," I said.

"I've tried to be nice about it, but Gilly has the skin of a rhino! In the end, I had to be really blunt. I mean, she can be good fun sometimes, but I don't want her as a girlfriend in the romantic sense." He looked at me.

"How did you manage to get through to her?" After all, it wasn't as if this was the first time he'd tried to say any of this to Gilly and she'd never taken any notice before.

"I told her there was someone else."

"Oh!" He hadn't mentioned anyone else to me. I felt hurt and, for some reason, more than a little disappointed.

The others waited by the limo for us to catch up. The journey back to the hotel had a frosty atmosphere. Gilly was mad at Rob and not altogether thrilled with me, either. Marco and I weren't getting on and Marco disliked Rob anyway. Only Fiona and Paul remained oblivious to it all.

We trooped into the reception area at the hotel. Gilly collected her key and announced that she was off to bed. Paul and Fiona had already gone.

"I need to make some calls." Marco turned on his heel and went to join Gilly at the elevator. It was pretty clear he didn't want me around while he held his mystery conversations and to tell the truth, I didn't want to be there.

"Looks like you and me," Rob said.

"Both Billy-no-mates."

"The bar's still open," he suggested.

I shrugged and followed him to an empty table.

"Do you want another brandy?" Rob asked.

"I feel pretty far-gone, but what the hell."

Rob ordered two brandies.

"So, you're an official Gilly-free zone?" I lifted my glass to toast him.

"And you'll soon be a Marco-free zone?" He chinked his glass against mine.

It didn't feel like much of a celebration, but brandy is a good anaesthetic. Even though it was warmer in the bar, I still felt cold and huddled a bit further into Rob's coat.

"Who has Marco gone to phone?" Rob helped himself to some of the peanuts which had appeared at the same time as the brandies.

"I don't know and I don't care. He was with another woman down by the marina earlier today." I told Rob what I'd seen.

"You can stay in my room tonight, Em, if you don't want to share with Marco." Rob's blue eyes locked onto mine.

My breath caught at the back of my throat. Heat pooled in my stomach and I don't think it was just brandy warming me up.

"Um." My mind went blank. Okay, it wasn't blank, but the images that flashed across my mind rendered me incapable of coherent thought or speech.

"You're right. I shouldn't have suggested it." He leaned back in his seat and took a swig of brandy.

"You shouldn't have?" My voice sounded squeaky.

"Forget it."

I finished my drink and put my empty glass down carefully on the table. My hands shook and I rubbed them on my dress to stop the quivering. "I should go upstairs."

Rob finished his drink and stood up. "I'll walk you."

The lobby looked deserted except for the pretty girl in uniform behind the reception desk. The lift doors opened as we approached.

"It's Marco." I grabbed Rob and we dived for cover behind a massive potted palm.

Marco had changed into dark casual trousers and a black shirt. His mobile phone was clamped to his ear and he didn't look around as he walked out through the front doors.

"He's going out. Come on!" Rob took a step forward, grabbed my hand and tugged me across the lobby.

"What are you doing?"

"Let's follow him, see where he's going."

"We haven't got a car."

Rob waved his hand to shush me.

Marco spoke to the commissar while the car valet bought the rental car round. "I won't be back until later. I'm meeting some friends at the marina."

"Very good, sir." The valet hopped out of the Mercedes and held the door open.

We watched from the door of the hotel as he roared away without a backward glance.

Chapter Twenty

"Now what?"

Rob frowned. "We can get a cab."

Before I could stop him, he stepped through the doors and held his hand up to summon one of the taxis from the rank outside.

"We don't know where he's gone."

Rob ignored my protest as he bundled me into the back seat. "Puerto Banus marina, por favor, Señor."

"At least you haven't asked him to follow that car."

Rob grinned. "Hey, that's an idea."

"This is stupid," I said. "We don't even know for certain that this is where Marco's going. And what do I do if he's at the marina?"

"Aren't you curious about what he's up to?"

Okay, he had me there. I admit it, I was curious, but my instincts told me that there were some things about Marco I might be better off not knowing.

The taxi dropped us off at the street that led down to the waterfront. There were still people about, but the bar crowds had thinned and the waiters were clearing some of the tables, preparing to close down for the night.

"This is crazy. Let's go back to the hotel." I hung on tightly to Rob's hand. As people dispersed, the marina took on a different atmosphere. I wasn't exactly dressed for a covert surveillance operation, either. I was in my best silk summer sundress, kitten heels and Rob's coat. I felt sure Nancy Drew would have been better prepared.

Rob gazed around the waterfront. "Okay, maybe this wasn't a good idea. Still, we're here now. Let's just walk down by the boardwalk near *The Lady Crystal*."

"And if we don't see him, then we go back?"

"Okay," Rob agreed, although his tone still sounded reluctant.

I shivered, and Rob draped his arm around me, hugging me in closer to the warmth of his body. We walked along past the line of boats bobbing gently on the sea. As we drew further away from the bars, it became darker and quieter. Soon, the only sound I could hear was the rhythmic slapping of the water on the hulls of the yachts as they rocked in their moorings.

A few of the yachts had chinks of light glowing from inside their cabins. *The Lady Crystal* was accessible via a chained-off section of the narrow wooden boardwalk. She lay in darkness. No light shone from her deck or from the yachts moored either side of her.

"What was that?" Rob's whisper tickled warm in my ear.

"What?" I strained my eyes to see.

"I saw something. Someone's moving about on *The Lady Crystal*."

A gentle breeze blew from the surface of the water to ruffle the silk of my skirt against my legs. "It could be Paul's crew?" I suggested.

"If it was the crew, they'd have the lights on. This is someone who doesn't want to be seen," Rob murmured.

"Then we should go. They could see us." I tugged at his hand urgently. Then I saw the figure on *The Lady Crystal's* deck and it was one I knew all too well.

"Someone's coming—quick!" Rob shoved me backwards into the darkened archway of one of the now-closed boutiques. I heard footsteps on the boardwalk and a low whistle. Rob lifted my skirt and tucked it up under his jacket so the white material was out of sight. Acting quickly, he pushed me

Things To Do

back so I was tucked in tight against the wall, his body shielding me from the view of anyone passing by.

It felt scarily arousing to have the rough plaster of the archway against my bare legs. Rob's fingers lingered on the exposed bare skin of my thigh while the weight of his body pressed against me.

"Do you have the merchandise?" I heard Marco; he sounded close. God, I hoped he couldn't see us. I was so frightened I could hardly breathe. What if he recognized me?

"No worries. It's done." Another voice, male, answered him.

"We'd better make the exchange." Marco's voice.

"You've done well. I will tell Tony I'm pleased with the goods."

"The drop zone is set. My dear Emma's family has been very useful."

"We'd better go. Your woman will be looking for you, Marco," a woman's voice called from further away. I heard footsteps begin to retreat and wondered if it was the same woman I'd seen him with earlier.

"Emma won't ask any questions, and if she does I'll take care of her." Marco's voice sounded low with menace.

Rob fingers pressed into my thighs, a mute warning not to move in case we attracted their attention and they saw us.

"I thought I saw someone in the shadows." Marco's voice again. The footsteps paused and then began moving our way again. Rob squeezed my leg more urgently. I thought I would faint with fear.

"Kiss me," Rob whispered.

"What—?" I began, and then he pressed his lips against mine, hiding my face from view not to mention shocking the glorious living wits from me—just as the footsteps came to a halt nearby.

"One of the girls with a punter. Come on, we don't want to be seen," the woman whispered. The other man gave a catcall and made what sounded like a ribald remark in Spanish. I heard Marco laugh.

217

Rob kept kissing me until we heard them move away. Once we were certain they'd gone, Rob stepped back, looking awkward as he helped me pull my dress back down. "Sorry, Em."

My body shook like jelly. I knew we shouldn't have followed Marco. What was worse—even though I'd been convinced I was about to die, being half-naked and kissing Rob had been disturbingly arousing.

"It's okay." I wasn't sure what he was sorry for, or what was okay. I wasn't sure about anything at all.

"We need to get back before Marco realizes you're missing."

"Back?" I squeaked. He didn't seriously think I was prepared to go back to the hotel and Marco after what we'd just heard. I scrubbed at the tears trickling down my cheeks.

"You have to. If he thinks you know something it'll put you in danger." Rob didn't sound happy.

"I can't, I'm no actress." I was hopeless at lying.

"You don't have to be. Look, he already knows you're mad at him. Just stay out of his way and give him the silent treatment until we get back to England." Rob pulled a clean white hanky from his pocket and wiped all the smeary mascara off my face. "We'll try and get Fiona and Paul to bring us down to the yacht tomorrow. They already said they probably would. If we find anything suspicious, we can go to the police. If not, well, we go home the day after tomorrow."

I sniffed miserably, knowing he was right. "How are we going to get back to the hotel?" The bars had closed and the harbor looked eerily deserted.

Rob frowned. "We'll have to head toward the main road and hope we can pick up a cab. If not, I reckon it's about half an hour's walk." The look on my face must have been enough. "Look out for a call box. There might be cab numbers."

"And what if Marco and those other thugs see us?" Knowing my luck they would probably drive right past.

"It's a chance we'll have to take, Penfold."

Things To Do

"Coming here was a shitty idea." Just for that moment, I think I managed the family death glare, because Rob's optimism definitely wilted. "And it was your shitty idea!" I added.

"Okay, I'm sorry."

We started to plod along towards the main road. I've never been a church-going kind of person but I'd willingly become one if a taxi was to show up at this point in time. How come with a wardrobe full of shoes and clothes, I'm always dressed and shod inappropriately? Pointy-toed kitten heels are not the footwear of choice to wear while hiking alongside Spain's equivalent of a Grand Prix track.

Since all the traffic passing us moved so fast it was a mere blur, identifying any kind of vehicle—let alone a cab with a lit-up vacant sign would be a miracle. I resigned myself to blisters and walking.

We reached a crossing point, ready to play chicken with the traffic before the start of the climb into the exclusive hills in which our hotel was set.

"Wait," I said.

Rob paused a few feet ahead of me while I pulled my shoes off and stuffed them into my bag. "What are you doing? You can't walk with bare feet."

"Well, I can't walk any farther wearing them." I wanted to cry. No—correction—I wanted to throw myself on the ground and howl, except the pavement didn't look very clean.

We stumbled along the street until Rob stopped suddenly at the corner, next to a street lamp.

"Em, have you got your phone?"

"Yes." For all the good it could do me. I wasn't even sure it worked in Spain, as I still hadn't heard from Sara.

He fumbled in his pocket and pulled out a business card. "Lend it to me a minute."

I rummaged about in my bag and passed it over. He held the card up to the street lamp then punched in some numbers. There was a rapid

219

conversation in Spanish, then he handed my mobile back with a triumphant grin on his face.

"What?" I asked.

"I called the hotel. They're sending a cab to pick us up."

"And you thought of this only now?" I glared at him.

"I thought you'd be pleased."

I wasn't sure if I wanted to kiss him or beat him to death with the shoes I'd stuffed in my handbag. The cab turned the corner after only a few minutes wait and we arrived back at the hotel as the first fingers of dawn poked over the horizon. Rob paid the cab driver and walked with me to the elevator.

"Do you think he's back?"

Rob shook his head. "No, I checked with the commissar."

Relief flooded through me. The elevator doors opened and Rob got out at my floor and came with me to the door of my room.

"Just in case," he murmured.

Cautiously, I opened the door. The room was just as I'd left it earlier, with no sign of Marco.

"It's okay." Suddenly I felt a bit awkward.

"Get some sleep," Rob said. "I'll see you later and if there's any hint of a problem, come and find me." He smoothed my hair gently with his hand.

"I'll be fine." I wished I felt as confident as I sounded.

Without saying another word, he kissed me briefly on the lips and strode off toward the stairs, leaving me with aching feet and an aching heart.

✔ ✔ ✔

I woke up to sunlight flooding the room and Marco sitting in a chair in front of the window, hands templed together as he watched me.

"Whew, guess I overdid the celebrations last night. What time is it?" I pushed my hair out of my eyes and struggled to sit up. My heart thumped like a bass drum.

Marco glanced at his watch. "Almost eleven. You missed breakfast."

I couldn't tell what kind of mood he was in or if he suspected I'd been out late last night. "Sorry, have you been waiting for me?"

"Gilly and Fiona were concerned about you. Paul has offered to show us his yacht." Marco seemed to be choosing his words carefully.

"I'd better hit the shower then." I slid out of bed and headed for the bathroom.

"What have you been doing to your feet?"

Marco's question stopped me in my tracks. I'd been so tired when I'd closed the door on Rob that I'd just hung up my dress and crawled under the covers. I looked down at my feet. The soles were black and my heels red from where my shoes had rubbed.

"My feet hurt last night so I had my shoes off in the restaurant and in the bar. Then I walked back up here last night without them. Those floors must be dirtier than they look." I did my best to feign a puzzled look and headed into the shower before he could question me any further.

As I started up the water I heard Marco's voice. At first I thought he must be talking to me, but as I had my hand on the bathroom door ready to answer him, I realized he was on the phone.

It was hard to hear above the sound of the running water so I tried to listen through a glass on the door like they do in films.

It doesn't work. I only made out snippets of the conversation. I heard Marco say "She doesn't know," and "The merchandise has been placed."

I heard him hang up the phone, so I darted under the water and began to shampoo my hair.

"Emma, I'm going downstairs. The others will be by the pool." Marco rattled the bathroom door handle impatiently.

"I'm almost done," I shouted, and I heard the bedroom door shut. I turned off the shower and reached for a towel.

I raced to get dressed. Marco's mention of breakfast had reminded me I was hungry. I didn't bother to dry my hair. I figured it would probably look better if it dried naturally and I didn't want to keep everyone waiting for me yet again.

Gilly, Fiona and Paul were at a table by the side of the pool in the shade of an umbrella. They all wore linen suits and looked like they had been posed for a *Vogue* fashion shoot.

"Well, good afternoon." Fiona made a point of looking at her watch. She rolled her eyes when she noticed my wet hair and distinctly last-season Capri trousers and tee-shirt.

"Where's Rob?" I asked.

"On the fruit machine in the bar." Gilly didn't appear happy with how this weekend had turned out.

"Now that you're finally here, we can go." Fiona stood and picked up her bag.

"What about Marco?" I hadn't seen him since I'd come downstairs.

"He said he'd meet us out front. He's going to give you, Gilly and Rob a ride. One of my crew will collect me and Fiona." Paul placed his chair tidily back under the table.

"I'd better go and get Rob." Gilly adopted a martyred tone and marched off toward the bar.

No one mentioned going for lunch, so I hoped my tummy wasn't gurgling too loudly as I followed Fiona and Paul inside the hotel.

Marco lounged against the front desk, talking to the receptionist as we entered the lobby. Rob and Gilly were behind us as we walked over.

Marco straightened up at our approach and switched on his "Mr. Affability" persona again, reaching into his pocket and smiling congenially at all of us. "Ready to go?" He jingled the keys to the rental car in his hand.

Things To Do

"You all go on ahead. Fiona and I will be along shortly. One of my crew will be on board and he's expecting you." Paul gave a nod in Marco's direction to indicate we could go.

Dismissed, the four of us trooped outside to wait for the valet to bring the car around. Rob yawned loudly, causing Gilly and Marco to turn around in surprise.

"Sorry, I think the late night and travel are catching up with me."

Marco turned away as the rental car came into view and Rob lifted his eyebrows in silent apology to me.

Gilly and Rob climbed into the back of the car and, prompted by the commissar opening the front passenger door for me, I took my seat in the front next to Marco.

"What are we doing for lunch?" My stomach gurgled as Marco swung the car along a narrow side street towards the coast road.

"I'm full from breakfast." Gilly still sounded miffed.

"I'm sure Paul's crew will have something on board for lunch," Rob suggested.

Marco left the car in the small parking area where we'd stopped the day before. It was a beautiful day. The waterfront appeared busy once more with tourists and the bars and cafes looked cheerful and welcoming.

It was a far cry from just a few hours earlier, before dawn, when the harbor had shown the other, darker side of its personality. Not unlike Marco, really, when I thought about it.

"Oh, I want to go in that shop!" Gilly announced as soon as we arrived at the harbor edge, and she disappeared inside a boutique selling very expensive fashion jewelry. I left Rob and Marco studiously ignoring each other and went inside to see what had caught Gilly's eye.

"Look, Emma, aren't these sweet?" Gilly had forgotten she was cross with me and stood admiring tiny dog collars studded with Austrian crystals that twinkled and sparkled in the halogen shop lights.

My heart sank. I didn't want to be the voice of doom, but there was a possibility she might not get Robbie the dog back from the dog-nappers.

"Lovely," I said.

"I've got to get one of these for Robbie. He'll be so excited when he comes home and sees what his mummy's got for him."

Some things there are just no answers for, so I left her to it and went back outside into the sunshine.

"What's she doing in there?" Rob asked.

"Buying a bling-bling collar for Robbie the dog."

"Christ!" Rob muttered and kicked a loose pebble into the harbor water with a splash, scattering the shoals of little fishes which flitted around the hulls of the boats.

Marco wandered further down the marina and was busy on his mobile. Every time I saw him use the phone, I felt uneasy. I couldn't help remembering the man with the horrid laugh who I'd spoken to the day before.

"How has he been?" Rob jerked his head in Marco's direction.

"A bit weird, but things are just frosty between us. He noticed my dirty feet this morning but I managed to pass it off." I broke off as Gilly crossed the pavement toward us, carrying a posh little stripy carrier with a crest on it.

"Which one did you choose?" I felt sorry for Gilly.

"I got a blue one for a boy." Her mouth wobbled a bit and I hugged her.

Rob wandered off in the opposite direction to Marco. I think he was worried in case Gilly might whip those doggy photos out again.

"I'm sure you'll get him back, Gilly." I tried to sound reassuring. "The police were pretty confident, weren't they?"

"I suppose so." Her face brightened a little. Perhaps the thought of the nice-looking policeman calling to see her again as well as the prospect of getting her dog back had cheered her up.

"We'd better go down to the yacht. I expect Fiona and Paul will be along in a minute," Gilly called to Rob.

Things To Do

I beckoned to Marco; he was still on the phone. We made our way to where *The Lady Crystal* lay at anchor at the end of a narrow wooden jetty. I noticed faint scuff marks on the side of her hull and wiggled my eyebrows at Rob. I expected Marco to show some kind of reaction—I thought criminals were supposed to when they returned to the scene of the crime—but he didn't even blink.

Chapter Twenty-One

An elderly man appeared from inside the yacht and welcomed us on board. Gilly had forgotten Fiona's warning about wearing suitable shoes, so she moaned when she had to take hers off.

Once we all sat down under the canopy on the cockpit with a pot of coffee and a big plate of biscuits in front of us, I began to feel more cheerful.

Marco stowed his mobile away and recovered his good humor. Posing in his sunglasses, he looked as if he should be the owner of the yacht.

"This is a very nice boat. We had a lovely time on here yesterday," Gilly remarked.

"I'm looking forward to seeing around it. Paul promised to give us the grand tour." Rob yawned again. I watched Marco from behind my sunglasses but he didn't bat an eyelid.

I know Rob planned to use the tour to look for some sort of clue as to what Marco had been doing on board *The Lady Crystal* last night. I wasn't sure what to look for. Footprints? A large label saying "evidence"? The outline of a body in chalk on the deck?

Paul's crew were the people best placed to know if something looked odd or wasn't right on the boat. Since neither Rob nor I knew a poop deck from a yard arm, I couldn't see how we would notice anything out of the ordinary.

Paul and Fiona came along the boardwalk accompanied by an older woman, who I assumed from her clothes, to be another crew member.

"Has Tom been looking after you?" Fiona asked as she stepped down into the cockpit. I helped myself to another biscuit and she frowned. "You'll never fit into that bridesmaid dress, Emma, if you keep eating biscuits."

Rob raised his eyebrows sympathetically and Gilly looked smug. It's alright for people who are naturally skinny or who don't like food. But I like chocolate biscuits and puddings and even when I've dieted really hard, I still have a big bust. I just look out of proportion then, like a pre-surgery version of Dolly Parton. If you can imagine a version of Dolly with brown curly hair, that is.

Paul disappeared inside the yacht with the two crew members. Presumably he wanted to check what they were doing. With any luck it included feeding us; something smelled delicious and I hoped it was lunch.

Fiona sat down gracefully on one of the empty chairs.

"How long will it take you to sail back to England?" Marco asked her.

"I'm not sure. We're going to have to fly back with you tomorrow, after all. Paul's had a lot of urgent business phone calls so Tom and his wife are going to sail her back instead. They have to do the work on the boat first anyway, before it can go anywhere."

Fiona didn't sound too disappointed. I suspected she preferred the yacht moored somewhere nice as a kind of floating hotel rather than actually sailing in it. Fi had once been sea-sick on the car ferry from Dover to Calais.

I wasn't sure if I imagined a flicker of annoyance flitting across Marco's face.

"You'll be kept busy organizing the wedding once you get home," Gilly said.

"Oh, I know." Fiona sighed.

"You can always have your honeymoon on board." Rob stretched out on his chair and I knew he had his eyes fixed on Marco to gauge his reaction.

"You could sail around the Greek Islands," Gilly suggested.

"Mmm." I could tell Fiona had imagined herself in a tiny bikini with a gin in her hand on board *The Lady Crystal* around the Med.

"So, when do you think the boat will be back in England?" Marco asked.

"Paul's finding out. There's quite a bit of varnishing to do and apparently the engine has to be checked. We aren't in a hurry, so it could take a few weeks."

Marco's fingers twitched and I suspected this news had interfered with his plans in some way. Paul came back into the cockpit to join us.

"Thomas has suggested he give the engine a full overhaul. It makes sense as I haven't moved *The Lady Crystal* for quite a while." Paul reached for Fiona's hand and squeezed her fingers tenderly. "Sorry, darling."

Fiona did her best to look disappointed. "Oh, it's all right. After all, we'll have plenty of other sailing opportunities."

"Marco, you wanted a tour? Come, I'll show you around before we have lunch." Paul smiled at Marco.

My stomach gave a gurgle of appreciation at the mention of lunch.

Rob sat up in his seat. "Do you mind if I tag along? This is such a beautiful boat. I'd love to see the rest of her."

Marco scowled as Paul beckoned Rob to join them, then he led them both inside the yacht.

"Em, is everything alright with you and Marco?" Fi waited until the men were out of earshot before she leaned forward to whisper across the table.

Gilly made a noise that sounded suspiciously like a "huh."

"I'd rather not talk about it." I didn't want to discuss anything personal with Gilly listening in and besides, what could I say? My husband might be a gangster and if I dig too deeply, he'll kill me? Oh, and by the way, I think he's hidden something illegal on board your fiancé's yacht?

Thomas's wife laid the table in front of us with fresh linen and silver cutlery. Fantastic smells came from the galley kitchen. The men arrived back as Thomas was about to open a bottle of chilled white wine. I glanced at Rob and he shook his head, so I guessed he hadn't found any clues.

Lunch tasted as delicious as it smelled—fresh bread, grilled sardines and salad with lovely baby potatoes. If I hadn't been so anxious about Marco, I'd have really enjoyed it.

"Did you like your tour around?" Fiona asked Marco. "*The Lady Crystal* is Paul's pride and joy."

"It was very interesting." Marco leaned back in his seat and took a sip of wine.

"I hadn't realized it was so big," Rob said.

Paul laughed. "Oh, there's plenty of room. Even when the crew are on board, there's still a lot of space."

"I'm amazed you don't get stowaways," Gilly said. "There must be plenty of hiding places on board."

Marco's head snapped up and he fixed his gaze on Gilly, who carried on innocently eating her salad.

"There are regulations in place regarding passengers and customs," Paul said. "Just because you're on a yacht doesn't mean you get a free rein, although it's rare for a yacht to be searched from stem to stern. It would be impossible—Gilly's right. Look how many hiding places you could have." He gestured expansively with his fork.

"You mean you could smuggle things?" Gilly's eyes were like saucers.

"I suppose some people might, but it isn't really a risk anyone sensible would run, although the odd extra case of spirits occasionally makes its way over," Paul reassured her.

I chanced another glance at Marco. He was back to being Mr. Affability again, but I sensed tension emanating from him whilst Paul talked.

I felt glad when lunch ended and the conversation moved onto more mundane things. We left Fiona and Paul on board finishing the bottle of wine. Gilly wanted to go shopping and worryingly to me, Marco offered to go with her. Rob planned to go back to the hotel for a nap and I longed to do the same, but felt obligated to offer to stay with Gilly.

"Don't be silly, Emma. Marco and I will have a lovely time." Gilly waved me away.

"You might as well go and catch up on your sleep. We'll see you tonight." Marco looked at me and a shiver ran up my spine. Whatever he had planned, I was not a part of it.

I couldn't see Marco intending to harm Gilly. More likely he wanted to find out where her comments about smugglers had come from. I pasted a smile on my face and joked about them spending too much money before I set off with Rob to take a taxi back to the hotel.

"Do you think Gilly will be okay?" I pounced on Rob as soon as we were out of sight.

He moved my hands from where I had a tight grip on the front of his T-shirt. "Em, he's not likely to bump her off or kidnap her when she's on a publicity jaunt for an international charity."

"Well, why was he so keen to go shopping with her?" He had to have an ulterior motive; I had learned lately that Marco always had one.

"I don't know. Maybe it's as cover for something else?" Rob said.

I pondered his suggestion as we strolled along in the sunshine. He still had hold of my hand.

"He didn't seem happy when Paul said the yacht wasn't sailing tomorrow. You didn't notice anything when you looked around?" I asked.

"Nothing unusual, but there are so many possible hiding places on board, plus we don't know whether he'd hidden something or intended to pick something up."

We'd reached the taxi rank. I still felt uneasy about Gilly, despite Rob's reassurances. "You are sure she'll be okay?"

"I'm certain of it. Whatever Marco may be up to, it certainly isn't anything that he wants to draw attention to. So he's not likely to risk that by allowing something to happen to Gilly."

I knew he was probably right, but the Marco I'd come to know over the past few weeks wasn't the Marco I'd fallen in lust with on a sunny Antiguan beach.

"Do you want to go back to the hotel?" Rob took a step toward the waiting taxi.

"I'm not following Marco again."

"I wasn't going to suggest it. This trip hasn't been much fun for you, has it, Emma?"

That was an understatement if ever there was one. "What do you have in mind?" The way Rob looked at me when I spoke, I didn't know what he would suggest. I knew what my mind had imagined and it involved a naked Rob and a double bed. The way my body leapt to attention from the touch of his hand in mine, whatever he suggested I would probably go along with it.

"I thought we might go into Marbella and wander around for a while. Why, what did you think I had in mind?"

I never knew that your whole body could blush. Evidently, Rob's mind worked the same way mine did and I wasn't the only one with naughty thoughts. "Nothing." I couldn't get any redder and Rob knew it was a lie anyway.

"You sure?" He teased, enjoying my embarrassment.

"Quite sure."

His face sobered for a moment and I thought he might be about to suggest we put our fantasies to the test. Instead, he took hold of my other hand and pulled me toward him.

Rob is much taller than me, so standing toe-to-toe, I managed to hide my red face in his chest. He wrapped his arms around me. "Look at me," he whispered, and when I did, he kissed me. My heart began to perform crazy back-flips and I forgot we were in a taxi-rank.

"Let's go to Marbella." Rob took hold of my hand again and pulled me into the back of a taxi.

Dazed, I climbed in beside him. Why Marbella? I mean, we had perfectly good bedrooms at the hotel and after that kiss, I really wanted to put one of them to good use.

"Where are we going?" I felt a bit irritated. If he didn't he fancy me, what was with all of the kisses lately?

"Wait and see." He flashed me a grin and slid his arm around my shoulders. Feeling a bit more reassured, I snuggled up against him, and enjoyed the nice solid feel of his body against mine.

The taxi dropped us off in the old part of the town and Rob took me wandering through narrow cobbled streets with courtyards filled with trickling fountains and orange trees. The green shutters of the houses were closed and we strolled along hand-in-hand with not another soul in sight.

The air was warm and still. Every few yards, we stopped to kiss. It felt truly magical, as if we were the only two people left on the planet. I didn't really understand what was happening between me and Rob, but I knew that things were changing rapidly—and in ways I didn't mind at all.

Eventually we stopped at a café in one of the courtyards with orange trees in the centre of the square. Only a couple of tables were occupied so we sat down in a quiet corner and ordered some coffee.

Rob let go of my hand when the waiter reappeared with our drinks.

"Thank you for this afternoon. It's been lovely." I took a sip of my latte and revelled in the feel of Rob's leg pressed intimately against mine under the table.

"I thought we needed a break."

I placed my cup down carefully on the table and tried to think how I could ask him what was really on my mind. "Why didn't you take me to bed?" Okay, so tact isn't something I'm good at.

Rob raised an eyebrow. "Because everyone would know and with your situation being like it is with Marco, I didn't think it was a good idea."

He was right, mores the pity. I'm hopeless at keeping secrets and if we had spent the afternoon bonking I might just as well have had "adulteress" tattooed across my forehead.

Things To Do

A clatter of heels sounded in the square and Rob shifted the weight of his leg away from mine. Startled by his abrupt withdrawal, I looked across to see Gilly and Marco coming towards us, accompanied by Paul and Fiona.

"Hi, you two!" Fiona called and waved.

Marco appeared to be burdened down with numerous carrier bags and he had the stunned, dazed expression that too much time spent with Gilly appeared to induce in men.

"I thought you were going back to the hotel?" Gilly sat down and picked up the drinks menu.

"Changed our minds." Rob sipped his coffee. "I see you bought a few things."

Gilly beamed happily as Marco dropped the pile of carriers at her feet and then pulled his chair up next to me. "Marco's been so helpful."

Fiona and Paul sauntered up and took a seat. "We thought we'd take a look around Marbella and Marco kindly gave us a lift. Where have you two been?" Fiona asked, looking at me and Rob.

"Just wandering about." I was sure my face had gone red. I could hardly say I'd been too busy snogging the face off my best friend to notice my surroundings.

"You haven't bought anything?" Marco asked me.

I shrugged. "Didn't see anything I liked."

Marco looked suspiciously at Rob. I wished Marco wasn't so close to me. It made me feel uncomfortable.

"What's everyone got planned for tonight?" Paul asked.

"Well, the flight is quite early tomorrow, so I'm going to get an early night." Gilly rustled busily through her carriers.

"Yeah, I'm pretty tired too." Rob glanced at me.

"I might go to the casino. I heard it was supposed to be good." Marco didn't ask me what my plans were and thankfully didn't suggest I accompany him.

233

"I'll probably have an early night." I took another sip of my coffee. "What about you, Fi?"

"Oh, we're having dinner on the yacht with some friends of Paul's who live along the coast." Fiona admired her engagement ring as it glinted in the sunlight.

Gilly finished rummaging amongst her purchases before draining her coffee cup. "Would you be an angel, Marco, and give me a lift back to the hotel?"

"No problem. Does anyone else want a ride?" He looked at me.

"Yes, please." Fi finished her drink.

"We'll get a cab later. There was a shoe shop Emma hasn't looked in," Rob said nonchalantly.

I let out a subconscious sigh of relief as they left. With any luck, by the time I got back to the hotel, Marco would have gone out for the night and I wouldn't have to spend time alone with him.

Even so, his being in the café had left a shadow. I might have had a nice afternoon with Rob, but Marco being here in Spain with me was a reminder that I wasn't a free woman and that I had unfinished business to deal with.

Things to do:

Separate from Marco.

Have wild passionate sex with Rob.

Persuade Fi to lose the bridesmaid frock from hell. Again.

We ordered more coffees and some cake and sat chatting. Rob didn't touch me again. Somehow the mood had gone and I felt awkward.

"How long do you think he'll be gone?" Rob asked.

"Marco? He loves a casino. I've known him be out all night in the past." I wished he would stay out all night.

"When are you going to tell him you want a divorce?"

"As soon as we get home. I'll feel safer then." I didn't need to spell out why I used the term "safer." Rob had heard the same conversation.

"Why did you marry him, Emma?" Hurt showed in Rob's eyes as he asked me the same question I'd been asking myself all weekend.

"Because he was sexy and charming. Because he said he loved me." I blinked back tears. "And because he asked me."

A tear escaped and rolled down my cheek to plop onto the table top. Rob reached across to cradle my face in his hands, stroking away the wetness with his thumb.

"I'm sorry, Emma. Don't cry."

"It's okay." I sniffed and pulled one of the paper serviettes from the dispenser in the centre of the table to wipe my eyes.

"I didn't mean to make you cry, I just…" He trailed off.

I understood what he meant. He'd just wanted to know why I'd gone to work in the Caribbean and married a man I barely knew without telling anyone.

It had been the magic of the island, I suppose. Part of my job there had been arranging weddings for couples who'd come out from England to get married on the beach in glorious golden sunshine. I'd been responsible for ensuring they had the flowers, cake and music they'd ordered.

Surrounded by sun and romance, Marco had, I realized now, used his charm and sex appeal to make me feel special. Wanted. A bit like Fiona, I suppose. Our wedding had been organized in a hurry. Marco had arranged the registrar because the lady who normally came to perform the weddings at the hotel had been ill.

At the time, the rush had seemed romantic. I had been flattered that this handsome, desirable man couldn't wait to be married to boring old Emma Morgan. It was as if by me marrying one of the golden people, I'd become one of them, too. Except I hadn't; I was still just Emma.

"We should go back to the hotel." Rob's voice interrupted my train of thought.

We walked back through the streets towards the seafront. The town came bustling back to life, ready for the evening trade. Rob hailed a taxi and we were soon at the hotel.

"I'll see you in the morning." Rob walked with me to the lift.

"Aren't you coming upstairs?" I went hot when I realized what I'd said, even though I hadn't meant it in that way.

"I'm going to sit in the bar for a while."

The lift pinged and the doors opened.

"I'll see you tomorrow, then." I got in and the doors shut. He didn't attempt to kiss me goodnight.

I opened the door of the room, praying Marco had already gone out. I'd just sat down on the bed with a sigh of relief when my mobile beeped in my handbag and frightened me half to death.

I dived in to see who had text-messaged me and recognized Sara's number on the display. There was a short message:

"Sara's okay. Shay."

Where was Sara? And why was Shay answering her messages?

Chapter Twenty-Two

Marco arrived back as I was due to go downstairs with our luggage to meet the others. I'd thrown his stuff into his bag, not sure if I'd done the right thing by packing for him.

"Good night out?" I wasn't being sarcastic, although it was now four in the morning.

"Yeah," he mumbled and moved into the room toward to the bedside lamp.

"What's with the sunglasses?" As he came closer, I saw why he had them on. It looked like he had the start of what promised to be a huge black eye.

"Nothing." He picked up his bag. "Did you pack?"

"Yes, everything's in and I checked the cupboards." I didn't expect to get an explanation for the shiner. To be honest, if I'd been around when whoever it was had taken a pop at him I'd have probably joined in—on his opponent's side.

"I said we'd give Gilly and Rob a lift to the airport. Fi and Paul are making their own way there."

Marco didn't look very thrilled. Maybe it was the thought of being in the same car as Gilly at this ungodly hour of the morning, but he didn't have much choice.

"We'd better go, then." He opened the door.

I waited to see if he would offer to carry my bag.

"What are you waiting for?" he asked.

So much for that. I picked up my bag and followed him along the corridor to the lift.

Rob was already in the lobby. I handed in the room key while we waited for Gilly.

"What happened to his eye?" Rob asked as Marco went out to get the car.

"I don't know. I asked but he wouldn't say. Where's Gilly?"

"Bribing a porter to carry all her luggage downstairs."

The lift doors pinged open and Gilly emerged, shepherding a sullen-faced, uniformed bell-hop with a laden luggage trolley.

"Honestly, it's so difficult to get good staff!" Gilly has a very loud whisper and her comment was rewarded by a scowl from the beleaguered bell-boy.

"Are you ready to go?" I eyed the luggage mountain. I couldn't imagine that she'd forgotten anything.

"All set," she answered brightly and collared the bell-hop as he was about to sneak off. "Wait! You need to take these outside and put them in the car."

She waved a bundle of Euros at him, which appeared to sweeten his disposition and he maneuvered the trolley outside.

Marco didn't make any kind of move to get out of the car to help, so Rob and the bell-boy loaded up the boot with our bags and cases. My bag wouldn't fit, however, so I balanced it on my knees all the way to the airport.

Marco dropped us off at the departure gate and went to return the rental car. He had his own ticket and passport so Rob commandeered a luggage trolley for Gilly and we went inside to check in.

The departure lounge was full of package holiday tourists. Gilly looked more than a little put-out when she realized she hadn't been booked to get the VIP lounge treatment for the return leg of her journey.

There was no sign of Marco, so we walked upstairs to get a coffee from the restaurant.

"Why is Marco wearing his sunglasses this morning? It was still dark on the way here," Gilly commented, as she snaffled the only free table in the restaurant from under the collective noses of a German family dressed in matching check trousers.

"He's done something to his eye." Rob gave the Germans an apologetic smile and strolled off to fetch our drinks.

"Emma, I'm really not one to interfere, but you and Marco seem to be having problems. I know you didn't want to burden Fiona with them yesterday, so if you want to talk about things, you know I'm here for you." Gilly leaned back in the aluminium chair and tried to look sympathetic.

"That's very kind of you, Gilly." As if I wanted to tell Miss Nosey all my business. I desperately wanted to talk to Sara; she'd be able to give me some advice. I just hoped she was okay. The weird text from Shay had bothered me.

"Is it the sex?" Gilly leaned forward and patted my hand. The two teenage girls sitting at the table next to us burst into a fit of giggles.

"No." I felt my cheeks start to heat up.

"Because that's where a lot of relationships fail, you know, in the bedroom."

"Gilly, I have good sex."

"Oh, yeah?" Rob slid a coffee cup in front of me. "Who's having good sex?"

I really need to master the family death glare. Gilly accepted her cup of herbal tea and gave Rob a pitying look. "It's a private conversation. I was helping Emma with her…" She dropped her voice to a piercing whisper. "…sexual problems."

Oh, God, just let me die now. Half the restaurant had turned to look at me. Gilly has a whisper that can shatter glass. You know how they say "in space, no one can hear you scream?" Well, you could hear Gilly whisper. I'd place money on it.

"I do not have sexual problems," I hissed back at her.

"Well, I guess that's good to know." Rob took a bite out of the chocolate chip muffin he'd bought to go with his coffee and winked at me.

"Oh, there's Marco." Gilly waved to attract his attention and Rob passed me a muffin.

Marco's arrival put a halt to the conversation, which was about the only good thing I could say about his appearance in the restaurant. Even Gilly lost the urge to chat and finished her drink in silence.

"I'm going to look around the shops. Anyone want to come?" Gilly gathered her hand luggage and looked expectantly at us.

"I'll come with you. I want a paper to read on the flight." Rob stood up.

I moved to join them, but Marco laid his hand across my arm. "Emma and I will catch up to you."

I sank back down on my chair, my palms all sweaty and my heart bumping as if it was about to leap out of my chest.

"I think we need to talk." Marco leaned forward, his eyes still hidden behind his dark glasses.

My voice deserted me, so I nodded in agreement.

"I'm going away for a while when we get back. If anyone asks for me, you don't know where I am."

"But I won't know where you've gone! Marco, how much trouble are you in?" I thought I'd been frightened when I'd overheard the conversation by the harbor, but now he was seriously freaking me out.

"It's nothing, just a little temporary problem." He leaned back again in his seat.

"Marco, I think we should go our separate ways." The words came out in a rush. "I want a divorce."

He frowned. "It's Rob, isn't it?"

"Marco, answer me honestly, do you love me?"

The silence while he made up his mind gave me my answer. He didn't care about me. He never had. The funny thing was, I'd known all along, I suppose. But for a while, I'd fooled myself into believing in a fairytale and now it was over.

The handsome prince was a frog once again. Cinderella was back in rags and my marriage had fallen to bits in an airport departure lounge full of holiday-makers.

"I'm going to move back to the flat at the end of the week," I said. "Do you want me to pack your stuff for you?"

The question snapped him back from wherever it was his mind had wandered off to.

"Thanks. I'll have someone come by and pick up my bags." He sounded preoccupied or bored. Clearly, the end of our relationship held no great emotional impact for Marco. I and my family had reached the end of our useful shelf life. Whatever he'd been using us for must be finished. At least that part made me feel a little relieved.

"I'm going to find the others." I shouldered my handbag and stood up. Marco continued to look past me, as if watching something or someone at the far end of the restaurant.

"I'm going," I repeated, struggling with the urge to thump him.

Marco looked up as if surprised to find me still there. "Yeah, see you around, babe."

Was that it? The end of my marriage was marked by nothing more profound than "see you around, babe?" Gritting my teeth, I pulled together the remnants of my pride and stalked off, past the giggling teenagers, my head held high.

Rob had waited for me just out of view around the corner.

"Is everything okay?" He opened his arms and I stepped into them. I needed that hug. My legs were jelly after the conversation with Marco.

"He's going away, moving out. It's over." I started to cry. I must have got mascara over so many of Rob's shirts lately.

"Hey, come on. They just put out the first call for our flight."

I scrabbled in my pocket for a tissue and dabbed at my eyes. "Where's Gilly?"

"She's gone ahead to the gate with Paul and Fiona. We met up with them in duty-free." He stroked my hair gently. "Come on, Penfold, I'll race you to gate thirty-one." Rob has a way of making me smile even when I feel crap.

Gilly, Fi and Paul had waited for us, but I couldn't see Marco anywhere. I didn't even know where he would be seated on the plane since he hadn't checked in with us.

"It's so crowded in here. I'll be glad when we're on board." Fiona glared at a passing toddler with a chocolate-covered face who'd looked as if he might touch her beige linen trousers.

"Never mind, darling. I know how much you were looking forward to sailing back but we'll be able to do that another time," Paul soothed.

Eventually, we made it on board. Gilly bagged a window seat; I got the seat next to her and Rob sat next to the aisle. Fiona and Paul were at the front of the plane near the cabin crew. I tried to look for Marco, but it was hopeless. The air hostesses had started to do the seatbelt check ready for take-off and I couldn't see past them.

Gilly had a heap of magazines, so at least I was spared the pictures of Robbie the dog on the way home. She opened *Harpers and Queen*, put on her headset, then promptly fell asleep. I borrowed her copy of *Cosmopolitan* and tested the quiz questions out on Rob.

By the time the plane started to descend, we'd worked our way through most of Gilly's magazines and two lots of brandied coffee.

I hadn't thought through what I would do when we landed. It was a typical, murky London morning and the Spanish sunshine seemed a long way away. We trekked through the airport corridors down past passport control to the baggage carousel. Gilly checked her text messages all the way down and moaned about how far it was to walk.

Rob went with Gilly to find a trolley while I waited for the bags. I switched my mobile on more in hope of a message from Sara than any expectation of there actually being one there.

Nothing! I'd convinced myself while I was in Spain that the reason I hadn't heard from her was because I was abroad. I'd even convinced myself that the text from Shay had been sent before we'd left for Spain and had been held up in the ether over the Alps. Somehow I had fully expected the minute my feet were back touching English soil that my phone would spring to life and there would be umpteen messages from Sara.

Our bags took ages to come onto the carousel and we were amongst the last of the passengers to leave to go through customs. Marco's bag still traveled round and round on the belt with no sign of its owner as I followed Gilly and Rob through the green channel and out into the arrivals area.

Much to my surprise, Mummy and Mr. G stood waiting for us.

"Hello," I said, deciding that 'What are you doing here?' would sound a touch ungrateful.

"Darling, we had to come and meet you." Mummy enveloped me in a huge, Chanel-scented hug. Given that we're not a family who are massively affectionate in public, I felt worried.

"What's the matter?" I half-expected her to say the burglars had returned or the flat had caught fire judging by the expression on her face.

"Oh, darling, it's Jessie. She's in hospital."

"There's been an accident," Mr. G explained.

"Oh, my God! What kind of accident? How bad was it? Is she going to be alright?" I looked from Mummy to Mr. G, desperate for reassurance. Poor Sara—no wonder she hadn't answered any of my messages. It explained why the text had come from Shay, but why would he have said Sara was okay and not mention anything being wrong with Jessie?

"She'll be okay, they think. She's through the worst now and they've moved her from the intensive care unit," Mummy said.

"Why didn't anyone let me know?"

"You couldn't do anything and Sara was in such a state that we went along with what she wanted. She didn't want to spoil your trip. Or Rob's," Mummy added as if suddenly noticing that Rob was still there.

Gilly had already gone to claim her taxi and I assumed Paul and Fiona had left before us.

"Is Sara at the hospital now?" I couldn't think straight.

"Yes. I knew you'd want to go straight there. That's why we came to meet you."

"Could I come too?" Rob looked as stunned by the news of Jessie's accident as I felt.

"No problem." Mr. G took my bag. "Is...erm...Marco not with you?" He coughed, clearly embarrassed at having to ask.

"No. He's gone."

Mummy didn't look surprised. "We'd better hurry then, or Ian will have to pay a huge parking fee. We left the Volvo in the short-stay car park and you know how horrendous the fees are if you go over the time limit."

It began to drizzle as we walked across the car park. "What happened to Jessie? You didn't say how she got hurt." I scurried to keep up with Mummy.

"They were crossing the street. It was wet like today and a car shot around the corner and hit them. Jessie's buggy took the brunt of it but Sara got hurt, too. She's broken her leg."

We'd reached the Greenback mobile and I jumped in the back seat next to Rob.

"Did they get the driver of the car?" Rob asked.

"No, he ran off before the police got there. Apparently, the car had false number plates so they haven't tracked him down yet. Honestly, the things that go on today!" Mummy tutted.

A chill ran down my spine. "It was an accident, though?"

Mr. G peered at me in the rear-view mirror; his eyes bulged with astonishment behind his steel-framed glasses. "Of course, Emma! There are lots of witnesses, so hopefully they'll catch him. A photo-fit picture was in the local paper and there were shots of him on the CCTV cameras."

I felt a bit more reassured. With the events of the past few weeks, I had begun to search for a sinister motive behind everything that happened in my life.

Mummy and Mr. G dropped us off outside the hospital after giving us directions to Jessie's ward. Rob and I stood on the pavement for a moment, staring up at the building before we went in.

"I hope they're going to be alright." All I could think of was the last time we'd seen Sara. When she'd been with Shay after the fight had started at the nightclub.

"Sara's pretty tough and your mum said Jessie was getting better." Rob gave my hand a squeeze of reassurance.

Hospitals have a smell to them that's all their own. It's changed slightly. It's no longer as chemical as it had been when I was seven and had my appendix out. But they still have that certain odor that tells you even if you're blindfolded that you're in a hospital.

We followed the signs until we came to a set of double doors decorated with pictures of Winnie the Pooh. A nurse answered the buzzer and directed us to a small side room. Sara sat on a chair next to a cot. She had a big scrape on her cheek and her leg was in plaster.

Jessie was asleep. A drip hung from a metal stand next to the cot and all I could see of Sara's baby was a fuzzy little tuft of hair peeping out from under the blanket.

I bent down to give Sara a big hug. Obviously she couldn't stand up very easily because of her leg. "We came straight here."

Rob pulled two spare chairs forward from the other corner.

"Emma, I'm sorry I didn't text you but it's been a nightmare. I've been so scared…" Sara's face crumpled and she burst into tears.

"I'll get us a drink," Rob murmured and slipped from the room to leave us together.

"Sara, I would have got the first flight home."

"I know, but by the time they'd put my leg in plaster and Jessie got rushed away… I thought I'd lost her, Em." Sara wiped her eyes with the sleeve of her cardigan and looked around for some tissues.

"Mum said you were hit by a car."

Sara found a packet of tissues inside the bedside locker. "It came from nowhere. All I remember is a screeching noise and a bang. We were thrown up in the air. I tried to get to Jessie but my legs wouldn't work." She blew her nose.

"How's Jessie doing?" I glanced at the cot.

Sara followed my gaze. "They think she'll be okay. She broke her arm and had some internal bleeding so they had to operate, but they've reduced her medication a little now and she seems better."

Rob came back in with a small round tray and three plastic cups of tea. He passed one over to Sara and handed one to me before balancing the tray on a nearby sink and taking a sip from the last one himself.

"How's Shay?" I looked directly at Sara. She hadn't mentioned him up to now and after what had gone on before I went to Spain, I wasn't sure if he was still in the picture.

"He swaps shifts here with me so one of us is always with Jessie." Sara flushed and I knew she'd kept something back.

"And?" I asked.

"I'm pregnant."

Rob choked on his coffee.

"Oh, my God!" I exclaimed, and then I blinked at Sara, abashed. "I…well, I mean…" My voice faded. I thought of the beautiful girl in the nightclub with the Jimmy Choo shoes. What did I mean?

"It's okay, Em," Sara said. "We're both really pleased about it. Everything's fine between us now. The woman at the club turned out to be a friend of Shay's. He's known her since they were kids. I've met her now and everything is okay. She's been having a rough time of things lately, her husband had been slapping her around, and she needed a shoulder to cry on," She smiled at me. "You know Shay, always a sucker for a sob story."

"Well, in that case, fantastic!" I said, and Rob nodded in agreement.

Sara's bright grin faltered somewhat. "So what about you and Marco?"

"We've split up. It's over. There's a lot to tell you." I explained what had happened in Spain. Sara's eyes grew bigger and rounder with every word.

"Bloody hell!" Sara looked at Rob for confirmation of what I'd been saying. "Where is he now?"

"No idea. He's obviously bitten off more than he can chew this time, so he's in hiding."

"Blimey, Em. I didn't want to say anything before but I will now. Thank God he's gone. I've been so worried about you. The things Shay told me that he heard about that friend of Marco's, Everton the gangster, well..."

I think I was better off not knowing.

A doctor came in to see Jessie so we said goodbye to Sara and left the hospital.

"I need to drop by my flat and collect my mail," I said. "I want to make sure everything is okay." The conversation with Sara had stirred uneasy feelings again about Marco and his cronies. Maybe I should get my locks changed again, just in case.

"I'll call you later," Rob said.

I waited for him to kiss me goodbye but he didn't. It was almost as if Spain had never happened.

Chapter Twenty-Three

Rob grabbed a passing cab, so I wandered along on my own down the road toward a bus stop. On the one hand, it felt quite nice to be on my own, just to get lost in the people on the streets. On the other, I was really hurt. I mean, I'd been dumped by my husband and the man I'd fallen in love with all in one day.

Whoa, hold that thought! Where had that come from? When had Rob moved from being my best friend to being someone I wanted to have wild, passionate sex with to being in love? Where on the sliding scale was that?

And what had changed for Rob? When we'd been in Spain, he'd seemed as keen on me as I was on him. Unless it was being back home, or the mystery girl he'd mentioned in Spain that had given him guilt pangs. Or, I suppose he could be like me—not sure about Marco and the mess my life had now become.

The bus pulled into the stop and I got on. The third possibility was that he didn't fancy me after all, that it had all just been the atmosphere combined with alcohol and sunshine. He could regret risking our friendship for a leg-over. Yet that afternoon together had been so magical…

By the time I'd changed buses and made my way across town to the flat, I'd worked myself into a deep depression. I knew Steven and Toby were out, because the blinds didn't move as I walked up the path. If they had been home, they would have met me at the front door, wanting to hear all the gossip.

Things To Do

I let myself into the house and into my flat. It felt cold and unloved like me. I found a pile of letters on the mat, most of them circulars and bills. They were all addressed to me. No more mystery mail for Marco.

I dumped the letters on the kitchen worktop and put the junk mail in the trash. There wasn't much to eat in the cupboards, as usual, and my stomach had started to rumble. Eventually I unearthed a Pot Noodle from behind the tins of spaghetti hoops and put a kettle on to boil.

The flat warmed up once the gas fire was on and I sat down in front of the TV to eat my lunch. Lack of sleep caught up with me and I nodded off during a quiz show re-run.

A strange scraping sound woke me. I couldn't momentarily remember where I was. The room had grown dark while I'd been asleep. The lounge was lit only by the glow of the fire and the commercials playing on the telly.

The scraping noise stopped and I heard the murmur of voices outside the flat in the communal hallway. There was a sudden bang and my lounge door flew open. Before I had a chance to move or grab my phone to call the police, there were three very large men standing in my living room.

"Where's Marco?" The largest of the men stood directly in front of me. The others flanked him. They clearly meant business.

"M-Marco's gone," I stammered. "I...please, I don't know where he is!" My heart started to pound so fast I thought I would have a heart attack.

"Well, I suggest you tell us where the double-crossing son of a bitch has gone or your pretty face won't be quite so pretty," the man said, in a very reasonable, pleasant tone. He straightened his shoulders and cracked his knuckles as he spoke.

"But I...I promise! I really don't know where he is!" I bleated. "He wouldn't tell me. I left him at the airport this morning." Oh, God, what if they didn't believe me?

One of the men produced a thin blade from the sleeve of his jacket like a conjurer performing a card trick. It glinted bluey-orange in the firelight.

"Perhaps you need a reminder." The man with the knife lifted it up toward my face so the flat of the metal pressed cold and hard against my cheek. I noticed a spider's web tattoo on his wrist with three red spiders on it.

"I'm telling the truth!" I cried, shaking with fear, my eyes filling with tears. "I really don't know where he's gone!"

The leader's mobile rang and he flicked it open, his eyes still fixed on my face. "The girl says she doesn't know where he is, claims she left him at the airport." He listened for a second then held the phone out to me. "The boss wants a word."

He nodded to the man with the knife, which he moved away so I could take the phone.

"Emma, how are you?"

"Everton?" Everton had sent these three to find Marco?

"As you've heard from my employees, I'm rather anxious to talk to Marco."

"Everton, I don't know where he is. He wouldn't tell me anything about what was going on. He told me he had a few problems and planned to be away for a time." I kept my eyes glued on the knife as I spoke. I had to convince Everton to call off his henchmen.

"Your husband has something which belongs to me," Everton told me mildly. "It's rather valuable and I'd like it back."

"Marco never told me a thing. He said he would be away for a while and wouldn't say where. He said he'd send someone to collect his things but he didn't say who or when. We've split up, and I'm getting a divorce." I was desperate for him to believe me.

There was a moment's silence. "It's lucky for you, Emma, that I've always liked you. If Marco contacts you, tell him I want to see him."

"I will, Everton, yes," I said, nodding my head like an idiot. My hand trembled as I held the phone. "I'll tell him."

"You promise, Emma? I'd hate to think you might let me down." Everton sounded as if he'd just invited me to dinner, all nice and polite.

"I promise." I'd promise anything to get rid of Everton's thugs—my firstborn, my last Kit-Kat, anything.

"Give the phone back," he said. "There's a good girl."

I handed it back to the leader. He listened for a second then gave a slight shake of his head to the man with the knife, who in turn made the blade disappear back into his coat sleeve.

"No police. Marco shows up, you let the boss know. Or we'll be back." The leader grinned. He snapped the phone shut and they departed, leaving all the doors standing open behind them.

I listened to them leave; I couldn't move a muscle and terror still had me pinned to the settee, but through the lounge window I saw a black BMW glide away from the curb.

As soon as I thought it safe to move, I grabbed my mobile and locked myself in the bathroom. Once I'd finished throwing up, I called Rob.

God knows how quickly he drove to get to me. I hadn't shut the doors. I felt too frightened to move from the relative safety of the bathroom. It was only when I heard Rob's voice call my name from room to room that I managed to get up off the floor and unbolt the door.

"What the hell?" Rob caught me as I fell into his arms.

"They came looking for Marco."

"Who did?" He gripped my arms and pushed me a little way away from him so he could see my face. "What happened? Are you hurt?"

I managed to shake my head. "Everton's men came. One had a knife." I couldn't get my voice to work properly.

"Jesus Christ. I'll call the police." He went to pick up the phone.

"No!"

He looked at me in bewilderment. "You've got to call the police, Emma. Look at the state of you."

"No. Please, Rob, I can't."

He put the phone down and hugged me tightly. "If you'd been hurt, Em..." His breath gusted against my hair, blowing warm against my cheek.

"They just want Marco. He's got something of Everton's."

"The 'something' that was on the yacht?" Rob asked.

"Who knows? I don't think Marco will come back while they're looking for him." I felt much better with Rob holding me, stroking my back soothingly.

"You can't move back in here. You should stay on at your mum's for a while longer." Rob looked around my flat as if he half-expected to find more gangsters hiding in my cupboards.

The sound of a knock on the front door made me leap in Rob's arms. My heart rate only slowed down again when I heard Toby call my name. "Emma! Are you here?"

"We're in here," Rob called.

Toby opened the lounge door. He was in his cycling gear. "What's happened? The door lock's broken again."

"Emma's had unwelcome visitors." Rob's face was grim.

"Burglars?" Toby glanced around the room.

"Everton's thugs," Rob answered.

"Shit, Emma." Toby moved back a step.

"I'm taking Emma to her mum's. It's not safe for her here. Everton's looking for Marco."

"I'll get the flat secured. Do you want me to call you if Marco shows up?" Toby asked me.

"No. Call me," Rob said.

Normally, I would have argued about Rob making decisions for me, but I let him stuff me into my jacket and bundle me into his sports car without a murmur.

Rob jumped in beside me and started the engine.

"It was Everton's men in the BMW, the one that you kept seeing and the one Gilly noticed." I suppose I thought they might still be hanging around. Perhaps they might even follow me.

"Makes sense."

"You don't think they might threaten Gilly?" Maybe Everton was behind the dog-napping. I didn't know. Nothing made sense anymore.

"I wouldn't have thought so."

I wished I could be as sure as Rob sounded. My stomach was still queasy with what had just taken place and I couldn't stop peering in the rear view mirror.

"No one's following us, Emma."

Rob hadn't suggested I stay with him. I know he only has a tiny studio flat, but I was still hurt.

"I was just making sure," I said.

"I'll feel better once you're at your mum's house. You'll be safe there. Mr. G will bring you into work and I can run you home, so everything will be fine. I'm sure Everton will manage to recover whatever it is that Marco has taken without involving you."

We pulled up outside Mummy's house. There was a strange car parked in the spot where Marco normally left his car and my pulse started to race.

Rob got out and came around to open my door. "It looks as if your mum's got company." He saw the expression on my face. "It's okay, Emma. It's not one of Everton's cars."

I didn't think Everton would send his goons around in a silver Astra, but I wasn't up to being logical. "I promise everything will be okay, Emma," Rob said. "Marco's gone."

His words reassured and comforted me. "Come in with me." I didn't want him to drop me off and leave. I didn't plan to tell Mummy what had happened, as she would insist on involving the police and I didn't think that was a good idea. If Everton heard, then I might get another visit from the thug with the knife.

Rob smiled at me. "I won't leave you until I know you're safe, Penfold."

253

I heard voices coming from the lounge as we opened the front door. Mummy came out into the hall to meet us. "I'm glad you're back, Emma. There are some people here to see you."

I thought I would pass out. We'd been wrong. Everton had sent his henchmen round in an Astra.

"They're from the police and the immigration department," Mummy added.

Rob helped me off with my coat and followed me through into the lounge to sit beside me on the sofa.

"This is my daughter, Emma." Mummy introduced me and sat down.

The two men in the room glanced at Rob.

"Rob's a friend. It's alright to talk in front of him," I said, worried they might send him out.

"Miss Morgan, I'm afraid we're here to talk to you about your…ahem…husband." The older of the two men phrased his words carefully.

"Marco and I are no longer together," I said quickly.

Mummy exchanged a glance with the other man and he nodded almost imperceptibly.

"Your mother told us that you were under the impression that you and…ahem…Marco were married," the official continued.

"We were married in Antigua." What did he mean, 'under the impression I was married?'

"I'm afraid you've been the victim of a serious deception, Miss Morgan."

Rob moved forward on the edge of his seat. "What do you mean?"

"I mean, the marriage was not legal."

"What?" Rob and I both spoke together.

"The man you believe to be your husband married you under false pretences." The official looked sympathetic.

Things To Do

"I don't understand." I looked from the older man to the younger one. I'd been there, in a wedding dress with a wedding ring. We'd had a band, cake, everything. I should know. I'd paid for it.

"The celebrant used at your ceremony was not licensed to perform marriages. In addition, the groom has not divorced his first wife, or indeed, any of the other young women he has duped in the same fashion over the last few years."

"You mean I'm really not married?" I couldn't believe what they were telling me. There had to be a mistake. I know Marco had lied over many things but the marriage was real, wasn't it? And what other women?

"I'm sorry, Miss Morgan. The gentleman concerned has been operating under a number of names; it's taken us a while to track the full extent of his activities."

"I think I need a drink." The business of the passport with the different name made sense now. God, I'd been stupid. What the hell had I got myself into?

Mummy passed me some brandy in one of her best goblets. She poured herself a generous measure and after a quick glance at Rob, she poured him one, too. She waved the decanter in the direction of the officials but they both refused with shakes of their heads.

"Is that possible, Em? I mean, you helped arrange weddings for people while you were out there." Rob took a swig of his drink.

"Yes, but for our wedding Marco arranged everything. The registrar who usually came to the hotel was ill, so he got someone else in. I know when I saw his passport, he said there'd been a misprint on his name and…" I was a lousy travel agent. I hadn't even rumbled that lie.

"Do you have a marriage certificate, Miss Morgan?" the official asked.

"I'm not sure. Marco kept it. I left Antigua in a hurry, so…" Everyone looked at me with a pitying expression.

"Oh, Emma." Mummy sat back down with her drink.

"Do you know where Marco is now?"

"I've no idea. He said he was in some kind of trouble and had to lie low. He said someone would collect his things. There are people looking for him who say he has something of theirs."

The younger of the two men made notes in a small black notepad. I assumed he must be the policeman. "What else has Marco done?" I had a feeling I would regret asking, but I had to know.

The men exchanged glances. "We believe that Marco is, or was, a key figure in a gang involved with international drug trafficking," the younger of the two men explained.

"The investigation into the Spiders has been on-going for some time and involves a number of different departments. A number of other gang members are also under surveillance," the older man added.

"Can't you arrest them?" Mummy asked.

"At present, we are still obtaining evidence. We have enough to convict junior gang members but to nail the big fish, we have to have more proof. You appreciate that this information is confidential, of course," the older man added.

"You mean people like Everton?" I asked.

"We're not at liberty to disclose further information or to be more specific."

I took that to be a "yes." "This gang, do they all have a spider's web tattoo on their wrists?"

Again, there was the exchange of glances. "From our information, an empty web is a junior gang member, a red spider signifies a murder, and a black spider is a high ranking official." I felt sick. The knifeman had three red spiders on his web.

They asked a lot more questions about Marco's friends, his routines and his hangouts, though my meager answers weren't much use. Marco let me see so little of his activities, that I wasn't able to tell them much at all.

Eventually they left, telling Mummy they would keep the house under surveillance to track whoever came to collect Marco's belongings.

Things To Do

Rob looked happier when he heard someone would watch the house. I think he hoped they would whisk me off to a safe-house somewhere until Everton and Company were under lock and key, but they didn't make the offer.

"I think I need another drink," Mummy said after she'd waved them off. "Anyone else?"

"No, thanks, Mrs. Morgan," Rob refused.

"At least you won't have to get a divorce, Emma. Although, I do think we ought to check your legal position with a solicitor. I'll go and ring Mr. Blackman." She tootled off into the kitchen to ring the lawyer who'd handled her divorce from Daddy.

"You must think I'm really, really stupid." I finished the last of my brandy. I was scared to look at Rob. He must wonder how on earth I'd not known the truth about Marco.

"No. I think you're Emma. Life is certainly never boring around you." He draped his arm over my shoulder and hugged me close.

My eyes started filling with tears. "How could I have been such an idiot?"

"You heard the police—Marco's an accomplished con man. You weren't to know. I just wish I'd hit him harder when we first met." Rob flexed his fingers thoughtfully.

I revelled in the comforting weight of his arm across my shoulders and the faint smell of his cologne.

The front door opened and Rob immediately pulled his arm away from me as we heard voices in the hall. Fiona was home and talking to someone on her mobile. She flung into the lounge and dropped her bag onto an empty armchair, still talking as she moved.

"For the last time, Niall, I don't care if you're miserable." She sat down, rolling her eyes at me and Rob while she listened to whatever Niall had to say.

"Look, you made your bed, you lie in it! You bonked Glenda behind my back and were stupid enough to get her up the duff! It's hardly my fault it's twins." She crossed her legs, one foot waggling irritably in the air.

257

"Oh, for God's sake! I'm getting married in three weeks time to Paul. No, I will not pay you back any money, or have sex with you, so get over it." She snapped her phone shut and dropped it into her bag, then leaned forward expectantly. "So, what's new with you two?"

Chapter Twenty-Four

"What did Niall want?" Rob asked. He'd pulled away from me so quickly at the sound of Fiona's voice, I felt hurt. It made sense of course, I realized. He'd always had a thing for Fiona. Whatever had happened between me and him in Spain had been a fluke, nothing more. He meant for us to resume our customary status quo now that we were home again—Dangermouse and Penfold, with Dangermouse still mad for Penfold's beautiful, if not unattainable sister.

"News travels fast!" Fiona said. "Niall's heard I'm marrying Paul and he's decided he's made a terrible mistake by leaving me for Glenda. Glenda is having twins and presumably his nookie's stopped. The rat!"

"Does he still want his money back?" I asked.

Fiona produced a small file from her bag and began to study her fingernails. "No idea! He didn't mention it much. He was too busy whining on about Glenda nagging him and how much he missed me."

"Have you and Paul set a date for the wedding?" I was sure I'd heard her tell Niall it was in three weeks' time. I would never be able to lose enough weight to fit into that hideous bridesmaid frock by then.

"Paul's sorted it all out. He's very efficient and there's no point in us hanging about. I've already got my dress." She blew some imaginary dust from her nails and eyed me speculatively. "I think you'll need your dress in the larger size."

I gritted my teeth. "Fi, I don't think that dress would look good in any size."

"Rubbish! It's perfectly adorable and fits my theme. Besides, at such short notice, I haven't time to mess around. Obviously Sara's had to drop out as she can't be a bridesmaid in a wheelchair."

Lucky Sara. I bet it was the one thing she'd be thankful for about breaking her leg.

"Gilly's going to take her place. Fortunately, they have similar figures." Fiona finished her mini manicure and slid the file back in her purse.

Mummy came back into the lounge, her cheeks flushed from the brandy. "My solicitor's looking into it for you, Emma, but it should be straightforward providing no false documents have been lodged in Antigua."

I should have been pleased by the news, but instead, I felt numb about the whole debacle. Mummy told Fiona what had happened. Fiona didn't look fazed by Marco's history at all.

"I'm sorry, Em, but he was a smoothie."

How come no one ever said to my face what they'd all apparently thought behind my back? I knew why, really. One—I wouldn't have listened, and two thinking about it, they had all tried to hint at what they'd thought of Marco, Rob more than anyone.

"Has Paul sorted out your wedding plans?" Mummy asked Fiona.

"Yes, the invitations are being printed and sent tomorrow. The announcement is in *The Times* and we've two magazine interviews booked for Wednesday." Fiona smiled smugly and admired her engagement ring.

"You'll need a bigger size for your dress, Emma," Mummy said.

Okay, so I'm fat and stupid! If I'd had an inkling of a chance with Rob up until that moment, this constant reminding of my overabundant size had surely squashed it. I'm also doomed to wear a satin, ruffled crinoline tent for my sister's wedding. Provided, of course that another knife-wielding mass murderer didn't try to kill me first. God, I needed another drink.

✔ ✔ ✔

Things To Do

Paul and Fiona dropped me off at work the next morning. Mr. G had stayed out all night seeing Esme. It felt very peculiar walking into work knowing Rob would be there and how I had come to feel about him. I wondered if any of the other staff would notice, or guess. I kept trying to tell myself that if he could act like nothing had changed, as if Spain had never happened, then I certainly could, too, but then my head would flit full of these naughty little thoughts of the two of us together, groping and snogging in the stationary cupboard at the office, and I'd feel strange all over again.

Much to my surprise, Mr. G was already in, yet there was no sign of Rob.

"Good morning, Emma," Mr. G said. "Glad to see you're on time. It'll be all hands on deck today. Stephanie's called in sick and I've had to send Rob off to look after the Jackson Street branch. Everyone's going down with this wretched bug."

My spirits fell into my shoes. A whole day with no Rob and with Mr. G on the shop floor. I hoped there were some Kit-Kats left in Rob's desk drawer.

I phoned him at lunchtime but he was busy with a customer, so I left a text on his mobile asking him to pick me up from work so we could visit Sara and Jessie at the hospital.

The afternoon was quiet so I spent a lot of time fantasizing about me and Rob and the stationery cupboard. I also got a lot of tidying done. Mr. G prowled about the shop like the proverbial toad on hot bricks. I wanted to know how things had gone between him and Esme, but he never talked about personal matters in work-time.

It was nearly time to close up when the phone rang. Mr G had gone to cash up in the back office, so I took the call.

"Emma, it's Gilly. I've had another letter!"

I didn't need to ask who from; I could tell by the uncharacteristic wobble in her voice that it had to be the dog-nappers. "Have you rung Gavin?"

"He's coming around later."

"Well, what does it say? Does it tell you when to pay the money?"

261

"I can't talk now!" she hissed dramatically down the phone. I wondered why she'd bothered calling me then.

I lifted the receiver away from my ear a little. "Why? Where are you?"

"I'm in the changing room at the spa."

"What's Gavin going to do? Is he setting a trap?" I remembered an episode of *The Bill* where they'd done that.

"I'm not sure. I can't risk anything happening to my little Robbie."

"Call me after Gavin's seen you and let me know what he says."

We closed shortly after Gilly had hung up. As it was getting dark, Mr. G wanted to wait with me until Rob came, but the street was busy with people so I told him to carry on home to Mummy. I had to start to reclaim my life. I couldn't keep jumping at every strange noise or looking at every black car as if it might hold a member of the Spiders.

I loitered about in the high street and browsed in the shop windows while I waited for Rob. Despite my best intentions, I still kept looking for the black BMW but thankfully there was no sign of one.

Eventually Rob arrived, double-parking long enough for me to hop in before the traffic behind him could begin to protest. We set off for the hospital.

"Any problems today?" Rob asked and swore under his breath as a minicab cut us off.

"Gilly called. She's heard from the dog-nappers. Gavin, the policeman, is going to see her later."

"She's mad about that dog," Rob said. "She'll pay the ransom."

I waited for him to say he'd missed me, but he didn't. No kiss hello, or anything. I guess it was more than I could have hoped for. It took us ages to find a parking space at the hospital and Rob was in a foul mood by the time we got to Jessie's ward.

Shay was there in his usual garb: Bob Marley T-shirt and faded jeans. He sat with one arm around her and his other spread protectively across her tummy. I got a big lump in my throat just seeing them together.

Jessie was sitting up in her cot, playing with a shape sorter. As soon as she saw me and Rob, she let out a big squeal of delight.

Shay stood up to greet us both and to pull chairs out for us. I was so glad Sara and I had been wrong about him deceiving her.

"Hello, Jessie." I reached into the cot to stroke her fuzzy hair.

"The drip's down and we might be able to go home tomorrow." Sara smiled.

"That's good news. Better not tell Fiona or she'll have you back in that bridesmaid's dress," Rob joked.

Sara rolled her eyes at me. "Please, no! She told me she'd recruited Gilly."

I nodded. "She's planning a country theme. I hope Mummy managed to talk her out of the shepherds' crooks and sheep."

We spent a nice hour talking to Shay and Sara and playing with Jessie, then Shay walked with us down to the hospital entrance.

"Word in the clubs is that Everton's disappeared. Things are a bit hot for him lately." Shay looked at me.

As far as I was concerned, Everton and his cronies couldn't disappear fast or far away enough for me.

"You know Marco's gone, too?" Rob said.

"Yeah, and apparently, he's gone with two million pounds of Everton's money." Shay chuckled.

My mouth fell open. "Two million? No wonder he said he was lying low."

"Steer clear of them both, Em. Things will get nasty if Everton catches up with Marco." Shay's face sobered and a chill ran down the length of my spine. I'd experienced firsthand how nasty Everton's men could get.

As Rob and I walked back across the car park together, we heard a noise like a car backfiring and a black BMW suddenly pulled out from nowhere, racing straight for us.

"Holy shit, Emma!" Rob pushed me out of the way and we sprinted for his car. Well, I ran as fast as the skirt of my stupid uniform would let me. I yanked the door open and dived inside. If I was to die because of Esme Grebe's lack of fashion sense, I decided then and there that I would come back and haunt her relentlessly.

The BMW screeched around the corner and there was another loud popping sound, like a firework. Rob sprawled across the driver seat and shoved my head down under the dash.

"What the…?" I heard shouts and then the screech of tires as the BMW drove away. Cautiously, we raised our heads and looked up. There was a hole in the corner of the windshield on Rob's side.

"Those bastards shot my car!" Rob straightened up and glared after the disappearing BMW. He delved in his pocket for his phone and punched in a number.

"They were shooting at us?" I stared at the hole and brushed little bits of glass from Rob's shoulder as he spoke to someone.

He closed his mobile and returned it to his pocket. "I just spoke to the detective we saw at your mother's house yesterday. We've got to get you out of town for a while."

"Where am I going to go?" I still couldn't quite take it in that someone had tried to kill me. And quite possibly Rob, too. The contents of my stomach revolted and it took a massive effort of willpower to keep from being sick.

"I'll work something out. The police will meet us at your mum's." Rob turned the key and started the engine. I didn't think you were supposed to leave a crime scene but presumably it might be more dangerous for us to hang about.

I noticed Rob had a tiny trickle of blood on his brow; a little piece of glass must have cut him when it shattered. We drove back to Mummy's, ignoring all the speed restrictions and earning ourselves lots of horn blasts and hand gestures along the way.

Things To Do

Three cars were outside Mummy's when we arrived. The younger man from the day before met us on the pavement. "A bit close for comfort." He looked at the car and at the blood on Rob's face.

Mummy and Fiona waited by the front door. "You're to come and stay at Paul's house in the country," Fiona announced before I even set foot in the hall. "I'm going anyway to get everything ready for the wedding and you'll be safe there. Paul has staff and a good alarm system. They won't be able to get near you."

"The sooner the better," Mummy added with a horrified glance at poor Rob.

"But what about work?" I asked. "And my flat? And Sara?" This could not be happening to me. I'd changed my mind about a career as a spy. Espionage and crime were far too dangerous. At least my fed-up travel agency customers never went as far as trying to kill me. Not even the vicar I once accidentally sent to stay in a red-light area.

"Emma, are you bloody daft? You were almost killed!" Mummy exclaimed.

"I've packed your things. The police are going to take us down there now in an unmarked car." Fiona's voice was firm.

I noticed the pile of luggage behind her and realized I had no choice. As we drove away. I had tears streaming down my face.

"Here." Fiona handed me a tissue from her bag.

I blew my nose and tried to settle back for the journey. I don't think I've ever felt so miserable in my life. It was bad enough that I'd got myself into this mess, but endangering my friends and family—not to mention the man I loved—was something else entirely.

265

Chapter Twenty-Five

When Fiona said Paul's house was miles from anywhere it wasn't a joke. Not only was it miles from home, it was also miles from the nearest chocolate-selling shop.

Fiona planned to commute back and forth into the city with Paul in his helicopter. That left me and the policeman assigned to protect me with the housekeeping staff, Paul's DVD library and no snack food. Even his daily papers were the worthy broadsheet kind, not a good red-topped scandal rag amongst them.

It came as a shock to find a picture of Gilly with Robbie the dog plastered over page five of one of them. The banner headline read "Dog-nappers Foiled." I sat down in Paul's library and read how Officer Gavin Howes had tried to set a trap and catch the notorious band of dog-nappers. Apparently, it had almost worked, but they'd escaped at the last minute, abandoning Robbie the dog and leaving the ransom money behind.

I was pleased for Gilly, but it would have been nice to find out if the dog-napping gang was connected to Everton. Although we'd suspected they might be, I got the impression from the police that Everton had bigger projects on the go; dog-napping wouldn't have provided the Stick Insect with pin money.

After a week passed, I started to go stir-crazy. Now I knew what the contestants on *Big Brother* went through. Rob wasn't allowed to contact me in case his phone fell into the wrong hands, so I had no idea what he'd been doing. The only relief was when the dressmaker flew in with Fi for a day to fit me up with my bridesmaid dress. Thank Heaven she opted for ice-blue fabric, not that it helped much. I still looked like one of those hideous dolls that old ladies stick on top of their spare loo rolls.

At last it was the eve of the wedding. Mummy flew in with Mr. G and Fiona, and the heli-pad was busy all day with caterers, florists and stuff. I'd been instructed to stay out of sight, just in case, although PC Plod, as I'd come to affectionately think of my police guard, told me privately that they planned to downscale the risk to me after the wedding as nothing had been seen or heard of Everton's men since the shooting.

Gilly, Rob, Sara, Shay and Jessie were all due to fly down in the morning. All the other guests were to arrive by car. Private security had been employed by Paul to screen arrivals at the gatehouses to foil paparazzi and homicidal knifemen.

The wedding chapel was on the far side of the grounds from the main house, and Fi had organised a Cinderella-style carriage to take us across. Everything was planned on a "country" theme. I had a sinking feeling that sheep still featured somewhere in her plans.

I watched the helicopter land and saw Gilly and Rob get out. Paul's staff helped Sara into a wheelchair and put Jessie on her lap. Shay pushed her off in the direction of the chapel and the others headed toward the house.

I waved as hard as I could to Rob but he didn't appear to see me. I was banned from going downstairs until it was time for the bridal party to set off, as Fi didn't want anyone to get a sneak preview of her color theme. I hoped he would be allowed up to see me by the security guards.

I was struggling with the zipper of the horror frock when Gilly came in.

"Emma! I've sent you a load of messages! Rob told me on the way here what happened." She pounced on me with a perfumed bear hug.

"I saw your picture in the paper" I told her. "I'm so pleased Robbie is okay."

Gilly lifted her bag from her shoulder and popped it onto the floor. Robbie jumped out wearing the little sparkly collar Gilly had bought for him in Spain. "I've got a little jacket for him, too. It'll match our dresses," Gilly cooed, scooping him up and kissing his furry head.

Poor Robbie. I'll bet he was just thrilled about that.

"Your dress is hanging up over there. Could you give me a hand with the zip on mine, please?"

Gilly moved to help me and I couldn't help remembering Valentine's night, when Rob had zipped me into my fairy outfit. I wished he was here with me now instead of Gilly.

"These dresses are so cute." Gilly finished with my zip and went over to her dress.

"Yes, they're wonderful," I said. If you liked to look like a satin-covered member of the Teletubbies, that is.

"And these are a lovely touch." Gilly reached behind her dress and pulled out two shepherdess crooks decorated with large satin bows. I thought I'd talked Fi out of them but clearly I'd failed. Great, I'd look like not-so-Little Bo Peep.

I helped Gilly into her dress and we pinned corsages of imported wildflowers into our cleavages. Gilly brushed Robbie's fur and fastened him into a sparkly little blue jacket to match his collar. "Don't you look a smart boy?" she trilled.

"Where did you get that coat from?" I'd never seen anything quite like it before. Robbie looked like a canine version of Elton John. He only needed some little doggy specs to complete the look.

"Marco helped me find it when we were in Spain. He spoke to the woman in the shop about shipping it and it arrived in the post yesterday. It was his idea. He thought it matched the collar." Gilly gave the fur on top of Robbie's head a last brush.

There was a knock at the door and one of the dressmaker's assistants came in to check if we were ready. After a last glance in the mirror, we trooped along the landing with our crooks to join Fiona.

She looked fabulous, like a true fairytale princess, with flowers carefully pinned in her hair and a sparkly cloak around her shoulders that shimmered in the light. Mr. G had agreed to give her away. She hadn't bothered to ask Daddy as he couldn't have come anyway. The Inland Revenue have some outstanding matters they wanted to clear up with him, apparently.

We followed her down the broad oak staircase to where Mr. G waited in the hallway. His chubby little face beamed with pride when she took his arm and I found it strangely touching. I'd promised myself I wouldn't cry but I had to have a little sniffle when I saw how carefully he looked after her, almost as if she was his own daughter.

He handed her into the lead carriage and Gilly, Robbie and I got into the second one.

"Ooh, look at the sheep!" Gilly squealed as we neared the chapel. Tied to small pegs at strategic positions around the field surrounding the chapel were sheep wearing ice-blue ribbons to match Fiona's theme.

Robbie the dog eyed the sparkling-clean, woolly creatures with interest and I hoped Gilly had a tight hold on him. Not that he was big enough to be a sheep-worrier, but maybe his Elton John outfit had given him ideas of grandeur.

We were helped down from the carriage by Paul's staff. We posed for photographs with our shepherdess crooks next to a convenient sheep. Gilly kept Robbie tucked firmly under her arm throughout the session. I was surprised Fi had agreed to Robbie being in the pictures—or even at the wedding—but apparently his appearance in the press had given him celebrity status.

The chapel had been lit with hundreds of white wax candles and when Paul turned to see Fiona walk up the aisle toward him, I started to feel sniffly again. Rob sat next to Sara and Shay and he winked at me as I walked past. He looked good in his suit. Dangerously sexy.

Mummy wore a hat that made her look like a giant mushroom that had lost a fight with a chicken. She cried all the way through the service. I must admit I had a nervous moment when they asked if there were any objections; I half-expected Niall or Glenda to pop out from behind one of the pillars.

Fortunately the ceremony went off without a hitch and Robbie the dog was as good as gold in his spangly coat and collar. Once the register had been signed, we all dutifully went outside for more photographs.

The shepherd had moved most of the sheep, leaving just a couple tethered near the carriages so the photographer could use them as background. Dodging some of Paul's elderly aunts who were flinging rice around with gay abandon, I sidled off to find Rob.

"Emma!" I found him loitering near the chapel porch, where we were partially screened from the rest of the guests. He smiled to see me, and hugged me fiercely.

"I've missed you so much," I said breathlessly. "They wouldn't let me call you."

"I know." He made no move to let me go, and when I looked up at him, our faces were so close, our noses nearly touched. My heart raced to feel his breath against my face. "I missed you, too, Penfold," he said softly, still smiling. He lifted his hand, brushing his fingers against my cheek, and my heartbeat quickened all the more.

"Can we have the bridesmaids again, please!" The photographer's voice cut across my happy daydreams.

"You're needed. I'll see you back at the reception," Rob promised. I trotted back to pose next to the sheep with Gilly.

"Paul and Fiona are sending the helicopter to bring Gavin down for the reception. He wasn't able to alter his shift so they offered to have him collected," Gilly confided, eying the sheep nearest to her a little nervously as Robbie struggled in her arms.

"So, you and Gavin are together, then?" I asked.

Gilly flushed. "Well, yes. Oh, Emma, he's lovely. I really think he might be the one." Her color deepened.

"I'm so pleased for you, Gilly."

Fi huffed across the grass toward us. "Will you two please come and finish the photos? I want to get back to the house. Paul just heard that security have intercepted Niall and Glenda at the gatehouse."

"He hasn't heard of anyone else trying to get in, has he?" I helped Fi lift her skirt clear of the grass as we were regrouped by the carriage.

"No, thank goodness, but did you know I had a death threat?" Fi smoothed the silk of her dress.

All at once, I wanted to throw up. "No."

"A note left for me at the hairdresser's. It said 'pay up the money, you hard-faced bitch.'"

Everything went swimmy. Why hadn't she mentioned it before? "Did you tell the police?"

"There was no point. Glenda—that silly cow—had signed it." Fi fluffed her veil out around her shoulders.

I inhaled a big gulp of air. I had to stop thinking everything was connected to Everton. Mr. G had a hip flask; I wondered if I could get across and persuade him to give me a slug of brandy before he went up to the house.

Gilly and I finally finished the photo shoot and went back to the house in a carriage with Mummy and Mr. G. I hadn't needed the brandy after all, which was lucky as I think he might have given it all to Mummy already.

Fiona hadn't invited huge numbers of guests, but somehow the hall, ballroom and library were full of people. Uniformed waiters cruised through the rooms ensuring the guests were all well-supplied with drinks while they waited for the return of the bride and groom.

Rob got talking to Mummy and Mr. G while I hung around near the entrance. As soon as he noticed me, however, he excused himself and picked his way through the crowd.

"Busy in here, isn't it?" He smiled at me and my pulse quickened again.

"Yes, I—" I began, but then a scuffling noise and a scream from the group of guests standing opposite us cut me short.

"Stand back!" Marco stood in the center of a space which had abruptly cleared as if by magic around him. Tucked under one arm was Robbie the dog and in his other hand was a gun. One of Paul's aunts fainted, causing a ripple of consternation in the crowd.

271

"Marco!" Instinctively, I stepped forward—what for, I'm really not sure—but Rob's hand fell against my shoulder to hold me back.

Marco looked directly at me. His eyes were hard and cold. "Keep away and nobody will get hurt." He fired a shot up into the ceiling and everyone screamed, ducking as a shower of plaster dust fell. Robbie began to whimper and Marco edged back toward the door.

"You bastard!" I struggled against Rob's arm. Anger overtook my common sense and I wanted to fasten my hands around his throat for everything he'd put me, my friends and family through.

Marco leveled the gun toward me. "So long, babe," he said, dropping me a sly smile and a wink. He was almost out of the door.

"You're not stealing my dog!" Gilly appeared from behind Marco like an avenging angel in blue satin. Before he had a chance to react, she whacked him hard across the back of his head with her shepherdess crook.

Taken by surprise, he went down like a sack of potatoes. The gun flew out of his hand. Gavin raced into the room behind Gilly and grabbed the fallen pistol as it skidded across the hall floor. Marco stirred as if attempting to get up and Rob lunged forward, punching him hard in the chin, knocking him out cold.

The guests applauded as Gavin rushed forward, pistol in hand to slap Marco in handcuffs. Gilly scooped up Robbie and cooed endearments into his little furry ears.

Marco groaned and opened his eyes as Gavin hauled him to his feet.

"You miserable shit! Why me? Why did you do this to me?" I screamed at him. Shay caught me by the arm and held me back before I could launch myself at him, intent on causing as much damage as a short woman in a satin crinoline frock possibly could.

"Because it was so easy." Marco sneered as the policeman started to march him away.

I broke away from Shay and slugged Marco hard on the other side of his jaw. He hit the ground unconscious for the second time that day, and Gavin had to haul him, limp and lolling to his feet. Another plain-clothed policeman joined him, and together, they hustled Marco away before I could inflict any further damage.

"I should have hit him like that the first time," Rob murmured, as people started to mill about, patting us both on the back and sympathizing with Gilly.

"How did he get here? And why did he want Gilly's dog?" Marco's last jibe had hurt almost as much as my knuckles. Robbie the dog yapped excitedly around my ankles, enjoying the attention of the guests.

"Emma, what was Marco doing here?" Mummy elbowed her way through the throng. I don't think she really thought I had any idea of what Marco's intentions had been but she had been as shocked as the rest of us by his sudden appearance.

"I don't know, Mummy." I was baffled too. I couldn't think why Marco would have been anywhere near here.

Gavin picked up Robbie the dog and started to examine the sparkly dog collar Gilly had bought in Spain.

"What is it?" Rob joined him as Gavin carefully took the collar from around the dog's neck and unfastened his little coat.

"I'm not sure, but these don't look like crystals to me. I think we need to get a jeweller's opinion on them." Gavin held the collar up to the light so the beams from the chandeliers splintered and rainbowed through the stones on to the wooden floor of the hall.

"Diamonds?" Mummy asked, as we all stared open-mouthed at the doggy accessories.

Gilly fumbled for the little pochette bag trimmed with lace that went with our bridesmaid dresses. "There was one bigger one on the coat. I cut it off this morning because I didn't like it." She drew out her hand and nestled in her palm was a rock rivalling the one in Fiona's engagement ring.

"Of course," I whispered. The police had told me that Everton and Marco had been involved together in drug trafficking. I realized that Marco had probably used the trip to Spain as a front to buy drugs for Everton, and that they had planned to ship them back to England hidden aboard *The Lady*

Crystal. That would explain Marco's persistent interest in the yacht—and why he'd been so dismayed to learn the boat would be delayed in leaving Spain.

"I guess we know what happened to Everton's millions," Rob said with a low whistle, his brows raised.

"Marco used them to buy diamonds," I said, my eyes widening. He must have seen his opportunity to fleece Everton, and rather than try to sneak away toting a bundle of cash, thought it would be easier to invest in diamonds. Easier to conceal—and lots easier to disguise—the small fortune in jewels had passed unnoticed into the country, and undoubtedly, Marco had thought it would be no problem whatsoever to get them away from a twit like Gilly once they'd arrived. Desperation must have forced him to come to the wedding that day; I imagine that if Everton's goons were gunning for me, they were after Marco even more relentlessly.

Gavin went to inform his police colleagues about our discovery. I began to think being a spy or a sleuth like Nancy Drew might be good fun after all. Then again, the knife and gun bit had scared me. I hoped the rest of the Spiders would be rounded up now that Marco was in custody.

The rest of the reception felt a bit anticlimactic after all the excitement. Mr. G made a speech, Paul's aunties got tiddly on champagne, Jessie was a little angel, and Robbie the dog ate so many titbits, he got sick on the best man's shoes.

"So, like I was saying earlier, it's a bit busy in here, isn't it?" Rob said. "Before we were interrupted with all of that excitement, I had been about to suggest we slip away for a few minutes, go somewhere quieter, just the two of us."

I blinked at him in surprise and my heart did this little happy pitter-patter thing. Had I just heard him right? "What exactly do you have in mind, Dangermouse?" I asked.

He smiled and leaned forward, kissing me. I closed my eyes, unable to breathe, my heart pounding in my ears. "I was hoping maybe we could find someplace where we could be on our own for awhile," he murmured as he drew away.

Things To Do

At that moment, I was ready to pounce on him across the nearest buffet table—crushing canapés and miniature quiches beneath us, if need be but I saw his point. Sometimes discretion really was the better part of valor. I peeped around his shoulder at the crowded reception. Everyone seemed to be busy on the dance floor. Gilly danced with Gavin; Fi was oblivious to everyone except Paul; Mummy had taken off the hat from hell and tangoed with Mr. G. For once, my boss looked untoadlike.

"There's always my room," I whispered. I tried to remember if I'd left it tidy.

We crept to the door, helping ourselves to some more champagne on the way, before sneaking off up the stairs. Thankfully the maid had been in and cleaned my room. Rob put the glasses and bottle down on the dressing table while I clicked on the lamp. The room was filled with a soft golden light and Rob took me in his arms.

"I've waited a long time for you, Penfold." He unzipped the back of my dress so that the satin slid to my waist, and he lowered his head to kiss me.

It felt like something out of a fairy tale, meant to be and perfect. I couldn't believe it. Everyone else had found their happy ending—Fiona and Paul, Gilly and Gavin, Mummy and Mr. G, and now I was going to get mine, too. My heart was racing and so were my hands as I began to tug Rob's shirt loose from his trousers. "I've waited a long time for you, too, Dangermouse," I said.

He started to ease the dress down over my thighs. "I love you, Emma."

And, just before his fingers and tongue left me speechless, I managed to murmur, "More than Kit-Kats?" Then he touched me someplace wondrous, rendering any further conscious thought completely impossible.

About the Author

To learn more about Nell Dixon, please visit www.nelldixon.com. Send an email to Nell at helen@nelldixon.com or visit her blog at http://nelldixonrw.blogspot.com

A man who thought he had life figured out...just met a woman who proved him wrong!

Last Thing I Expected
© *2006 Heather Rae Scott*

Kindergarten teacher Grace Adams wants to turn over a new leaf. She's hoping a new school and a new apartment will de-magnetize the loser magnet she seems to possess. According to a student's mother, she's cursed. All it would take is a simple ceremony, some friends and a teeny-tiny bonfire in a coffee can to shake it...

Within a few moments her apartment is engulfed in smoke, her fire alarm is blaring, and she can't stop laughing because she really should have known better. The next thing she knows someone is busting through her door to "save the day".

That someone is firefighter Eddie Mancilla. He has one thing on his mind—fire chief. It's been a family tradition for generations. He's not about to jeopardize it for his former high-school crush. Eddie doesn't believe in curses or have time to rekindle a relationship with Grace. But as the reunion combusts, Eddie has to douse a lot more than structure fires, now he has to quench the fire he has blazing for Grace.

Once they unite it's going to be a four-alarm situation. Grace is under his skin and unfortunately **her bad luck seems to have spread.... to him!**

Available now in ebook and print from Samhain Publishing.

Meddling landladies, fashion-tortured canines, psychotic best friends - is that what it takes to bring two love-jaded people together, or will they be killed with good intentions?

You'll Be The Death Of Me
© 2006 Stacia Wolf

Allison Leavitt is great at living in a make-believe world - she'd created one in her best-selling mystery novels, home of her fantasy man, a hard-nosed detective with a granite-encrusted heart. It's taken years for an artist to finally capture his image, the one she's lived with in her head for far too long. Imagine her shock when she discovers him standing in her living room!

When the shock fades, one question remains: now that she's found him, what is she going to do about making fantasy reality?

Displaced Los Angeles detective Jay Cantrall isn't happy with his Spokane, Washington assignment, and even more disgruntled with his whacked-out apartment house. The landlady runs around in muumuus whispering sweet nothings to her bizarre canine companion, who hates Jay but has romantic tendencies toward his leg. One tenant thinks nothing of staging mock murders, another is a man-shark, and his next-door neighbor, Allison, although incredibly delectable, seems to be incapable of little more than fish imitations.

Besides, he learned his lesson where women are concerned: nothing can bring a man's downfall faster than a woman's lies.

It seems that whenever Jay and Allison are near each other, disaster strikes. And when one of the disasters leaves Jay injured, guilt-ridden Allison decides to nurse the cranky cop back to health. But will her ministrations heal the wounds deep inside both of them, or will it end in yet another disaster?

Warning: this title contains hot, steamy sex explicitly described.

Available now in ebook and print from Samhain Publishing.

Fly Away

Discover the Talons Series

5 STEAMY NEW PARANORMAL ROMANCES
TO HOOK YOU IN

Kiss Me Deadly, by Shannon Stacey
King of Prey, by Mandy M. Roth
Firebird, by Jaycee Clark
Caged Desire, by Sydney Somers
Seize the Hunter, by Michelle M. Pillow

AVAILABLE IN EBOOK—COMING SOON IN PRINT!

Samhain Publishing

WWW.SAMHAINPUBLISHING.COM

GREAT CHEAP FUN

Discover eBooks!
THE FASTEST WAY TO GET THE HOTTEST NAMES

Get your favorite authors on your favorite reader, long before they're out in print! Ebooks from Samhain go wherever you go, and work with whatever you carry—Palm, PDF, Mobi, and more.

Samhain Publishing

WWW.SAMHAINPUBLISHING.COM

Printed in the United Kingdom
by Lightning Source UK Ltd.
116664UKS00001B/112-120